Wishing you cosmic journeys.

Sandra Fox Murphy

A Thousand Stars

Sandra Fox Murphy

Author's Note and Acknowledgement

This novel is purely a tale of fiction and imagination. The reader will find within actual historical events and genuine historical figures intertwined in a story that is fabricated fiction. The light of inspiration that spawned this story came to me through a family tree; however, the names, characters, places, dates and geographical descriptions are all either the product of the author's creativity or are used fictitiously. Any resemblance to persons, living or dead, or to actual events or locations is entirely coincidental.

*

I want to thank Serena Guin and my writing group at the Baca Center in Round Rock, Texas, for their insistence, upon hearing my short story "Ann," that a novel must reveal all of the details, the love and loss buried beneath the lines of my original short piece. Without their belief in me and in the story of Ann Hill, I never would have imagined this grand tale of love and grace.

I am indebted to the books, the websites and the multiple genealogies filled with the tribulations, successes and gifts of our ancestors, storytelling at its best. I thank my friends and family for cheering me along the way, and I am indebted to Karen Mead and Jean Stanley Goad (a descendant of the Tallman and Durfee families) for their invaluable feedback and encouragement. I am grateful to author Daryl Buckner for answering my questions and cheering me on. Many thanks to Jenny Quinlan of Historical Editorial for the beautiful cover she created. I especially want to thank Charity Singleton Craig, co-author of *On Being a Writer*, for her detailed, spot-on feedback, spurring me on to make this story into a more polished creation.

In memory of my father, Thomas Chandler Murphy, who chose me as his daughter in spite of my rebellious ways, and in memory of my grandfather Russell Brown, the ultimate storyteller.

O, thou art fairer than the evening air

Clad in the beauty of a thousand stars;

Brighter art thou than flaming Jupiter

When he appear'd to hapless Semele;

More lovely than the monarch of the sky

In wanton Arethusa's azur'd arms;

And none but thou shalt be my paramour!

"The Face That Launch'd a Thousand Ships,"

from *Dr. Faustus*

Christopher Marlowe

Prologue

Ann

1667, Rhode Island

The center yard in Newport is crowded; the citizens of this town have come to see me. It is the 15th day of May in the year of our Lord 1667, and the crowd has gathered to see justice, but it is not justice they will see. Standing before me is Constable Emery, a short man, his face ruddy and thick, with narrowed eyes reflecting his binding judgment. His sergeant, reedy in his disheveled uniform, has sympathetic eyes, but, I am certain in accord with his given orders, instructs me to remove my blouse and unlace my chemise. I do as instructed, unlacing and removing my cotton blouse, holding it tight in my hand, and pulling the ribbon at my back waist to loosen the smock I wear under my dressing, all the time looking the constable direct in the eye. The sergeant places my wrists in the grips on the whipping wagon and screws tight the locks to hold me still. From the corner of my eye I see Constable Emery, with a slight smile of satisfaction, take his cat of nines from a leather holster. At once I hear the whistle of the air around me, and the first strike startles me. Then, as if with a cadence, one comes after the other, stinging my bare back. By the time ten lashes smite my back, I can feel the warm blood, wet on my muslin. Five more are to come, as the judge had deemed fifteen. I will not cry. I try with all my wit not to wince as the drawn crowd watches and gasps. I close my eyes and know that this shall soon pass. I will soon be free as I have not been free since my youth. Yes, my youth; let me begin my story there, though my memory may be ravaged by time.

Chapter 1

Ann

... and the purple throated bird flies free
amidst blooms of the tranquil island waters
as far as one can see ...

1647, Christ Church Parish, Barbados

The blue-green Caribbean waves washed onto the nearby beach, with the rhythmic resonance of a soothing arrival; the sun was low toward the west. A tall ship with a Dutch flag swayed, newly tethered at the docks.

"Mama? Have you ever been to the colonies? Those to the north?"

"No, Ann," she said, staring toward the docks along the shore. "Since your father and I sailed to Jamestown with Captain Powell, I have never left the island. Your pa sailed to New Amsterdam and to the Virginia and the Massachusetts Bay colonies during his trading voyages. He said the land is wooded and full of wild animals and savages."

Amused by my own visions of unfamiliar wild animals amidst tall green trees thick on hillsides, I continued gathering the fruit into my bag as the market closed for the day. Mum worked as a seamstress during the week, but on Saturdays we would vend our orchard fruit here at the open market. Last year, my pa had died of tuberculosis, a disease likely contracted during one of his voyages. Pa had taken me aboard docked ships when I was a child, and I found them dark and filled with unpleasant smells. The foul odors of excrement mixed with the sweat, sweat from both man and beasts. On one occasion I saw a rat skitter across the deck and through a break in a wall, a break so small I did not think my fingers would fit. I grabbed Pa's hand.

After Pa died, Mum and I managed well due to the goodness of Mum's friend Maria's husband, Antoine. Antoine had a tailor shop where Mum did the stitching and fine work. Moreover, we had our abundant home orchards where I had played as a young girl. Pa's trading company here in Barbados was gone now, as he had been unable to travel and barter during his long illness.

As I gathered the oranges into my bag, a well-dressed gentleman walked, rather hurriedly, toward me, while Mum was visiting with her friend Adelaide, who was selling sugar cane and raw sugar next to our table. He was tall and lean, with sandy-colored hair beneath his cap, and his jacket a deep blue of a fine fabric, as if he were a man of means.

"Miss, may I get two of those before you finish packing them away? " His voice was strong, and I noted a twinkle in his eye. He looked to be about twenty-seven or twenty-eight.

"Yes, you may. I will give you these four for one pence. Will that be good?" I said, returning a reserved smile as I admired his blue eyes. "We will only have to carry them home."

"Well, let me lighten your load, Miss ..." He paused, awaiting a response.

Hearing his hesitation, I looked up and saw his expression of anticipation and realized he was asking for my name. "It is Ann, sir."

He nodded his head and beamed a smile, handing me two pence. "Here is an extra for your trouble. Ah, my ship just arrived in port. I can wait no longer to taste these oranges after months at sea." He began peeling one of them and bit into it, the juice running down his jacket. "You have a good day, Miss Ann." As he gathered his remaining oranges and began to walk away, he paused and slowly turned back. "This isle is such a charming place. The sea calm and blue. I imagine it would be quite pleasant to wake here each day with the sea breeze. Are you here at the market each day, Miss Ann?"

"No, sir. We market the fruit only on Saturday. I help my mother at Antoine's Tailor Shop during the week. However, there will be other vendors here on Monday."

He smiled again. "It was not the oranges I was hoping to see when I return." He winked at me, turned on his heel and walked toward the docks.

My mum had witnessed this exchange as she returned to our table. "Well, well. That was a nice-looking gentleman who winked at my daughter. You will be married and gone in the blink of an eye, my dear. Gone, and me all alone in my orchards, what with your brother out to sea now. Maybe you are too pretty to have out here at the market," she mused.

"Oh, Mum, don't be silly. I'm not going anywhere. And you have so much more to teach me. You must school me in the fine embroider work you do."

"Yes, I do." We loaded the unsold produce, mostly oranges, a few grapefruits and lemons, into our buggy and rode silently back to the edge of the town of St. Michael and to our sweet home in the village near the sea, surrounded by the trees of our orchards and, and beyond that, fields of sugar cane. I wondered often of other places, and the British Isles whence my parents had come. They had spoken often of the Thames River in London, as well as the bustling city of Bristol, where they had once lived. Our home sat in a small fishing village where the calm blue waters met the sandy beach when the skies were clear. The sailing ships passed back and forth with goods from across the sea, if they were able to get past the pirates, and the many sailors drank heartily at the town's pubs. Yet our home was quaint, with a quiet view of the sugar cane fields and our orchards at the foot of the hills. I had known no other life than living here.

Chapter 2

Ann

Mum spent Tuesday demonstrating her simple embroider stitches, making me watch and in turn watching me copy her work in hopes that I would assist her at the shop, and with full confidence that Antoine would sometime in the future offer me compensation for my work. He had plenty of work coming in, with the growing population of traders and plantation owners. Since coming to the shop with Mum, I had been stitching straight seams and pressing dresses for her; on certain days I would cover the front table when customers arrived. Antoine would tell me that my sweet smile enchanted his customers, and I would giggle in embarrassment.

Antoine had left, as was his custom, at lunchtime, and I sat at the front table, stitching the cuffs on a shirt, as Mum was working in the back room. Alma, who was a servant for Mrs. Hitchcock at one of the large plantations, came in the front door with two of her mistress's dresses for alteration. As I recorded the pick-up in Antoine's journal and folded the dresses, the gentleman I had met on Saturday walked in and smiled at me. He held the door for

Alma as she exited, and I am certain I blushed when he turned to speak to me.

"Well, good morn, Miss Ann. What a surprise to see you again." He smiled.

"You too, sir," I said, knowing well that it was not likely a surprise at all. "I hope that you are enjoying your time in Christ Church. Can I be of some help?"

He handed me a jacket made of a luxurious wool fabric of deep red. He said it needed repair at the sleeve where the seam had pulled loose. I picked up the journal of accounts from the shelf and wrote the repair as he had described, yet I was aware his eyes watched me. I noticed he was quick to smile, a smile that lit his face, and his eyes were a shade of blue like the calm ocean on a sunny day.

"And your name, sir?"

"Peter Tallman. Tallman of Newport. Or, at least, Newport is my destination."

I carefully wrote his name. "And when might you need this finished, sir?"

"Please, Miss Ann, you may call me Captain Tallman. I am not old enough to be called 'sir' by such a captivating lass." Again he beamed his broad smile and again I blushed. "I sail again next Wednesday. Can you have this done by Monday?"

"That will not be a problem, sir." He cocked his head, staring at me. "Captain Tallman," I added.

"My thanks for your kindness. Since I am just arrived to Barbados and have never set foot here before, I would relish the opportunity to learn about your island and its settlement. Have you lived here for many years?"

"I have lived here all my life."

"Well … I would fancy the honor of escorting you on a promenade through your village, where you might familiarize me with the sights. May I possibly have your father's permission to escort you on Thursday evening and have you home by sunset? I can meet with your father this evening to solicit his blessing."

"I am flattered. It would be Mum's permission you will need. My father died last year."

"I am sorry to hear about your father, Miss Ann." His smile vanished momentarily and his visage reflected the seriousness of his words. "May I meet with your mother and ask her permission to spend some time with you? I am sure she would not approve absent meeting me."

"Sir …." I paused for a moment and smiled. "I would be honored, with permission, Captain Tallman. My mum is here at the shop. I will get her."

Out of the corner of my eye I saw Peter watching the hem of my green dress as it brushed the frame of the doorway into the next room.

"Mum, remember that gentleman you saw visiting with me at the market last Saturday? Well, he brought in this jacket to be mended." I handed the jacket to Mum. "I have the order at the front table and will bring it to you. But he has invited me for a promenade and wants your permission and blessing." I paused. "I would like to go."

"Well, Ann. I told you, did not I, that you are catching the eye of many a young man. And you seem eager to go on this promenade. Precisely who is this gentleman?"

"He introduced himself as Captain Tallman. He neglected to say where he was from, though his English has an accent. He said he was on his way to Newport. Beyond that, I know nothing more of him or his family."

"Newport. Where is that? I do not recall your father traveling to a place called Newport."

"He is waiting out front."

"Yes. I will have a word with him. Let me see what sort of impression he makes on me." She laid the red jacket on her worktable and then winked as she rose and walked through the doorway. I followed her.

"Good day, sir. Ann tells me that you wish to keep company with my only daughter. I'm afraid we have not met."

"Forgive me. I am Peter Tallman. I hail from Germany, though my family is from Amsterdam, and I am en route to the colonies, with Newport to be my new home. I am a trader of goods and an apothecary. I met your delightful daughter on Saturday at the market and would be honored to escort both of you on a promenade through the town this Thursday, if that please you. As I told Miss Ann, I am eager to hear more of this settlement in Barbados."

"That is quite generous of you, Mister Tallman. I am Madam Hill; you may call me Elizabeth. My husband, Phillip, succumbed to tuberculosis last year. He and I immigrated here to this island from England many years ago, with the first settlers. Ann and I would be honored to accompany you on Thursday. My daughter, Ann, is but eighteen, and you are gracious to invite me, as I would have insisted on a chaperone."

Peter smiled.

"As is our custom here, we would welcome you to our home for refreshment following our walk. I would take great pleasure in preparing for you some of our local foods."

"That is kind. I would be honored to partake. I am finding that the people of Barbados are exceptionally welcoming." He smiled at Ann, standing in the doorway behind her mother. "I will meet you here on Thursday around four o'clock, if you are free at that time.

"Yes," replied Mum.

"Good day, Miss Ann." He tipped his head in my direction. "Elizabeth."

The door closed as he left. "Thank you, Mum."

"Well, he seems like a proper gentleman, and I'm sure you have noted he is strikingly handsome as well. I believe he has taken quite a liking to you. I'll finish that new brocade dress I am sewing and, if you like, you can wear that on Thursday."

"Yes, but he is leaving next week," I shared, with some anxiety.

"Well, dear, the ships sail both ways."

***

On Thursday evening I sat with an embroidery piece in my lap, practicing on a new stitch, the split stitch Mum had shown me. I had already put on my new blue brocade Mum had finished, with its tucks and pleats on the bodice and the velvet ribbon Mum had sewn at the waist. The shop would close in a few minutes, and I was fetching butterflies in my chest anticipating Peter's visit, while Mum was busying herself with cleaning up the sewing room and carefully folding her finished work. She, too, had worn her good dress, but, except for her flitting around the room putting away her cutting board and iron shears, she seemed calm, unlike myself.

"Mum, I am full of anxiety. What if Captain Tallman thinks I am foolish?"

"Oh, Ann, there is no good reason to distress. It is just a walk, dear. And a meal," she added as an afterthought. "As you said, he will be gone next week. Let us have a good time. You are a strong young woman; just be who you are and do mind your manners. I know that we live here in Barbados where our ways are more informal, but Captain Tallman seems otherwise."

"Yes, Mum." As I knotted my stitches, I heard the bell ring as the front door opened. I placed my piece and thimble in my wooden box on the shelf.

Antoine poked his head around the corner.

"Liz, you have a visitor. A Captain Tallman." He turned and winked at me.

Mum squeezed my hand as we left the back room, and we made our welcomes to Peter and introduction to Antoine as we bid him good day.

"Do not you both look splendid today." Peter smiled as we departed the shop, stepping onto the main street in town, a street beginning to bustle with workers heading for home and a few newly arrived sailors searching for their land legs.

"I have found the boardinghouse where I am staying to be quite pleasant. My family, though in Germany, are from the Netherlands, so I've learned a bit of Dutch along with my German and English, all the tongues being of use at the tavern." We continued walking, away from the docks. "After weeks at sea following years at war in the kingdom, this lush and tropical paradise of yours is a respite. I must admit I am a bit reluctant to depart this paradise, thus I am eager see your town and hear more about Barbados."

"Yes," said Mum, "but our community is yet small and will not take long to see. You fought in the war? I have heard of the struggles in the empire."

"Yes, we have been at war within Germany, invasions from the French and the Swedes, and throughout Saxony, with my family in Hamburg in the midst and suffering great loss. The church is much at issue in the fight, yet the Lord Himself has blessed me in my battles; but enough talk of war."

"Well, Captain Tallman, then let us walk toward the parish. The first church was built in Jamestown when we first arrived, and later this one in Christ Church. Jamestown is truly where the Barbados community began in 1627. That is when my dear late Phillip and I left Bristol and, with Captain Henry Powell, arrived here as new settlers."

We walked down the well-traveled road toward the only church in our village. Mum had told me I was baptized at the church in the parish of St. James as an infant. The sea breeze rustled through the leaves and played with my skirt. I was feeling more relaxed and could see the many hues of pink painted through the clouds as the sun lowered toward the horizon.

"So, you arrived with the first settlers here to the island?" he asked.

"Yes, my husband, rest his soul, and I came with the first settlers, on the king's ship *Olive Blossom*; Captain Powell saw this as a place of prospect, with the crops of tobacco and fruits, and now sugar cane. Of course, the blessing is the climate. I hear the winters are brutal in the colonies. And yet you wish to go there?"

"Yes, I do. But you are correct about the beauty of this place. I have sailed to Newport once, two years ago. It was the spring when I arrived at the shores of Newport and Plymouth, where the forests and waters were enchanting, and the English were busy building towns and governments. I found it to be a fortuitous place where I may bring my trades and skills to the growing colonies. There is great need for goods and medicines, so my services would be welcomed and I can grow my small endeavor; I am certain."

"Yes, I am confident of your prediction," answered Mum, "as such services are still welcome here. Our parish is still small and isolated, thus Ann and I are fretfully eager for new shipments from England that bring fabrics and threads for our work."

"So where is this place you call Newport?" I asked.

"Newport and Portsmouth are young settlements in the Island of Rogues, Aquidneck, an island on the sea. These towns have sprung from the settlements to the north at Boston and Plymouth. Aquidneck is a fertile land woven through with bays and rivers. The foundation of these new settlements is within their freedom of religious belief, as contrasted by the strict Puritans to the north; free thought being an attribute I am drawn toward after the Lutheran immersion in Germany causing so much conflict."

As they neared the parish building, Peter observed, "Your church here is simple and does not equal the grandeur of those in England and Germany. But what grandness do you need when it is all before you in the blue waters of this calm sea and the gilded sunsets. God's gifts are the grandeur of your church."

"Yes. You are a wise man, Captain Tallman, to see that. It is what we cherish of Christ Church." Mum paused, looking toward the cemetery.

"Our settlements are suddenly growing," Mum continued, "with the defeat of the Royalists in England. I am sure you have encountered them in your voyages."

"Yes. I have befriended one or two Royalists in my journeys. The empire is furthermore sending debtors to the new world. I hope to indenture one or two for my journey to Newport."

We turned and headed back down the road in the direction of the docks, the opposite end of the town. As we passed the tailor shop, Peter loosened the rein on his horse he had left tethered and led her behind us. He said the horse belonged to his generous landlord at the boardinghouse in the town of St. Michael.

"The general store, over there, did have an apothecary inside; but now there is only one in the port town," I pointed out to the captain.

"Ann, do you sing at the church?" Peter asked.

"Yes, how did you know that?"

"Well, someone as captivating as you surely can sing as pleasingly as these yellow canaries I see here."

I blushed and retorted, "Those are yellow finches, but yes, both Mum and I do sing with the parish." We passed the tavern, and Mum guided us inland from the docks toward our little house amidst the orchards.

Our home was clapboard with a clay-tiled roof, and surrounded by the flowering bushes my mum had planted so many years ago, now overgrown and full of blossoms. Inside the front door was a sitting room, with a stove for the rare cold days. Then there was the large kitchen, with a cooking stove and our grand pine table Pa had built near the stairs that led up to my bedroom. Mum's room was on the lower floor beside the kitchen. Pa had added a door from the bedroom, at the side of the house. He built these about five years ago as a gift to Mum; the doors opened out into Mum's gardens, where she grew vegetables and flowers.

At home in our cozy kitchen, Mum served us glasses of juice from the pineapple; Peter was astounded by its sweetness and delighted by the unexpected nectar. Mum baked pones and saltwater trout with a tart citrus sauce, and we dined, talked and laughed at the table until late into the evening. Peter's laughter filled the house, laughter such as we had not heard since Pa died. As we ate and drank, the captain shared tales of his adventures in Germany and his voyages at sea. He was a fine storyteller. Finally, making note of the late hour, he made his thanks and took my mum's hand, bent down and kissed the back of her hand gently. He then took my hand and kissed it so gently, a gesture I was not familiar with but found charming. As he walked to the door, Mum invited Peter to join us again the next evening and he eagerly accepted, nodding his head, and smiled at me before departing.

"Well, dear," Mum said as we cleaned the dinner table, "that is a generous and enchanting man. And he is quite ambitious in his plans, and likely a much better husband than you could find here on the island." She said this with a tinge of sadness in her voice, and then giggled when she saw she had made me blush at the mention of a husband.

Chapter 3

Ann

Peter made the decision to remain in town, to delay his trip to Newport, telling us how impressed he had become with the island; he was eager to take advantage of trading opportunities in the nearby seas, evidenced by the many ships arriving and departing. He boarded at a room near the Roebuck Tavern, near the docks; and as the weeks went on, Peter continued to visit our home several evenings each week, eager to partake of Mum's cooking and conversation, and often playing a game of whist until we could no longer be silent and laughter ensued. One evening Peter brought a large, unbroken conch shell he had found on the beach. He displayed the delight of a boy, astonished by the shell's perfection, its natural beauty. Peter was enchanting.

He appeared to feel at home in our parish, and he had not hidden his affection for Mum and myself. He had acquired his own horse for travels, and on several occasions he had even attended the parish services with us; the local citizens came to know him as part of the community. At the docks and the Roebuck Tavern, where he favored sampling our varied rums, he continued to barter with incoming ships and merchants and even added some local tobaccos and rum to his inventory as he became acquainted with the plantation masters. His liaisons with the plantation owners and gentlemen traveling from England had only strengthened his status on the island, as well as his desire to stay. Peter contracted with a warehouse at the dock to store his goods while in Barbados, but he was yet determined to journey to Newport in the Isle of Rogues.

With my brother Robert gone often to sea, Mum and I were fortunate to have Jeremy nearby. Jeremy had been a servant Pa had indentured at the docks, many years before. He had been a godsend to Pa, to Pa's trading company, and to us as well. He had been like another brother, and when his indenture had ended, Jeremy stayed on to help for three more years before moving to a cottage he had built on adjacent land Pa had gifted him. We shared the barn between. When Pa died last year, it was Jeremy who looked after us as well as our properties. Though Mum and I were respected in our small community, Jeremy was ever present to chase off rogue sailors or beggars, usually unbound slaves, pillaging our orchards.

It was the Christmas holidays when Peter came to join Mum and me for dinner on the evening before Christmas Day. But Mum was feverishly ill when he arrived, and I was panicked. When the sudden, loud knock came, I caught my breath and opened the door, praying that Peter or whoever it might be could help.

"Mum is not well and so feverish. I am frightened for her," I said, my words stilted between my distraught breaths.

"Let me see her," he said as he shut the door against the stormy winds. "I have heard the yellow fever comes and goes here often on the island. Is she partaking of food and liquid?"

"No, but a mere drink. She is so warm. Hot, truly. I know you have dispensed medicines. Please, can you help her?"

Peter took my hand and squeezed it gently. I led him to Mum's bed. She was fitfully asleep and wet with fever.

He placed his hand on her head, holding it momentarily yet showing no expression of concern. He sat in the chair I had placed by Mum's bed, watching her as the moments passed in silence. I stood there watching and waiting, unsettled inside.

Suddenly, Peter rose from the chair. "You get some drink in her. I am going to get my medicinal case. I will be back quickly, as quickly as I can ride."

He was gone as suddenly as a ghost, and I went to the kitchen to get some water and juice from a fresh citron. I poured some in the vessels and took them to Mum. It was not easy to wake her, as she seemed delirious. She took a few drops of the citron and more water than I had expected.

She looked at me. "Dear Ann, I will fight." Her voice weak, she added in a whisper, "I cannot leave you."

I cooled Mum's face with a wet rag, pressing it gently, and then her neck, so hot.

"Mum, the captain is bringing some medicines. He will help. I know he will, Mum," I said softly as she fell back into a fitful sleep.

I sat with her, waiting for the captain. My mind wandered. Had Peter really been here? He had arrived and left so quickly. Was his presence but a vision? So many had died here on the island from diseases brought by outsiders; Mum could not be one of them. I prayed she would not be one of them. Just as night's darkness began to surround the house, Peter returned and came into the room with a small bag.

"How is she? Did she take some drink?"

"Still fitful, but she drank a bit of citron and some water."

He lifted some bottles from his bag. "This medicine is opium from the east and will help her fever. And this one is an herb," he said as he revealed a second bottle. "It will help make her stronger. Beyond that, we can only pray. Go get a small vessel for the opium, and I will need you to heat some water for the ginseng. Bring the vessel first so I may give her the drug for her fever."

I ran to get the vessel and took it to Peter. Then I started a fire and heated some water. Peter joined me.

"I gave Elizabeth the medicine. It will take some time to work. Here is the herb. Put this amount into the hot water and let it sit a bit. Then we will try to get her to drink this and wait."

He looked into my worried eyes. "She will be better. The sleep will do her well, and if she is worse tomorrow we will call upon the physician for a bloodletting. We do not want quacksalvers caring for her. I will be certain to find a reputable physician." He sat silent, almost as if in prayer, for a few minutes. "I know God has blessed us. She will not leave us."

With tearing eyes, I moved toward Peter, and he gathered me into his arms and held me as I held onto him tightly, filled with hope that he was right.

"Ann, I think it is time you started calling me Peter. You know my affection for you, as well as your mother. We are family and you need not call me Captain."

After a few moments, calmed by Peter's confidence and warmth, I took the warm drink to Mum and Peter woke her. She drank most of the water steeped with ginseng and, though weak, seemed aware of our presence.

"Bless you both," she whispered, her weakness evident and frightening.

I sat by Mum as Peter stood nearby, and we watched quietly as Mum fell into sleep. It seemed a deeper sleep, less restless. As she slept, we returned to the kitchen, where I fixed some plates of breads and guava jam, and added some cheese that Peter had brought us earlier in the week. I poured some wine, and we sat, eating and drinking in an easy silence, at the table.

As I was cleaning up after our meager meal, Peter came and took me by the hand and led me to the sitting room. The room was dark, but Peter took his pewter tinderbox from a pocket and, striking the flint against the steel, lit the small candle on the table. With the shadows highlighting his cheekbones and thick lashes about his pale eyes, he appeared so handsome in the flickering light. It was difficult for me to call him Peter; he was tall and strong and was still Captain Tallman to me. As I sat in the chair that had been Pa's, Peter sat near to me on the wooden stool. He rested his hand on my arm, sending an unexpected warmth to my very core.

"My sweet Ann, I have come to love you and your mother as family. I regret that your mum is so ill, but we will get through this. I will be here for both of you. Tomorrow we will prepare a small feast for the holiday and, as God answers our prayers, Elizabeth can partake of some. I will bring some staples from the tavern tomorrow. But for now, it is the holy holiday. God has blessed me, and, to show my affection for you, I have brought you this gift."

He picked up a small, engraved wooden box he had set on the floor, handing it to me. The box itself was oddly elegant, carved with flowers and a bird pattern on the lid. I looked into Peter's blue eyes as he nodded for me to open it.

I lifted the lid and there was the most exquisite ruby necklace, more elegant than anything I had ever owned, had ever seen.

At first my face was stilled by awe at the beauty of his gift, and as I revealed my surprise, Peter said, "This is near as beautiful as you are to me."

"Oh, what can I say? I have never worn anything as grand as this."

"But, Ann, you are worthy of such jewels. You shall wear it as if a queen in Barbados and look beautiful, as ever, at my side."

I put the necklace around my neck and Peter helped me clasp the silver chain.

"See. As stunning as you," he said, and he kissed my hand, then my cheek.

"Thank you, Peter. I cannot wait for Mum to see it."

"Tomorrow, dear. She will be well enough tomorrow."

I prayed he was right. No amount of jewels in the world could make up for not having my mum.

Peter lit his pipe and sat in a chair near me. I did relish the smell of his tobacco, a fragrant leaf he purchased at the tavern. I pulled out my linen piece with my stitching and went to work to keep my mind otherwise occupied, and Peter told stories of his life in Germany. We checked on Mum periodically, and when she seemed, finally, to be resting better, Peter said he would leave for the evening, adding that he would stay if I liked or, otherwise, would be back to see us in the morning. I told him that he should go and get some rest and, because of Mum's illness, we would not be going to parish in the morning.

"We will have a quiet day. I will send Marianne, a servant at the tavern, to help you cook. Ann, it is good your mum is sleeping soundly, but if you need help, send Jeremy for me." He leaned in and kissed me softly on the cheek. My fingers went to the necklace at my nape.

"I do not need a servant to help tomorrow; I can prepare the meal. Thank you, Peter, for everything you have done tonight. And for the gift." As I leaned in to kiss him on the cheek, he turned his head and my lips softly met his.

Despite my objection, Marianne arrived in the morning and we prepared a small meal for Jeremy, Peter and myself. Mum had slept through the night and her fever had lessened. We prayed at the meal, thankful for our Christ, our food and our family. As Peter said "Amen," Mum walked into the room and said she would like a bit of nourishment. We all laughed as we rose to hug Mum and welcome her back from Death's door.

Chapter 4

Ann

Though Peter had continued to visit us for dinner and games several times a week through the year, he left the island in the midst of summer to trade and meet with persons of influence in Bermuda and then Antigua, where he added parcels of indigo and local ginger to his inventory. He returned to our island in September, and Mum and I were glad to see him again when he rode out to our village. Our home had been peculiarly quiet during his absence, but he wasted no time in resuming his regular visits for dinner, delighting Mum with the town's gossip and stories of the islands he visited.

It was a Friday in late November of 1648, and Peter walked through the front door as Mum and I were closing the shop for Antoine, who had gone down to the docks to gather a new fabric shipment. I was excited for tomorrow so I could see the new yardages and maybe choose one for myself.

"Good day, young ladies." He flashed a smile at Mum. She enjoyed Peter's charming ways and how easily he could make her laugh. I relished the sound her laughter; Mum had been quite somber during the years after Pa's death. Her former easy spirit, through God's grace, was returning, and this brought me much joy.

"Good day, Peter." I smiled as I reached for the keys to lock up the store. "Mum is making oyster soup tonight, and I think she has made a tart for dessert."

"I do love a good tart." He winked at me, as he oft did when he made me blush.

I had come to feel comfortable around Peter. Last week, as we walked in the orchard, he had kissed me. It was a soft, gentle kiss, unlike a more urgent one a month earlier as we found ourselves alone in the kitchen one evening cleaning the dinner table. In their own way, each kiss had taken my breath away. I'd never felt such warmth run through my whole being, but then, I had never been kissed before. I wondered if Mum had been watching, but she had said nothing.

I locked the front door at the shop, and the three of us walked toward our buggy. Peter rode his horse aside us and shared the stories he had heard at the tavern that afternoon, as Mum giggled and gasped when she heard a story about one of her friends or someone she knew. At the house, Peter gave Mum some ginger he had brought for her to use in the dishes she prepared, and we enjoyed a dinner of oyster soup and breads. Mum made cups of coffee for each of us and served her citrus tart as we sat at the table.

As we were finishing our coffee, Peter took on a serious look, prompting me to hold my breath. Peter seldom turned somber. I became full of anxiety for what news may come with his changed mood, for I had known, in my heart, that he would at some time depart for the colonies.

"Lizbeth, I cannot convey to you my gratitude, which is great, for how you have welcomed me into your home and into this community. You are like family to me. It has been almost two years since I arrived, and you and Ann have made this feel like home for me. But I must tell you that I have contracted with the *Golden Dolphin* in the harbor to take myself and my goods on to Newport. The captain has scheduled his crew to depart in six weeks, and it is time I start growing my wealth, as my trading has subsided here and my inventory sits idle. I hear that the Isle of Rhodes has collected a strong community, and you know I left Germany to be a part of these opportunities."

"Oh my" was all Mum could muster. Her jaw tightened and she exuded an unwelcome sadness. Seeing this, Peter reached across the table and placed his hand on hers, holding it there to comfort her.

"I have come to care for you both. Deeply," he continued. "I know that my affection for your daughter has been no secret to you, and to think I could begin a new life in the colonies without her disheartens me. Thus, in the absence of Ann's father, I am pleading for your blessing, Lizbeth, and God's blessing, to ask for your daughter's hand in marriage."

With this, he paused and glanced toward me. My heart was pounding in my chest. I had imagined this could happen, but was so easy with our current life I had not seen the suddenness of it upon us. I smiled, a tentative and awkward smile, and then looked down, awaiting, breathless, Mum's response. All I could hear was my heart beating within my chest.

The silence seemed endless, as I sensed that Mum was clearly taken sudden by Peter's plea. I looked up at Mum. The surprise on her face was clear, but surely she must have known this was to happen. Had not she teased me about Peter's making a suitable husband? She looked toward me and smiled a smile that was mixed with both joy and sadness, and then turned back to Peter.

"Peter, my dear Peter, you are like a son to me; and, therefore, I cannot refuse your request, and know that you are a good match for my Ann. May it be clear that even with my blessing, this will be Ann's choice. It remains that she is my only daughter and I will be heartbroken at her absence. Yet her happiness and future are hers to choose, nor should they be mine to deny."

"I understand, Elizabeth. Ann and I will talk, with your blessing. But you must know that I would want you to travel with us. You are welcomed in my home wherever it may be, as I have shared that you, too, are my family. I know you have your home here, but please consider my offer. It is from the heart. Though I hereby profess my love for Ann, I love you both."

"Oh, dear, this is so much." There were tears in Mum's eyes.

"I will let you take it in, Lizbeth. I know this is a heavy decision, and I know well how much you cherish your home of Barbados. May I speak alone with Ann?"

"Aye. Give me a few moments alone," responded Mum, sitting with her hand on her bosom. I watched Mum, knowing her heart must be pounding in her bosom, as was mine.

Peter took my hand as I rose from the chair, and we walked through the back door and toward the orchards. It was the dry season, and the sun was setting to the west over the mountains. In the midst of the symmetrically set trees, Peter took my hand in his and kissed it.

"Ann, you do not need to answer me at this moment, but I am making preparations for the voyage and time is of the essence in those preparations. I love you. That first moment I saw you at the market, my heart leapt. I know that Isle of Rogues, where I am going, is far, and I know life there will be harsher than your life here; but I cannot bear this life journey without you by my side." He paused.

Before I could say a word, he took me into his arms and kissed me softly, as he had done the week before. Then he kissed me as he had the first time, with the weight of his body against mine as I leaned into the orange tree behind me; I kissed him back with an urgency matching his own. The trees around us hung heavy with fruit, and the oranges, ripened for harvest, glowed with the promise of pure sweetness. Peter stepped back. "Tell me, Ann, before God, tell me you feel the same?"

"Yes. Yes, I do not want to be away from you. I treasure my home here, but I will go wherever, as your wife." The words slipped gracelessly off my tongue. "Yet there is so little time to prepare."

"I well know. Please forgive me my haste, but I have already spoken with the priest at the parish church. He can marry us on the second day of the new year." He winked at me and grinned. "Yes, my little one, I was presumptuous that you would agree to be my wife. With your blessing, I will arrange the documents."

Hands held, we walked slowly, silently, back into the house to see if Mum had recovered from the surprise of Peter's news. She had cleaned the kitchen and appeared cheerful. She walked over to us and hugged Peter, knowing by the glow in my eyes, without a word being exchanged, that I had accepted his proposal.

We sat at the table and talked excitedly through the evening. Mum wanted to go with us, but she was wavering, since this place was her true home and where Pa would forever remain. Yet I knew deep in my heart that she would not let me go alone, so there was much to prepare.

Mum decided that Jeremy could oversee the home and the orchards for my brother Robert, who would return to the island intermittently. In the mornings, Jeremy worked at the small tavern that sat between our orchards and the beach where the fishermen kept their boats. He was saving to purchase more land so he could grow and trade sugar cane.

"I want Jeremy to keep any profits made from maintaining and marketing the orchards, as it will be fruits of his own labor," said Mum.

"Since you choose to come with us, Lizbeth, that sounds fair," added Peter.

Jeremy, who had emigrated through his indenture from Ireland at only thirteen, had joined us for dinner a couple of times with Peter, and they appeared to get on well.

"I will find temporary quartering for us in Newport as soon as we arrive. It should not take long for me to open my apothecary." Peter could not restrain his excitement about the trading opportunities that would soon greet him in the colonies to the north.

"I have seen that the land is forested and woven through with bays, inlets and rivers. I have been told that the Indians there are friendly and trade with the settlements, so there is no need to be fearful," he added, sensing my wariness of this new place.

"Indians? You are speaking of savages?" I asked.

"They trade with the colonists. There is no need to fear," Peter assured me. My neck tightened, and my hands grasped and gathered the fabric of my skirt, hidden beneath the table.

Chapter 5

... the sun on the horizon peeks below
from clouds grown full and dark with night,
the winds approaching full of woe...

Ann

Mum wrapped her arms around me tight and hugged me as we readied for bed that night, after Peter had left.

"All will be fine, dear. I am certain of it. We will check the new fabrics tomorrow morning, and I will find an elegant yardage to make you a beautiful gown. I asked Jeremy to see if he will find us some trunks to pack our belongings, but I presume Peter has some at the warehouse we may use."

I lay in my bed, in my loose muslin gown, my hair brushed free, my eyes wide open. Before sleep found me, I was restless and my mind raced. What would my new life be like in this place called Newport, so far away? Then I thought of my wedding. I could not wait to see the gown Mum would stitch. Of course it would be special, as Mum's work is exquisite. Would my new home be dangerous? What about the Indians? Are the sunsets beautiful, as I see here? The thoughts would not stop racing on and on in my head, keeping me from sleep.

When sleep finally came, it was an uneasy sleep. Pa came home. He embraced Mum, and I followed as he walked through the orchards with her, holding her hand as I remembered when I was a young child. The vision was comforting; a sense of peace filled my dream. As the warm sun hung low in the sky, hazily throwing light through the trees, I ran to catch up with them. Pa took my hand, and then, leaving Mum behind, he and I walked toward Dover Beach. I told him about Peter, how we had met at the market, how handsome and strong and smart he was, and I told him of my betrothal. After telling Pa that we planned to leave Barbados, I took my shoes off and set them by the tree so I could feel the sand and the surf on my bare feet. I had not walked in the sea's surf with my Pa for so long. As the bubbling sea foam of the breaking waves played with my toes, the sun suddenly dimmed and the clouds blanketed the shore, but I still saw Pa through a sudden mist.

"Be careful, little Ann. Things are not always as they seem." His voice was fading, further and further away. "Trust God, dear Ann ... and be...." His words moved from whisper to disquieting silence. He faded away; I did not hear the last word or words. I ran faster and faster after him, toward where I had last seen him, through the mist and the waves breaking on the sand, suddenly cold, calling out "Pa? Pa?" But Pa was gone. I felt a chill.

I awoke suddenly and wrapped myself in my blanket to warm the chill that came from nowhere. I was saddened that this was but a dream and Pa was not here with us. Though my dream had felt comforting and full of Pa's presence, and though the smell of Pa seemed all around me as I sat in my bed, a sense of foreboding filled me with an eerie uneasiness.

Chapter 6

Ann

The new year had come, and there was to be a wedding at Christ Church Parish. After the wedding, Mum and I would be traveling with Peter to Newport in the colonies for the beginning of a new life. I prayed there would not be savages, and Peter had assured me that the town where we would live was civilized and growing. Peter could not contain his elation when speaking of the growth and community in the colonies.

For the past few days, I had helped Mum and Adelaide make tarts and prepare vegetables for the celebration after my wedding ceremony. Mum had asked Jeremy to purchase a lamb for slaughter, and he would help on the wedding day with grilling the feast. God blessed us to yet have Jeremy as a great friend beyond his years of indenture, but Pa had treated Jeremy like family. He had helped set tables in the orchard near our home. Mum pulled linens and candlesticks from her old trunks, washing and polishing as she readied for the occasion. The air was thick with excitement.

When I awoke on my wedding day, I found the sun rising bright in the sky, and I felt like both the girl I had been and the woman I was about to become, a confused mixture of a young girl and the grace and courage I had gleaned from Mum. I stood straight, a posture that betrayed my youth and folly. I knew in my soul that I would be saying goodbye to the carefree young Ann. Today was a bridge to my new life, my new life as Mrs. Peter Tallman. I went down the stairs to the back of the house and pumped fresh water into the pitcher, kissing Mum on the cheek as I walked back through the kitchen. "Well, don't you have a spring in your step this morn." She smiled at me. In my room, I poured the water into the basin and carefully washed my face, then my arms and legs, and powdered with the fragranced talc Antoine and his wife, Maria, had gifted to me. I took the crisply folded linens from the shelf and placed them on my bed, neatly tucking the edges and dressing the crisp cottons, sweet-smelling from the sea breezes. Thinking of my freshly dressed wedding bed, I filled with an apprehensive anticipation. I quickly put on my favorite red skirt and white cotton blouse, then skipped down the steps to breakfast with Mum. She had made some strong coffee and fruit, mangoes and oranges, with pones.

"Do you need some help with your dress, dear?" Mum asked.

"I may later, Mum. I will get dressed and call you when I am almost ready." After I helped Mum in the kitchen, I climbed the steps and gently unfolded my gown.

The dress was intricate and polished. There was a certain weight to it, giving it substance. Mum had worked on it at the shop when time allowed, and every evening at home. We had gone through Antoine's new shipment of fabrics and Mum had found a creamy silk damask with a tinge of green. She had said that the green would be a symbol of fertility, clearly something she had thought of but I had not. Another unknown: would there be many children? Contemplating this made me so grateful that Mum would be with me. I could not even begin to think of children, of larger responsibilities, not while my thoughts were of Peter and how his nearness made me giddy.

Yes, back to my dress. The embroidery Mum had stitched on the bodice was delicate, yet added depth to the pale background. There were red and gold flowers with green leaves, large leaves as well as some that appeared dainty. There were tiny embroidered birds of brilliant purples and deep greens flitting amongst the flowers on the fitted bodice, which ended in a low waist, where Mum placed soft gathers for the skirt. The colors were so intense and Mum's satin stitches so lush that it appeared as if these tiny birds were truly hovering about my dress, like a vision from the fairy tales Pa read to me as a child. A deep-purple velvet ribbon had been stitched and embellished with beads across the squared neckline, and Mum had added purple silk cord through the eyeholes in the back that laced up my gown. It was a dress worthy of this day, worthy of the gifted ruby necklace I would ask Mum to fasten at my neck. There was a fullness of gathered fabric at the back of the skirt. I believe Mum said it was called a bustle in England. Mum had even covered my shoes with matching brocade.

I braided and pinned my hair, and now I was dressed and waiting for Mum. As I stood there, before my mirror, waiting, I breathed in the beloved smells of the ocean beyond my window and silently took in the meaning of this most special day. Peter would be my husband; I, his wife. Mum walked toward me, dressed in a deep emerald. She looked serene.

"You are a most radiant bride, my sweet Ann. Oh, how I wish your Pa could be here to see you today, and your brother, Robert. My sweet young daughter will be a wife, and with a handsome husband who I believe will provide well for you. God has blessed us with Peter. Are you happy, dear Ann?"

"Aye, Mum." I gently hugged her so as not to muss my dress. "I am so happy. Mum, I do not know if I could have done this without you. I am filled with joy that you are coming with us."

"I believe we are all blessed at this moment. Yes." Mum looked at me up and down, smiling. "I suppose they will soon be waiting at the church. Are you ready?"

"Yes, but might you please fasten this necklace?" I handed her the ruby necklace Peter had given me.

"My dear, yes. We must not forget this," she said as she fastened the hook. "There, those rubies at your throat look as if they belong with the deep colors on your bodice. It does complete it. Your hair looks pretty, but let's find a winter blossom to add."

I was full of joy, yet there was a knot in my chest. This was the only life I had ever known. At the garden, Mum cut a late-blooming white dogbane and pinned it above my ear. Jeremy met us with the buggy. We rode in silence the short distance to the church. Once there, I walked with Mum past the cemetery, aside the church, where Pa was buried. Mum's hand reached for my shoulder and she hugged me before she walked into the church. I stood alone before the entrance.

As I approached the door of the Christ Church parish, I found the priest and Peter awaiting me. Peter stood tall and dapper in formal attire, with his deep-blue jacket adorned with gold braid and a crisp white collar beneath. I was glad he had not worn the wig, the style of many men. His head turned as I walked toward them and he smiled, with that twinkle in his eye, eyes nearly cobalt with the reflection of the hues of his jacket. The gleam in his eye made forgotten the knot in my bosom. The three of us entered the sanctuary, full of our dearest friends, and approached the altar, candlelit for the ceremony. As Father Hartley, the parish priest, cited the words of our troth, I could see the waves of the sea out the church window and could but imagine what life would be beyond here.

Chapter 7

Peter

This unforeseen aside in my journey to Newport, my staying here in Barbados almost two years, brought me to this day, this day that would alter the course of my life journey. *Da ist mein Glück gesegnet.* My happiness was truly blessed, a gift unexpected.

I was anxious to establish my freeman status in the Isle of Rogues and begin my trades. The stay here had indeed permitted my bartering to add to my apothecary staples that would expand my inventory, as well as my resources, for my shop. I had purchased as much rum as my trunks could hold, as well as tobacco. As gold in Newport. And, the day before, I made the purchase of three Negro slaves, two men and a woman, who had just arrived at the docks in St. Michael on a Dutch ship from Guyana. I had already contracted their transport on to Newport, along with my inventory and my new family. But, alas, the form and smile of a beautiful girl that had set this course two years before. My sweet Ann had glistening dark locks with lit throughout with auburn, and her green and hazel eyes drew me in.

When I first saw her at the market, I could not take my eyes from her.

Now we stood there, in the Christ Church parish. Ann was the unforeseen prize of my voyage; she would greatly ease my transition into life in Newport. She is a fine English girl from a good family.

"Dearly beloved, friends, we are gathered together here," recited the priest at the altar, "in the sight of God, and in the face of his congregation, to join together this man and this woman in holy matrimony, which is an honorable state, instituted of God in Paradise." There was a litany, recited by the deacon, with responses by the choir, praying for the gifts of chastity and of the blessing of children. Yes, I was certain there would be many children.

Ann was dazzling in her gown, with her thick dark hair pinned high and a simple white bloom. Suddenly, as a cruel interruption of graceful moments, I thought of the stories I had heard of the auctions of English women in Virginia, where they were sold as wives for wifeless settlers. I am a lucky man to have found such a wife, the beginnings of a strong family. I do hope the harsh climate will not be difficult for Ann and her mother. A new life is before us.

". . . the parents who have nurtured them . . . for the prayers of parents make firm the foundation of houses." I looked out the window and saw the blue-green calmness of the sea, knowing the Atlantic to the north is much more gray and wicked. The priest continued, *"for the groomsman and bridesmaid who are come together in this joy.*

"O Master, stretch forth Thy hand from Thy holy dwelling-place and conjoin this Thy servant Peter and this Thy handmaid Ann, for by Thee a woman is conjoined unto a man."

The priest took the two golden rings I had purchased in town, and he made the sign of the cross with Ann's ring over my ring, saying three times, *"The servant of God, Peter Tallman, is betrothed to the handmaid of God, Ann. In the Name of the Father and of the Son and of the Holy Ghost."*

The priest made the sign of the cross over us and slipped the ring on my right hand and then the other one on Ann's. We were now husband and wife.

"The right hand of Thy servants shall be blessed by Thy mighty word and Thine uplifted arm....

. *"Wives submit yourselves."* He addressed this to Ann. He passed a silver cup of wine to me. *"O God, Thou who hast made all things by Thy power, and hast established the universe and adornest the crown of all things that have been made by Thee, bless with a spiritual blessing this common cup given to those who are conjoined for the community of marriage."* I drank from the cup and the priest passed it to Ann, whereas she sipped of the wine. *"Amen."*

Taking the silver cup from Ann, the priest said, *"And thou, O Bride, be thou magnified as Sarah, and rejoiced as Rebecca, and increased as Rachel, being glad in thy husband, and keeping the paths of the law, for so God is well-pleased.*

"Be thou magnified, O Bridegroom, as Abraham, and blessed as Isaac, and increased as Jacob, walking in peace, and performing in righteousness the commandments of God."

The priest continued the prayers. *"Replenish their lives with good things, receive their crowns in Thy kingdom unsullied and undefiled, and preserve them without offence to ages of ages."* At this point I leaned in to kiss Ann, a soft and long-held kiss, and I felt her soft hand on the back of my neck. At this, the church filled with celebration and the priest blessed us as we left, walking hand in hand.

We departed, some walking, others in their buggies and on horseback, for Lizbeth's home, where there was planned a reception of local flavors with friends, as well as Jeremy and a trading companion of my own, Charles, who had arrived in Barbados last week. My friend Modyford, with his wife, was there. Tables were set through the orchard with white linens and candles. Elizabeth, Adelaide and her friends were placing food and pouring drink for the crowd, filled with laughter and happiness. I felt some trepidation at leaving this wonderful place for the unknown, but I had a fortune to build. Jeremy lit the candles at each table as the sun was setting, and the rum and ale flowed freely. The night was pure joy; tomorrow we would begin preparation for our journey.

My friend Charles stood and raised his glass. "Another round for good measure. My friend here, Peter, has claimed a most beautiful wife here in this paradise called Barbados. I do not quite grasp his hurry to leave all of this for the cold waters of the north. To you Peter, and Ann, may you have many children and great fortune in your new Rogues home. You are blessed. May we drink to ye both."

I took Ann's hand and stood as the crowd toasted and drank. "Charles, you are a true and blessed friend. And on this day, I am a blest man to have won the hand of Ann." I turned to Ann and kissed her on the cheek. "This is my prize from our treasured island. The last two years I have spent here have been the most blest of my life. And I have gained a mother here as well." I walked toward Elizabeth and took her hand, and, under the trees, danced with my new Mum as the celebrants applauded and laughter swirled about us.

I cannot recall the end of the evening, only a brief memory that Jeremy and Ann helped me into the house and up the stairs. I heard later that Jeremy had to take Charles back to town, as the libations had taken their toll on him as well.

Chapter 8

Ann

The gathering after our wedding was raucous and full of joy, with a bit too much drink. Even I, who seldom took much libation, felt light on my feet as the night ended. My hair tousled from dancing, I found that most of the guests had departed, and Mum and her friends were laughing as they put up the food still on the tables. Peter was, by now, unsteady on his feet, and Jeremy helped me get Peter to our wedding bed, because he had drank too much of the kill-devil and could barely stand. Jeremy, avoiding my eyes in an effort to conceal his unease, helped me remove Peter's boots and get him into bed.

"Ma'am, he will feel better in the morning. I believe we celebrated a bit much." And with those words said, Jeremy deftly departed to help Peter's friend Charles get back in town. Charles was in no better condition. I sat for a moment alone. Sitting on the side of my bed with its freshly tucked linens, I saw my gown creased and stained with wine. My eyes watered as my new husband lay sleeping, and I was unseen.

I had imagined this night differently; I had anticipated

the consummation of our vows, remembering Peter's tender kisses. Never had I envisioned this night as Peter drunken, in need of Jeremy helping him to bed, me sitting still and saddened. As I hung my wedding dress on the hook with care, there was no one there to embrace me. With the excitement of the day behind me, I fell into a deep sleep.

The winter dawn filtered sunlight through the window. It was quiet and I lay awake in stillness as the birds began deep-throated morning songs. It was then that Peter stretched his arm across my bosom and awoke, blinking at the light and finding his smile as he became aware of where he was. He reached for me and drew me to him. He kissed me long and hard, and I felt his manhood. My breath caught within my chest and was held as I took in the smells of soured ale mixed with unfamiliar desires. I had no chance to breathe anew as he kissed me long and drew me beneath him.

"Ann, I failed you last night. But I will wait no longer," he whispered, hoarse from the night's quaffing. He softly ran his fingers along my hairline, then even more gently over the nape of my neck. As my inhibition waned I kissed him as deeply, eagerly, as he had kissed me, and his eager hand reached, tenderly, below the lace of my cotton gown, touching my breast, and my whole being trembled. He held me tight for a moment, as if to ease my trembling. After a bit of fumbling with lacings, Peter and I haltingly melted into each other, becoming as one. When we were gloriously spent, we lay, amidst the applause of the birdsong. Peter's breath was warm on my cheek as he whispered, "I love you, Ann."

"Yes, ye do, Captain Tallman," I teased, and kissed him again.

He smiled and reached for the covers. With one grand movement of his arm he threw off the linens and ran his hand, gently, down the length and the curve of my unclothed body. "You are beautiful, my wife." He took in the nakedness and vulnerability of my figure and then pulled me close to him. "And funny as well." He laughed.

The morning sounds in the kitchen downstairs interrupted us. Peter smiled and pulled me back down beside him, and as he covered me with the linens, he said, "You are Mistress Tallman now. You can sleep as late as you like."

As the sun shone brighter through the windows, I fell back to sleep, and, when I awoke, Peter was gone. I donned my dressing gown and then found him in the kitchen with Mum, talking about his plans for Newport and arranging some help for her in packing for our journey. I kissed Peter on the cheek. Mum hugged us both and left for the shop to help Antoine with a few things.

***

I prepared a small dinner with Mum's fresh sweet potatoes and peas mixed with the meats from our gathering last night. Jeremy, with Mum's help, had tidied the yards after our celebration, and I had dinner readied when Peter returned from town.

"Well, ladies, I have arranged for Obbah and Miles to help with the packing and storage at the house. The best news is, the *Golden Dolphin* has a leakage and will be dry-docked for a few months for repairs. A gift of time."

Inside, I rejoiced with this news and saw my mum's face soften with relief as well. The delay in our departure was God's blessing, giving me more days in my beloved Barbados. And this meant that we would arrive in the colonies in the summer.

Peter chuckled. "I was certain this would not be bad news for my ladies."

"Let us celebrate that with a game of whist this evening after dinner," I suggested.

"We shall see later if there is time," retorted Peter quickly.

As we ate dinner, we spoke about what we would pack for the voyage and our new life, and what could stay at the house for Jeremy, and Robert upon his return. As I picked up the dishes, Peter grabbed me around the waist and kissed my forehead. "I have some paperwork to do." Peter lit his pipe.

"I need to see if I can contract the slaves out to Tom Modyford at his plantation before our delayed departure," Peter added as he walked toward the sitting room. Obbah was the female slave Peter had purchased here in the Barbados marketplace just before our wedding, along with two bucks, Zebediah and Mingoe. Miles was the English bondsman whose passage and services Peter had contracted.

Mum and I pulled out the cards and played a bit before Peter joined us for a brief time; then Mum, being tired, went to bed. She decided she would continue to work for Antoine as time allowed around our packing. I went up the stairway to undress for sleep, donning my embroidered muslin chemise I had stitched in December.

I poured some water from the pitcher into the washbasin and cleansed my face, and then loosened and brushed my hair, adding a bit of orange flower pomatum. As I turned down the bed linens I felt Peter's arms reach around my waist from behind. He brushed my hair to the side and kissed the back of my neck and shoulders. As I turned to face Peter, he gently pushed me onto the bed, where our lovemaking was urgent and eager, as two lovers first whetting their appetite for each other. My body spent and my heart full, we fell asleep in each other's arms.

The following months were full of preparation, with

mother anxiously going through trunks and finding what we would need in New England. She would leave the rest for Robert. The clothing and linens were held back to be packed last. At times, Mum would come across something, packed away for years, something that had come from England or had belonged to her mother or aunt so long ago. She would wrap these items carefully and pack them for our long voyage, hoping they would survive yet another trip. These were her treasures, and she hoped to pass them on to me one day, and eventually to her own grandchildren.

Peter traveled often to the growing plantations on the island, attempting to finalize his inventory for his apothecary in Newport, as his new friends at the pubs and the plantations would share stories of local remedies brought from afar, as well as those passed down from the old Arawak tribes, long ago fled to Trinidad. The time spent with the wealthy plantation owners was, for him, time well-spent in preparation for a future trade for tobacco, sugar and rum. His excitement about the future in Newport was contagious, and Mum and I were eager to see this new place.

My brother, Robert, returned from sea in early May, quite unexpectedly, and he was overcome with surprise by our preparations and upcoming departure. He fretted and pouted, knowing this had been our home for as long as he could remember.

"Little sister, I cannot believe you are now a married woman. How you have changed; my baby sister now grown into a woman, a wife." He hugged me, with awkwardness between us; disquiet between two siblings suddenly no longer children. "I do not know what I will do here without you and Mum. I am grateful that Jeremy is here and will help, what with my sailing. Our home will sit barren." Pausing, he looked sternly at me. "You love this man, Peter Tallman?"

"Oh, yes, with all my heart!" I exclaimed. "He will be home before dinner. I cannot wait for you to meet him. I am hopeful that you, sometime, will sail to the colonies, since I will miss you." Robert helped me move the chair and roll up the rug Mum had in the sitting room so that I could tie it for packing. "Here is a smaller rug over here that you can use in the room after we have gone." I told Robert all about Peter and how he had helped save Mum when she was sick, and Robert told me about his travels over the past two years to places such as Morocco and Spain, including a story of a fair young woman he had met in New Amsterdam. He seemed eager to return to New Amsterdam and see her again, but he shared that her father was rigidly Lutheran and strict. Her father would not be, likely, happy for his daughter to be taken away to another land, but Robert's passions appeared strong, and I imagined I might soon have a sister-in-law.

Peter had said we would board the ship in just three or four weeks. With the help that Peter had provided, most of our things were now stored with Peter's goods. Peter's servant, Miles, had been a blessing, and we had only to pack our clothing. Having never sailed, I was a bit apprehensive of the voyage before us. Mum had shared some of her memories of the hardships at sea, but she said we would not likely be so far out into the ocean as she had on her voyage from England. She had warned me of the seasickness and told me that it was better on the ship's deck, where one can see the horizon, than it would be down in the hold where we would sleep.

Peter arrived back at the house before sunset, and introductions were made. As we prepared the filets of kingfish with the ginger and citrus, and Mum warmed the beans from her garden, Robert and Peter spoke of trading at the table. Their sea travels were of interest to each other, and they found, through their stories, they had a few shared acquaintances and a fondness for Morocco. Robert was determined to stand on his own and aimed to recreate a business, such as Pa's trading company. The men appeared to get on well together. Robert expressed his disquiet over the well-being of Mum and myself. I found his protectiveness endearing. It was clear, in what I overhead, that Peter had encouraged Robert to travel to the new country with us. Peter's passion was contagious, and it would not surprise me if Robert changed his mind, in light of his heart being pulled toward New Amsterdam.

***

It was a warm morning in July when the day at the docks had finally come upon us. Our necessary goods were packed in our bags of leather and wool, and I stood there, next to Mum, a bit nervous but filled with anticipation for the journey and our new life. Peter and Robert, who had succumbed to Peter's persuasion and chose to move north with us, were in the depths of the ship overseeing that all of Peter's shipment was secure and naught left behind. Miles was safeguarding the slaves, Zebediah, Mingoe and Obbah, ensuring they were properly housed. The view of the town at St. Michael was so different from the ship's railings, and I watched the bustling on the streets afar and the church steeple and even the tobacco fields beyond, all that was familiar to me. My footing wavered as the ship rocked back and forth on the water. I braced myself for the journey as Mrs. Peter Tallman.

Chapter 9

Peter

The sun glowed golden. My goods were loaded in the hull of the *Golden Dolphin*, and I stood on the deck of the ship with my beautiful new wife and her mother. The journey was before us, the air full of excitement.

I took Ann's hand in mine. "Well, now is the beginning of our new adventure. Like your mum, you will be a settler. I have been so eager for this journey and pray we may see sights along the way besides the waves and horizons at sea." I kissed Ann's hand. "The captain said that we will stay over in New Amsterdam before going on to Newport."

Ann hugged me about the waist. As I looked into her eyes, I discerned a bit of apprehension in her smile, and kissed her forehead.

"Will the winters be terribly cold?" Ann smiled before I answered. "But I have you to keep me warm."

"I will find us suitable quarters, but you may have to remain on the ship for a day or two. I will arrange to store my goods immediately and then we can settle into a home." I looked at the busy crew on deck and the passengers bordering the deck. "In New Amsterdam we will visit my friend Pieter. With summer, I expect our voyage will not be tempestuous. I asked Zebediah to hang hammocks in our room below deck." I looked at Ann and assured her that the hammock might ease any seasickness.

The gangplank was finally pulled up and the anchors set free as we eased out of the narrow port. I saw tears on Ann's cheek and hugged her briefly, then went to find Zebediah, instructing him to show Ann and Elizabeth to our sparse room and carry the ladies' bags. After sending him on his way toward Ann, I found the captain to see if I could be of any help as the crew began raising the sails.

The seas were calm and the sun rising. The crew was armed in preparation for any chance encounter with pirates; though an encounter was unlikely, some pirates were known in the southern seas near Antigua, and our ship was laden with cargo. As we took to the open sea, it did not take long before some of the passengers were leaning over the rails of the ship. I soon found Ann in our room, sitting on the floor with a large bowl. I told her to go up to the deck; it was better to fix the eye on the horizon to ease her stomach.

Absent the busyness of work and chores, the days were long and tedious for myself as well as the family. To pass the time, I played some cards with Ann and Elizabeth on the deck. The women were more distressed than myself, with nothing to do, and Robert melded in with the ship's crew. Lizbeth and Ann had brought bits of stitch-work with them; and when the weather permitted, they spent time in the sunlight, sewing. On the eighth day, the waters became rough. The captain steered the ship closer to land but found no calmer waters, as it became clear the storm was large. Ann fretted as we sat in our dim room, and the ship pitched to and fro. I assured her that we would be safe and eventually pass through the turbulent waters, yet she suffered miserably with the sickness.

Elizabeth told stories as a distraction, stories about the sea voyage she and Ann's pa had endured when immigrating to Barbados. "We sailed through some bad storms in the Atlantic years ago when we left England, dear. Your pa and I were at first frightened, but your pa had both of us laughing through tears as he described dragons and sea monsters that we knew were imaginary villains. It is a passage to endure, and the captain knows well how to sail through this. I am certain we will be beyond this soon, God willing."

"I am certain God will protect us. I should be stronger, as the two of you are. But, I must share now, that it is more difficult now that I worry for another." She paused, looking toward us for understanding. "The nausea is more than the ship's swaying." She looked from her mum to me, her face pale and pitiful in its misery. "For I believe I am with child."

Robert walked in to join us, only to find a silence in the room, broken rhythmically with the waves crashing against ship's hull. The surprise of Ann's words took my breath as, at first, neither Elizabeth nor I could gather words to respond.

"Well, that is the best news I have heard on this day. And you, Lizbeth?" I said, breaking the silence. I rose unsteadily. "Are you as overjoyed as I?" I sat next to Ann and embraced her in my arms.

"Aye. Aye!" Elizabeth paused to share the news with Robert, then turned back to Ann. "But, Ann, how long have you kept this secret? How could you not have told me?" As I rose, Elizabeth took hold of my hand, moved close to Ann and hugged her daughter, both with joy and to hold tight as the waves rolled the ship. "Your child will be born a settler, on the Island of Rhodes."

"Mum, I had suspicions shortly before we left Barbados.

Oh my, I feel so ill," Ann said as she bent over in her agony.

Lizbeth turned to me. "Do you have a medicine, an herb, something that might ease Ann's stomach?"

"I may. My goods are stored deep in the hold, but let me look to see if there is a possible relief."

Touching the walls to keep my balance, I left the room, overjoyed at Ann's news, and I went up the precipitous stairway to the deck. The rain was hard and stung my face as I held to the ropes while the ship tossed and the seawater ran under my feet. I found the crew to see if there was anything at all that I could do. Some of the men were less concerned with maintaining their station than they were with not being thrown into the sea. The captain yelled in my direction that we were heading back out to sea; he thought we would be out of the storm soon. I waved an acknowledgement and yelled back at him that I had just learned I was soon to become a father; but he did not hear me, nor, I am certain, would he care, as the thunder roared and he turned to steer through the next wave.

***

Ten days after Ann revealed her secret, we docked in New Amsterdam. We would be at this town for two days, so I sent Miles to get some dairy goods for Ann while on dry land. Robert left the ship to visit with the family of the young woman, Hannah, who he hoped to court. Shortly after Robert left and Ann had eaten a bit, I contracted a buggy and, with Ann and Elizabeth, traveled to my friend Pieter Stuyvesant's home. Pieter, now general director of New Amsterdam, had come from the Netherlands. My family and his were friends in the old country, and I had traveled with him on one of my first voyages to the New World. Pieter had lost a leg to a cannonball in Saint Martin, and, as I remembered, walked unevenly with his wooden leg. He was generous to receive us and embraced me heartily in welcome. I was proud to introduce my family to him and his wife, Judith, who prepared us a most savory meal. Though Ann ate little, this visit in a civilized home was a good diversion from our sea voyage

"My friend Peter! You are fortunate, indeed, to be going to Isle of Rhodes, where I hear free conscience has taken root. It is an interesting concept Master Roger Williams has brought to this new colony."

"Aye, my friend. This very concept is what draws me to Newport. And the abundant prospects. The religious battles in the Habsburg Empire have worn me down. Yet these citizens of the isle clearly valued liberty more than all, and I want to be part of that."

The wars in Germany had been raging over the years since Pieter and I traveled to Plymouth, and then I heard of the Portsmouth Compact, which allowed religious tolerance. The dissidents who had colonized Newport intrigued me.

"You are a blessed man, Peter, to be settling there. But I must say that this damned democracy my people demand here is not productive. I have dealt with so much protest against taxation; yet it is just these taxes that provideth the people the security within the fort's wall and the new church. The Swedes have been troublesome as well. But the ill-tempered Kieft, who was here before me, Kieft who savagely battled with the Indians in this land, set the stage for our continuing battle. His brutal attacks on the Algonquins have hindered our relations with once-friendly natives. We are oft in greater danger," said Pieter.

I knew how Ann would react to this conversation. "I have been assured that such relations with the Indians at Aquidneck are more favorable. My family has had some concerns for safety, but, as they can see, your community here is flourishing and appears well fortressed."

Ann smiled in my direction, a clear knowingness on her face of my poorly veiled attempt to quell her fears and divert the subject of savages. I smiled and winked at Ann.

"Now that I am amongst dear friends, I must proudly share that on our voyage from Barbados, my beautiful new wife has revealed that I am soon to become a father," I boasted to my old family friend, in an attempt to change our topic of conversation. "This will be a wondrous gift, to have my first child born in the colonies, in Newport."

"Indeed," responded Pieter, raising his glass toward me. Judith smiled and added, "What a blessing for you, and you too, Elizabeth." With that news, Pieter and I toasted our good fortune and then retired for a smoke in the sitting room. I shared my plans to open the apothecary in Newport and discussed the trading contacts I had made in the islands. Pieter was well impressed with the resources I had availed and the coveted goods that might be available. We discussed the possibilities of getting some shipments of tobacco, sugar and rum to his forted city, and we discussed how soon I could travel and make such trades. As the hour got late, we wished each other well, and the ladies and I returned to the *Golden Dolphin*. Ann and Elizabeth both expressed some concern for their safety along the dark, wooded road after hearing Pieter's stories; yet, as I warily eyed the shadows around the dimly moonlit road, I assured them that we were safe and would, by the end of the week, be setting out for the final journey to Newport.

Chapter 10

Ann

The seas had been merciless. The accommodations were crude, although the hammocks Peter had installed in our room provided some comfort. The dank air and darkness, coupled with nausea, kept me on edge. I would find minimal relief lying in the hammock or going up on deck when the seas were calm and the sun warm. Some days I would come upon chickens or young goats running free on the deck, and, when the air was still, the underbelly of the ship would reek of its cesspools. To make the days and nights even worse, the lice managed to find their way into my hair, and then Mum's. Though Peter could do nothing to ease my nausea, Mum had brought a concoction from the herb quassia, a secret remedy the Indians had shared, to ease the discomfort of the lice. Mum would blend the herbal mixture with some saltwater, and we would wash our hair for welcomed, but temporary, relief. Nothing had prepared me for the hardships endured as we sailed to the New World on this God-forsaken ship toward what Peter called a better life. Each day I sprinkled a bit of my rosewater on a hanky and kept it near my bosom to veil the ship's hostile odors. The journey was oppressive, and I yearned for the sea breezes of Barbados. I was frail, beaten down.

As our journey neared its end, we stopped for supplies and discharge of goods in New Amsterdam, a place that Mum had once told me Pa had visited. The docks were meager, but the town was fortressed amidst glorious forests. I had never seen trees so tall, and the graceful animals Peter called deer would hide among the trees. Though my stomach was yet weak, I had been able to clean and dress well for a visit with people known by Peter's family. Pieter and his wife, Judith, welcomed us into their home, such a beautiful and large home in the forest. The furnishings were grand, and I imagined these were from the Old World, to which Mum whispered her agreement. The windows were draped in silk, silk of alluring hues and tied back with tasseled cords. Though I could eat little, their servants served the grandest meal of quail in succulent sauce, carrots, and jams made of the sweetest berries, with hearty breads. The meal, as well as the table settings, was much more formal than our customs in Barbados. Peter leaned in to whisper in my ear, instructing me to use the utensils from the outside in, and I shared a grateful smile with him. I was beginning to realize just how different my new life would be from the ways of my youth. I was intrigued, yet knew I would have so much to learn.

As we left the Stuyvesant home, Judith kissed my cheeks and wished me well with my journey and the birthing of my child. I wished she lived in Newport rather than here in New Amsterdam, for she seemed so charming and kind. Mum and I thanked her for her graciousness and expressed our hopes that we would see her again.

The buggy ride from Fort Amsterdam back to our ship was frightening after the story Pieter had relayed about the tribal attacks and Kieft's attempts to annihilate the Algonquin tribes. Once safe on the ship, I felt some comfort in its safety, which seemed strange after the prayers I had prayed each night for this journey at sea to be over.

With that, we soon set sail for the shores of Aquidneck Island, and I prayed for calm seas. The sun was shining, and we spent much of that day on the upper deck, where we could see, at times, forested lands to the west and dolphins dancing around the ship's bow. As the sun set, we enjoyed some delicious swordfish caught by the crew for our dinner; and my stomach was stilled, within these calm waters, permitting me to enjoy the meal and the company of my family and fellow passengers. Peter had purchased some dark, sweet grapes when we had been docked in New Amsterdam, which made a delicious finish to our blessed meal; unlike most we had endured on our voyage. My excitement grew for the end of this journey and our arrival in a new town and a new home.

***

Mum was beginning to show her weariness of this long journey, so it was with great joy that we finally arrived in the bay of Newport. As the ship approached the dock, I could see busyness everywhere, people going back and forth, great stacks of lumber. Skeletons of the foundations of new ships sat near the dock to the south. Peter could hardly contain his excitement, shouting directions to Miles regarding the unloading of his goods. He told Obbah to wait in our room below deck, readying our parcels and belongings, since he may not find lodging immediately. He shared that we may need to stay on board another night or two. Oh, how disheartening. I could not wait to bathe, and I know that Mum felt the same. The weeks of mingling with the grime of strangers and animals alike in a confined space immersed us in unbearable odors. But I knew Peter was a man of action, and I was confident that he would bring us some fresh produce from the docks if he could find any. Peter and several passengers took the skiff to shore, and I could soon see him scurrying around the docks with the others.

"Mum, I cannot wait to get to shore and, I pray, find some suitable lodging and bathe. Oh, to be surrounded by all of this water and to feel so dirty."

"Be patient, Ann. I am certain that Peter will find something quickly. He is not one to allow moss to gather under his feet."

"Oh, I pray I did not appear so soiled at the Stuyvesant house. Look at the farms over there! Maybe Peter can find a small farmhouse for us. We can get a cow for milking."

"One step at a time, dear. Peter will manage, with God's help."

As we sat below deck partaking of some dried pork and finishing the grapes, Peter came barging into the room.

"I have easily arranged for my goods to be stored, and I have arranged for a room at one of the lodges. I have been told of one or two leads for a dwelling. Come, gather your small parcels and we can disembark."

Turning to Obbah, he added, "Obbah, take down the hammocks and roll them. Tie them together and bring them along with our bags."

He hugged me with excitement and left as quickly as he had entered so he could instruct Miles and Zebediah on the unloading of his goods onto the docks.

"Well, dear, that did not take long. Not one more night on the ship. Obbah, I will take my bag, but you must gather Ann's things. I believe we are all longing sleep in a soft bed." Mum turned back to Obbah. "You, too, I am sure."

Obbah revealed a hesitant smile. That was the first time

I had seen her smile; it lit up her face. Pa had not believed in the ownership of other humans, thus I was not accustomed to slaves in my home. Though there were many African and Irish slaves in Barbados, a large number had been liberated. Pa had enlisted the services of Jeremy, whose indenture had given him the opportunity to come to a new land. Unaccustomed to being waited upon, I saw that I would have to learn how to oversee and make use of such service, to properly manage a household. God had blessed me with Mum to help me. I smiled at Obbah and trusted she, too, would be a blessing to me as I fashioned a new home and awaited the birth of the baby.

***

Under Peter's instruction, Miles had boxed many of our personal belongings from the ship, allowing us to retrieve those few items that we severely needed. He did this to eliminate the lice that may have leapt with us from the ship. Robert had found lodging with some friends at the docks. Our rooms at the lodge were small but clean, and Mum and I took advantage of the basins after Obbah pumped some water to bathe. We washed our hair, and Mum and I thoroughly combed out any remaining nits from each other's tresses. Peter cleaned up as well before he made arrangements to survey a farmhouse just outside of town. As he left, he shared that the owner of the house had died in the winter and his wife had returned to the old country, so it sat empty. I was hopeful that we could soon settle into a home, in time for Mum to start a winter garden. I had seen no fruit trees here in the dense forests.

"Mum, there are no citrus. No mango trees here. I am disappointed that we cannot preserve them for winter, for Peter said it would be cold here in a few months. Did you see a tailor shop on the street? The dress of the women I saw in town was so plain, without color."

"It is all so new, aye? I do not imagine there are citrus, but I am certain that there is something we can prepare for winter." Mum paused and looked out the window, watching the street.

"The women you saw are the Puritans. I pray their ways do not interfere with ours. You know Peter was drawn to this place for the freedoms. I fear such freedom may be sorely tempted." Mum paused as she gazed out the window. "I pray there are other Anglicans here, for it is certain Peter would not have brought us here if there were not."

Late in the afternoon, the door opened and Peter came in, smiling. "We have a home." Goodness, I thought to myself, this man, my husband, had a way of making the world come to him.

I ran to him and hugged him, filled with glee. "There is so much to do, and I know you are eager to open your apothecary," said Mum. "Is the house big enough for us all? Is there a garden?"

"Yes, I saw an untended garden. I will take care of all of this and send Miles to get some things for the house tomorrow. There is a fine well, so we shall have plenty of water. Let us spend the night here at the lodge. I have contracted the house, and in the morning I will purchase one or two horses and, with some luck, a buggy or cart."

In spite of our excitement, we all slept well that night, grateful for a bed that did not sway with the sea. The stillness of the land was welcomed after so many days on the water. Peter had made separate bunking arrangements for the slaves and Miles. Peter held me in his arms that night, both of us filled with great happiness that our journey was behind us and a new life before us. Sleep was a welcome gift, and the sun was high when I woke.

Peter was dressed and leaving before I sat up in my bed,

telling us as he walked out where we could find some breakfast across the street. There was a street market nearby, and Mum and I found some berries that were delicious. Mum questioned the merchant about growing the red and the blue berries. The woman sold her some strawberry plants and told her she would need to cover them for warmth in the winter. She told us that we could pick the blueberries and blackberries in the forests near town.

We found Obbah cleaning our room when we returned. She said that Peter had sent her to help with our things and that Miles would be meeting us with a buggy down on the street shortly. Obbah and Miles loaded our few bags into the buggy downstairs, and Obbah sat next to Miles on the seat in front. This was truly a work cart and not a buggy, but the seating was adequate. There was one beautiful white horse pulling our buggy, and Miles said that Peter had purchased another. The horse, which should have been two, strained pulling our load. Miles said there was a barn at the house, where we would stable the horses. Miles had clearly accompanied Peter to the house earlier, for he knew the way. As we rode out of town, I saw a small shop, pointing it out to Mum, for a tailor and cobbler. The ride was short, just beyond the edge of town. There, before us, was a small shingle house with a gambrel roof at the edge of the woods. A large barn sat away from the house, on the other side of a large overgrown garden. The house appeared to be only one floor, and I was eager to see inside. I did hope that the kitchen was well made.

Miles pulled the buggy to the front of the home, and we disembarked. Obbah gathered our bags and parcels.

"Ma'am," Miles addressed me, "Master Tallman has instructed me to ready the barn for our quarters … for me, Zebediah, Mingoe and Obbah. I will put the horse up and start on my task. If you need anything, please send Obbah for me." Miles turned toward the barn, leading the horse.

"Oh dear, is there warmth in the barn for them in the cold weather?" I asked Mum. "I had not thought of where they were to stay. What kind of mistress am I? I have so much to learn, Mum."

"You will do fine, Ann." Then Mum, with some force, opened the front door, and all I could see was darkness. It was so dark within this room; so dark I could see but colorless forms I would later find to be fine furnishings. I realized that it was the trees and the small windows allowing for so little light. Obbah found a Betty lamp and, near the oven, Mum found some flint. The light revealed a large sitting room that was well furnished. It seems the widow had left much behind and departed with only her most personal belongings. Upon exploring, I gratefully found many utensils and pots in the long and narrow kitchen, where a long wooden table, sturdy and appearing hand-built, sat waiting for dinner conversations. Nearby stood a large stone oven. There were shelves built in the kitchen and a tall and narrow table for preparation of food. The table sat under a large-paned window looking out into the woods, a sight I found spellbinding. I stood at the window peering into the thickness of the trees that shadowed this room. The scene beyond the glass was full of life, bursting with invitation.

Next to the window was a door leading out to the back, where I found the well. The yard behind the house was lush and overgrown, yet I was a bit apprehensive at what might reside in that forest. Oh how I would miss our orchards. There was a bedroom off of the kitchen and another one, on the opposite side, off of the sitting room. Both were small, but there was a bed in each room. This would do.

"Obbah, we do need to clean," said Mum. Obbah went through the kitchen and out back, looking for a broom. "I do not like how dark it is, but you know, we have been much spoiled by the sunny island of Barbados." Mum found a candle and lit it, and I set the lamp I held on the kitchen table for Obbah. "Let us start with the bedrooms and then the kitchen. I want to be certain the beddings are clean. Was it not blissful sleeping in a real bed last night?" Mum added, "Oh, what shall we do for dinner this night? I do hope Peter thinks to bring something. We have some of those berries left. Before nightfall I must find somewhere to plant these strawberries from the market." Then Mum passed her candle to me and was gone out the back door.

I sighed. There was so much to do in such a strange place. As I walked into the front sitting room, I felt an overwhelming sense of obligation to make our new home a safe and warm refuge for my family. The brick fireplace in the front sitting room was small, and on the mantel sat a small oil portrait of a young girl with yellow curls dressed in deep-green velvet and lace, a green silk ribbon in her hair. Oh dear, the widow must have left that. I picked it up and admired the painting, studying the girl's fair-colored eyes and wondering who she was and what story she had to tell; then I gently placed the painting in the bottom drawer of the desk in the corner. This was now my home.

Chapter 11

Ann

The sun was streaming through the trees as it neared the western horizon when Peter arrived at the house. He had thought to bring some goods for the kitchen. Obbah had been washing our clothing for most of the day, and Mum and I had changed the bedding and lit a fire in the kitchen oven to ensure the chimney was clear. I could not wait to make a pot of coffee with the beans I had brought from the islands, but such things would have to wait. Peter had brought a basket of two chickens for our meals this week and said he would send Miles to town for some layers once we made sure we had an enclosure to protect them from wild animals.

"I know the house is small, ladies, but I have been ensured that we can add on to it. I want to add at least one bedroom for the baby, an upstairs room is my plan, and I need to have Miles start a cottage for the help, near the barn. The day will come when I will build our own home on the land of our choosing, but that must come after the success of my shop. After my trades grow."

Mum took the chickens to Obbah, asking her to take one to the barn and prepare the other for dinner tonight. She found a pot, filling it from the well, and hung it in the oven to boil, and then joined Peter and me in the sitting room.

"We will have chicken tonight with some berry sauce, and I have some coffee I brought from home if Obbah can find a pot and some cups in the kitchen."

"Thank you, Mum," I responded as I sat next to Peter at the table.

"I have been looking for a shop and meeting some of the businessmen in town. I will spend tomorrow at the tavern getting to know more about the town and meeting new comrades. Zebediah and Mingoe will have my goods unloaded and stored by the end of the week. Miles has money to purchase a third horse. At the end of the week he will then go pick up the slaves and bring them home so they can get started setting up the barn and working a foundation for a cottage. I have arranged for a load of lumber to be delivered here tomorrow."

"Slow down, dear," I said, taking Peter's hand. "We cannot stay up with you since you are going so fast. It will all be done in good time." I turned to Mum. "I sound just like you, Mum." I laughed.

"Well, ladies, there is much to be done," he said impatiently. "I'm going out to the barn and check on Miles's progress. Let me know when dinner is on the table." He hurried out the door.

I found myself somewhat taken aback with his curt exit. Mum took my hand. "Let him have his eagerness, Ann. Let's go help Obbah clean that chicken and make the sauce. Peter is just excited and likely a bit overwhelmed."

Peter brought Miles back to the house for dinner, and Obbah quickly set a place for him. Except for a few comments Peter made to Miles about the barn, we ate in silence. Obbah would stay in the barn until the rooms could be added to the house, so she left with Miles after dinner, taking some food and bedding for the pallets in their sparse quarters. Thank our Lord it was a warm evening.

Though quiet, Peter satisfied his desires that night like a colt held too long in the barn. It was the first time since we'd left Barbados, with the exception of the one night on the ship, during the storms, when Peter had silently joined me in my hammock. But tonight, as we lay side by side, his strong hands explored my figure, still shapely, and though it was dark, I sensed the eagerness in his touch. He was not talkative, but his kisses and his urgency left me feeling treasured. I was his wife. A mother-to-be. I was mistress of his house. I did adore this man who had charmed me at the bustling market in St. Michael's parish not so long ago.

***

Over the next two months, Peter did not slow down. He had ensured, with Miles's help, that we had a dairy cow for milk, a rooster and chickens for eggs, and plants and seeds for Mum's garden. In addition to our buggy, he and Miles had built a cart for transporting goods for both the house and for his new shop. He had found a small space on the main street where he had set up his apothecary, a storefront where people could find herbs and medicines so rare in the colonies. He set up an area in his shop for sale of the rum and tobacco from Barbados. His tobacco sales were plentiful, and he was soon talking of going on another sea voyage back to the islands. Since the space in the barn had a small wood-burning stove and was satisfactory for Miles and the slaves, Peter had directed Miles to oversee the addition of a stairwell and two rooms upstairs in the house. He wanted to ensure they were done before winter and before the baby came, thus delaying the slave quarters.

My brother, Robert, had contracted a small house a bit north of Newport. After he was settled in with his friend from the docks, it was not long before Robert was at sea again, on a trading ship to Spain by way of the Virginia Colony. Though the girl who tugged at his heart was in New Amsterdam, he longed to explore the new Virginia Colony. I strongly suspected he would visit New Amsterdam at some time during his trip. Mum received a letter from Virginia telling her of the grand tobacco plantations and immense forests and rivers he found near Jamestown.

While Peter was so busy in town, Mum and I worked on making the house our own. We cleaned the webs from the corners, moved the furnishings and organized the kitchen and dining areas. We found our way into town and to the shop that carried fabrics, where we purchased some yardage to make drapes for the windows to bring some color into the house. I found and purchased some pieces to make new dresses to accommodate my growing waistline. After we cleaned the windows and hung the fresh-sewn curtains, draping them to the side to allow the light in, the house looked a bit more cheery. I still prayed for sunny days, yet the sun only shone in through the one window in the front of the house. There was one small window in each of the bedrooms, and the large window in the kitchen, all heavily shaded by the large trees and which, when opened, provided fresh air but little breeze. With all my being, I missed the bright sunshine and the sea breezes of our island.

I explored the forest, bringing Mum with me the first time, as I was fearful of what may hide there. We were excited to find blueberry bushes in the wilderness, and spent hours one afternoon filling two large bowls. Mum's garden was flourishing; Miles would hunt wild turkey and rabbit so our cupboards were not bare. Mrs. Lawton, from down the road, had come to meet us, and brought a dish of delicious cobbler made with the local berries. She shared her recipe, as well as telling Mum and me about the vegetables that grow well in Newport and those that are hardy as winter approaches. She brought some kernels of corn from her garden, corn that would soon be as tall as myself in our garden. She forewarned us to can and preserve as much as possible for the winter, and Mum shared that she had already preserved jars of blueberries. Mum made some coffee, which I believe Mrs. Lawton was unaccustomed to and found bitter. Of course, Mum was delighted with the gossip that Mrs. Lawton shared; and since the history of Newport was not long, she shared much about the town's beginnings. The story of Anne Hutchinson, with her strong personality and fervid outspoken beliefs, was fascinating. Mistress Hutchinson had been banished from the Bay Colony and led dissenters to settle on this island of Rhodes. The story of her massacre by Indians in New Amsterdam startled me, especially in light of our recent visit there.

"Oh, my. This is the story told us by Governor Stuyvesant in New Amsterdam," I responded to Mrs. Lawton and Mum. "He shared that the earlier governor, Kieft, had attacked the tribes and slaughtered many Indians, angering them, provoking retaliation. I am certain Mrs. Hutchinson and her family were caught up in this struggle of revenge. Oh, dear. For her to have done so much, and then to have these savages kill her family. This is heartbreaking."

"She would have been better off staying in Portsmouth," replied Mrs. Lawton. "As of present, we have a compatible relationship with the Indian tribes, and we trade and contract with each other. You have no reason to be fearful." Mrs. Lawton reached over and touched my hand, offering comfort.

"I am certain Peter will protect us, and Miles is here most of the time," said Mum, and looking toward me, she added, "Remember, we settled Barbados when there were natives living on that land. It will be fine, dear."

"But she was so strong, this Anne Hutchinson. She fought for these freedoms we have. Yet she was but a woman. I wish I could have met her."

"Much of our community is Puritan, but I know your husband said you are of the Anglican faith. We do not have a church here, since we are a small faction. Our Anglican priest holds services in our homes, as he travels from town to town. This Sunday he will be at my home, so I invite your family to join us. It is a blessing to have someone new in our small Anglican community."

"Bless you, Mrs. Lawton. We would love to come. I must say, we have been so busy that we have somewhat isolated ourselves here. I cannot wait to meet some of our new neighbors of common faith," replied Mum.

Mistress Lawton told us more about the town as we enjoyed cobbler with our coffee.

"I am glad you will come, but please, do call me Elizabeth," Mrs. Lawton replied as she left. She climbed into her buggy, waving goodbye. "I will see you on Sunday."

***

When Sunday came, there was a hole in our roof, at the edge of the sitting room, where Miles was working on the stairwell. The weather had a chill to it, and it was at that moment I realized we did not have clothing for the colder weather. Peter had decided to join us at the parish service at the Lawtons' home. Mum and I put shawls over our shoulders to break the chill in the air, my shawl thrown over a blue brocade dress I had tailored with a new higher waistline.

When we arrived at the Lawtons', there were six buggies and a tethered white bull sitting outside the large shingled house, a house much larger than our own. Peter and I looked, with eyebrows raised, at each other when we saw the white bull snorting amidst the buggies. We would later learn that our priest traveled from town to town on his white bull, an almost heavenly vision, one would imagine. Peter saw his new acquaintances Isaiah Taylor and Nicholas Easton when we entered the large front room. He had met them both at the town hall and told me he had liked Isaiah right away.

As Peter started across the room, I took his hand to alert him of Elizabeth Lawton's presence as she welcomed us into the house, and then Elizabeth introduced us to Reverend Blackstone. The reverend was from the Massachusetts Bay Colony and traveled through the communities to minister to small congregations. After the sacraments, we stayed a bit to visit with our neighbors, and Peter with his friends.

Several of the women welcomed Mum and me, offering their help as we faced the new obstacles of moving to Newport. They warned us of the frequent Puritan intolerance, mostly to the north, but expressed their hopes that our new government might overcome such division. Upon learning of Mum's skills in tailoring, they spoke much of weaving fabrics and clothing to suit our winters, and foods to store for preparation. Mum and I had already preserved berries and tomatoes. We had found a root cellar at the side of our house, where we were storing our turnip roots and preserves.

As we stepped into our buggy to leave, a comforting sense of welcome filled me. Peter guided our buggy toward home, and he shared with us his exhilaration in meeting Reverend Blackstone and Samuel Allen, a successful

Anglican trader.

"Did you know that Sam Allen has ownership in one of the plantations in Barbados? He is importing sugars from the islands and refining it here in Newport. We spoke of making a voyage together soon down south, but I will need to hire someone I can trust to manage my shop." Peter spoke excitedly of a trading voyage. I did not share his excitement. However, he said the indigo he had brought with us was unexpectedly gone, and he wanted to go to Antigua for more of the dye, as well as for the purchase of tobacco and coffee from his friend in Barbados.

"I cannot believe how popular the indigo is with the women here, as with the Indians too," he added. "The women are trying the ginger I brought, and I have had many requests. With the forests here, I am certain that I could find markets for quantities of lumber in the islands, thereby exporting and importing on my trip."

"Peter," said Mum. "You will go and return before the winter gales, won't you?" It was already September.

"Yes, we spoke of leaving early next month. It will be good," he responded as the buggy stopped near our barn.

"I will give Miles instructions in detail for finishing the house, and I will get him some help if he needs it. Then you will have Obbah in the house, and you will make better use of her. You are not to be doing the heavy work. Neither of you! I will make sure that Miles is able to oversee the work. And the slaves."

At home, Zebediah had milked the cow and brought a pail of milk in to Obbah. She had readied a small meal for us as evening approached.

"Will you be home before the new year, Peter?" I nervously asked.

"I imagine, or almost home then."

Peter smiled and continued eating. I knew that, with Mum's help, we would need to prepare for the winter and I would need to be responsible to be a good mistress of the house. Still, I felt it did not bode well that Peter was leaving so soon after our arrival in Newport.

Chapter 12

Peter

At the docks, Sam and I were about to board the *Lyon*, a French trade ship departing for the South Seas and Barbados. I was eager to be returning to the island, especially with the first chill in the air here in Newport. I purchased a shipment of lumber and had it loaded on the ship. There was little doubt that I could contract sales at a good profit where lumber was scarce, and I knew my friend Thomas Modyford, in Barbados, needed lumber. Sam was going to attempt to sell some of his local rum in the land where kill-devil was the day's drink, yet I imagine the taverns would be eager to add to their stock.

Miles was at the docks, since I had him bring me to town, and I gave him final instructions and some monies for specified purchases in my absence. He was good about accounting for his transactions; his indenture had been a wise decision, as I relied upon him heavily. I hired a young man, James, the son of a parish member, to run my shop in my absence and decided that, if he does a good job, I will keep him there. With my profits from this voyage I wanted to purchase some land, but I knew that I had not been here long enough to make that decision. I found out, through my friend Sam, that the Indian tribes may be interested in trading for some sugar, as well as the ginger and rum. Nonetheless, I knew that Sam had a corner on the local rum market.

"Let us go, Peter," said Sam. "The captain wants to set sail."

"Aye. I am eager to see the sunny islands again."

"You are leaving such a young wife, yet with child. Will she be all right? Is someone looking after your family?"

"Miles, my servant, is quite trustworthy. And the Lawtons said they would keep a watch over Lizbeth and Ann. We shall be back before my son is born."

Sam laughed aloud, a laugh rolling from his gut. "It is a son, is it? You have greater powers than I to know such a thing." We shook hands with the captain as we boarded the ship. It seemed like just yesterday that I was on the seas, and indeed it had not been long.

The trip was uneventful and the winds, with our good fortune, made the trip faster than most. We first stopped at Antigua, where I was able to sell a bit of my lumber and acquired a good stock of indigo and some ginger from my source. After two days, we left for Barbados and docked by morning. Sam was off to his own plantation, and I walked into the town that felt like home and boarded at the same lodge where I had once lived. It did not take long, as I sat drinking and sharing tales at the tavern, for me to sell all of the lumber save for the portion I had set aside for Modyford. Marianne was working the bar, so I walked over and, with a wink, sat down.

"It has been a while, Captain Tallman, since you were here."

"Yes, but I thought of you every day," I said as I sipped my lager. "I am here, upstairs at the lodge, the third room on the left, for the week. I am certain you can wander by for a visit this evening."

Marianne smiled and walked away with a tray of drinks to a table across the room. I stayed up late, hoping for a visit from Marianne, but there came no knock at my door.

The landlord had provided me with the use of a horse; thus, when morning came, I took a ride out to Elizabeth's house. I found Jeremy in the barn, feeding the horses.

"What a surprise to see you so soon." A worried look crossed his face. "All is well, I pray."

"Yes. Elizabeth and Ann are in Rhode Island, settled into our house. I have come down with Samuel Allen of Newport for tobacco and sugar. I had not thought about staying at the house, but I have already lodged in town."

"I have been working on expanding some of my tobacco fields. I have made some repairs to your house since the storms blew in this summer. If there is anything I can do for you while you are here, I have faith you will tell me."

"I will check the house before I leave and see if any other repairs are needed. I may stay here on my next voyage. For now, I am headed out to the Modyford plantation. But before I depart on Friday, I want to be certain that I receive from you any monies of profit from the fields and orchards that are due Elizabeth and Ann. You can find me at the tavern."

Before Jeremy could reply, I was on my horse, headed inland to the plantation. Modyford was in the fields, so I waited in his sitting room, lighting my pipe and perusing his books. I missed the access to good books, and remember that Ann, too, fancied reading books. There had been a library in my family's home in Hamburg, and Father's expectations had been high that I read the classics before I went to university. I was hopeful that he would be proud of my shop and my trading business. I knew that he had expectations that I would exceed the success of my older brother, now an official in Amsterdam. Failure was no option for *Vater*.

When Modyford walked in, I was reading a portion of a bound Homer, the *Iliad*, one of my favorites. "Hey, good man, why are you on the island? I thought you were in the colonies."

"Yes, I am. I have my shop established in Newport and have returned with lumber to sell and to restock my rum and tobacco. I am certain that you can sell me tobacco, as much as you can spare, and I would be bemused if you do not need lumber for your expanding plantation."

"Well, good man, I can sell you the tobacco. It has been a good year, and I have not yet shipped produce out to England. We harvested much before the fierce storms, and I am certain we can work out a good price, as well as for the lumber. How much do you have?"

"Half a ton of pine. And I have a small bit of fine maple. As a gift to you, I have brought this rum, a fine rum made in the Isle of Rogues, and some molasses," I said as I returned the *Iliad* to the shelf. "You know these books are hard to come by here in the New World. You are blessed to have these treasures."

"Yes, they are rare indeed. And I can use all the lumber you have. Let us negotiate a price and I can send my men to the docks." He lit his pipe. "Now, let us talk tobacco."

We negotiated an agreeable price on both, and I spent the day at the plantation. We were served a filling meal, and it felt good to be back on the island. When I departed, as the sun set, Modyford handed me a parcel.

"These are for you, good man. I have too many to read. Homer's book is in there. May you arrive safely home, and send God's blessings to your Ann and her mum."

"You are, truly, a good friend. I will share your message with my family, which will soon increase by one. And I will see you again. Send a message if you need anything from the colonies. God bless."

We shook hands, as Modyford shared his congratulations, and I mounted my horse and returned to town as darkness settled on the island. The weight of the parcel Modyford had given me was substantial, and I felt joy and anticipation to see the titles. I could now begin my own library in our meager home in Newport. One day soon I should have a large mansion with a library such as my friend's.

Back in town, I took my belongings to my room, walked down to the dock and marked the shipment for Modyford, telling the old man at the warehouse it would be picked up tomorrow. As I walked into the tavern, it was crowded, and I saw Allen across the room. We imbibed local ale and reveled in several laughs as I introduced Sam Allen to my many friends, and as the crowd diminished, I winked at Marianne at the bar.

"I will be at the ship tomorrow morn, Peter, loading my goods. I will see you there? We are leaving next week and the captain wants the ship loaded by Saturday."

"I will be there early. I have a shipment of tobacco coming in from one of the plantations, and am still negotiating my shipment of rum. I will stay a bit longer here and see you tomorrow. G'day, friend."

I drank another ale as the tavern slowly emptied of its customers. At the sight of Marianne going to the back room to store the tankards she carried, I shadowed her.

"I missed you last night, pretty lady," I whispered as she placed the tankards on the shelves.

"I worked late, Captain." She turned to face me. I reached for her face, tilting it up toward mine, and kissed her gently and long. I stepped back, waiting for her response; however, before I could even look into her eyes, she had her arms around my neck, pulling me back into her. Pressing her against the wall, I kissed her passionately and, in the darkness of the room, reached beneath her skirt with quick desire. Struggling to suppress our cries of fervor, we quenched our passions and were done well and straightway. Marianne's lips clung to mine momentarily, but she quickly smoothed her dress as we heard footsteps.

"Someone is coming," she whispered, pinning her hair where the locks had loosened. I stepped back and crossed the room as George, the innkeeper, walked in. Marianne was arranging the bottles on the shelf, and across the room, I picked up a bottle of rum.

"Hey, George, how much of this do you have to sell? I need a bit more for my shop in Newport."

George was startled at my presence in the dim light of the stockroom. He looked toward Marianne.

"I can pay well for a supply," I added.

"Tallman, I have some good rum down in the warehouse. Not much extra, but I can sell you some. And, Tallman, I am too old for you to be alarming me in the dark like this."

"Done. I'll be by tomorrow, in the morning, to settle with you and have it loaded on the ship." I walked out. "Good evening, George, Miss Marianne."

Back in my room, I slept deeply, with the sea breeze finding the open window, and, upon awakening, I looked forward to my journey home. Allen and I managed loading our goods on the ship the next day, with the tobacco arriving from Modyford's plantation early in the morning. I dropped by early to pay George for the rum and negotiated two more purchases at the dock, three more cases of rum and 260 bags of sugar from Allen's source. After all goods were stored on the ship, I rode out to the fishing village, found Jeremy at the tavern, and collected the monies he owed me. With our tasks complete, Allen and I stopped by the tavern as the sun set. Marianne smiled mischievously at me as she served drinks, but the tavern was crowded and no goodbyes or stolen kisses were shared.

As the ship negotiated its way out of the bay on the following Monday, I settled into my room below deck. After lighting a candle, I hung my hammock in the room I shared with my friend. Near the lit candle, I pulled the tomes from the bag Modyford had gifted me, one by one. There was Homer's *Iliad*, followed by three Shakespeare plays, *The Prince* by Machiavelli, *Tamburlaine* by Marlowe and a book of Marlowe's poetry, *The Essays* by Bacon, *The Lusiads* by Vas de Camoes, and a Dutch drama, *Mariken van Nieumeghen*. My heart raced. In my heart, these were the treasures of my voyage. I turned to the first page of *The Prince* and began to read in the dim light as the ship swayed and I could hear the winds snap the sails above.

Chapter 13

Ann

It was the first day on the calendar of December and the snow was falling again. The prior month revealed the first snow of winter, and I was beside myself with both the chill in the air and the beauty of the white forest. When the leaves had fallen from the trees and the forest was white, I could see the graceful deer walking through the trees from the window in my kitchen. It was a magical vision, with frozen ice sticks hanging from the eaves, as if from the fairy tales. Though Mum had seen snow in England, she was excited to see it again. For me, I delighted running through the yard, looking into the filmy sky as snowflakes fell onto my tongue, as if I were still a child.

The chill of winter was new to me. Our new friends helped me stitch new clothes with fabrics unfamiliar to me, and I found blessings in both the warm clothes as well as the new friendships. Miles had helped to clean and stage the fireplace and showed Obbah how to keep the fire going. Though the rooms upstairs were finished, Miles had not yet built the cottage for him, Mingoe and Zebediah. They had a small stove in the rooms in the barn, yet I could only imagine the incredible chilled winds that must come through the barn walls. Mum pulled old blankets she had packed in her trunks and gave them to Miles.

Mum and I had moved Obbah into the housemaid's room upstairs. We stitched bedding and linens for the pallet Miles had moved into the small room, and then I worked on dressing the large room upstairs for the baby. Miles later built two bedframes, one small and one large; and then he brought mattresses and bedding from town for the large bedroom, as Peter had arranged before his travels. Sweet Miles whispered to me that, as time allowed, he would build a bedframe for Obbah; I smiled broadly at his kindness. One morning I walked into the new room to find a cradle Miles had brought in from the barn, saying Zebediah had put it together and carved the spindles. I imagined I would be spending a lot of time there as I nursed the little one already kicking inside of me. Peter was due back soon. Oh, how I missed him. While he was gone, Mum and I had stocked the root cellar with preserves and jams and dried meats, ensuring that Peter would be pleased at our preparations for winter. I had made repairs to his jackets and clothing that he had left behind, and Mum had stitched a woolen cloak for him, as well as our own cloaks. The baby was due to birth just before spring arrived, and I was grateful that I would have Mum and Obbah to help me.

Obbah was a sweet girl and had been such help in settling into our home. I call her a girl, but she was but a year or two younger than myself. She was a quick learner and had become an excellent cook. She sometimes visited with Mrs. Lawton's servant, Susannah, and they shared information and learned from each other. Obbah dutifully ensured that food was prepared for Zebediah and Mingoe, and sent that out to them with Miles, who, in Peter's absence, often joined us for meals in the house. On other days, he ate in the barn with the slaves. Miles and Zebediah had cut and chopped a healthy stack of wood for the stoves in the house and in the barn, keeping us warmed as winter's gales fell upon us.

In Peter's absence, Mum and I would sometimes stop by the apothecary when we went into town for supplies. It appeared that his new man, James, was doing a good job, as the shop's shelves looked organized and clean. He said the tobacco was almost sold out, and he would be glad for Peter's return, as Peter's knowledge of the medicines and herbs was in great demand.

As I stood in the kitchen on a gray afternoon, watching the snow fall through the trees behind our house, I heard the front door open against the wind. Mum was in her room, so I walked into the sitting room and saw Peter, covered in snow, looking exhausted, yet smiling.

"Look at you! A sight for my sore eyes. I am pleased we have a roof in these gales," he said as he gathered me in his arms. "Whoa, there is something between us." He put his hand on my dress, where the fullness of my pregnancy was evident. "Our son is growing."

Mum, hearing Peter's voice, came hurrying into the sitting room to greet him just in time to hear his remark. "Well, Peter, someone is growing, be it your son or your daughter." She laughed as Peter hugged her and dismissed her statement, proceeding to share the details of his voyage.

"The islands are well and warm, while I see here the bitter cold winds have chilled us. The gales made it difficult to bring in our ship; bless the Lord, we are home. I sold all of the lumber and have sent Miles to store my new goods in the warehouse. I made a good profit on the lumber, and, since the house is done, I will put those monies into the business.

Obbah quietly came into the room and gathered Peter's parcels to take to our room and to pull his laundry.

"Obbah!" Peter's voice startled me. "Did I tell you to take those away?"

"No, sir," she responded in a whisper.

"You need to remember your place and do as told. Here, take these and I will take this one." He picked up a bag and laid it next to his chair. Obbah looked quickly at me, as if in apology, and then was gone.

"I hope you were not coddling these slaves in my absence. And James; have you checked on him at the shop?"

"Yes," Mum responded. "Anne and I have stopped by regularly and all appears well at the shop. James did say he was in need of tobacco at the store, but I am certain that you have brought plenty."

"Good." Peter pulled some coins from his pouch and handed them to Mum. "Here is your portion of the profit monies at the orchard and fields in Barbados."

Mum looked puzzled. "But I told Jeremy that any profits were his, as recompense for his help with the care of the property and horses."

"Well, that is not for you to decide. I am looking after you and Ann; looking after your interests. I shall settle in, and, when Miles returns, see where things stand in my absence. I look forward to a good meal at home and a smoke this evening before the warmth of the fireplace."

He walked out toward the barn, and Mum and I looked at each other, without words. After an awkward silence, I walked away and found Obbah in the kitchen, to make sure we had all we needed for our evening meal. She was quiet, and I apologized for Peter's sharpness, explaining his exhaustion from such a long journey. This would become the beginning of a pattern in our home, of a great deference and quiet when Peter was home as opposed to the warmth throughout the house when Peter was sailing. I was saddened for Obbah, as she had become trusting of us and, thus, shared her sweet personality as her confidence had grown. In one brief exchange, Peter had changed that. Mum sat at the table near the oven as Obbah and I worked in the kitchen, and I could see the distress on her face. She was very unhappy about the monies from Jeremy and what she saw as her broken promise. My emotions were conflicted. I was so saddened by the exchanges in our sitting room, while at the same time my heart was overjoyed at my husband's safe return and presence.

Dinner was good, full of conversation about Peter's voyage and his eagerness for new ventures. He shared that Miles, in spite of the weather, would begin building the cottage near the barn. I knew that Miles, Mingoe and Zebediah had already prepared the foundation, leveling the land within a drawn boundary. Miles had informed Peter that, during the past week, Mingoe had gone missing: Peter was angry, but said little about the missing slave.

"I made a grand choice in Miles's indenture. He is a smart man and a blessed asset. I see he has ensured the fireplace and stoves are in good working order both here and in the barn. This forest may block the sunlight from our home, but I can assure you it serves greatly in breaking the wicked gales from the sea."

"Yes, in spite of the shadows, I have come to be drawn into the forest, with its playful light and shadow, its shelter and berries. The snow has only enhanced its beauty, as if a fairyland," I shared, as Obbah timidly cleaned the plates from the table and Mum looked at me sternly.

"Be careful, Ann, not to go alone far into the woods," he said in response, and then changed topic. "I applied for my freeman status with Master Clarke in the governor's office before my journey, and Clarke expressed his gratitude for my bringing the apothecary to Newport. With the grand harbors for shipbuilding and the growth of this community, Newport will become a great city one day soon. Did Miles take his meals with you in my absence?"

"Yes, several times a week," responded Mum. "On other days, he will take food out to the slaves and eat in the barn."

After our meal, Peter retired to the sitting room while Mum and I played a game of whist at the table as Obbah cleaned the kitchen. When Mum retired to her room, the snow had stopped falling, yet the wind still whistled through the trees and rattled the windows. I did not know how the savages and the settlers of this land managed to survive this hardship. Not only was the chill to the bone, but also there was little food, and travel was treacherous. I had heard from others that the cold will last through March or April, when spring will start to warm the earth. It was now clear to me why the windows in this home were small, high and few, for when the wind and the chill came, the delicate glass proved to be an inadequate barrier. Mum and I had sewn some muslin curtains for the upstairs window, but we might better have considered a heavier fabric or lined a fabric with muslin. I was often saddened to remember my cherished Barbados now exchanged for this life, but I knew that Peter had a plan to better our lives. Yet for me, a better life would have included the sun's balminess, warm ocean waves, tropical flowers and fruits year round. My mind wandered to visions of my soon-to-arrive babe running and giggling on the warm beach sand; then, I remembered he or she would be bundled in layer upon layer of wool and cotton for warmth next winter.

Sitting at the table, in my reverie, Peter's voice startled me. "Modyford gifted me with a rare group of books with which I can start a library. This one is for you, Ann. I know you like to read, as do I, and you will cherish this Shakespeare collection." He handed me the book. "It is the printed collection of Shakespeare's sonnets."

The book was beautifully bound and, as I turned to the first pages, I found it full of verse on the delicate paper.

"Oh, Peter! This is a treasure."

"Yes, and there are more I will put in the sitting room. There is a collection of Shakespeare's plays, Marlowe's poetry, the *Iliad* and so much more. I will ask Miles to construct some shelves on the wall."

Books were rare, especially in the New World, I had heard, but in my few years of schooling in the island, I had come to yearn for my free time to read, and consumed the small pamphlets we were issued. Pa did have a small number of books at the house, and I had read them over and over as the years passed. But, the poetry of Shakespeare, the greatest poet of this lifetime, to have this was a precious gift.

As I held tightly to the tome, I rose and found Obbah to tell her goodnight, and then I joined Peter in our room. He lay in bed, watching me. I carefully lay the book on my dressing table and unbraided my hair, brushed it free and braided it loosely. In the mirror I saw Peter watching and I was filled with anticipation. Anticipation turned into carnal longing.

"Leave it loose, Ann. So that I can run my fingers through your hair," whispered Peter, smiling at me as I freed my braid.

Though Peter was exhausted from his long journey, we joined together, awkwardly around the unborn child between us, and I found solace in the warmth and comfort of his strong arms. Peter, still unshaven and smelling of familiar tobacco, was gentle with his expecting wife, but his gentleness roused in me a hunger that surprised us both. I craved more than his travel-weary soul could return. The wind outside blew the shutter sharply against the window, startling me, as we burrowed deeper under the blankets.

Chapter 14

Ann

... bending down as if to catch the wind,
the frosted trees seemed ghostly shapes
sheltering goodness as with leafless capes ...

The next day, Peter went into town early, saying he had much to do at the shop and at the warehouse. He was grateful for the new cloak that Mum had stitched for him. The snow started falling again, softly, and I made the decision to bundle up in my wools and new cloak and walk into the forest behind the kitchen. The woods were thick with green firs and barren maples, birch and old beech trees. The beauty of it fascinated me, and in the distance, between the trees, I could see a young deer and a slightly larger one. Miles had told me large or antlered ones were called bucks.

A bit of sunlight weaving through the trees made the snow sparkle; it was magical. I continued walking softly through the trees, toward the deer I had seen. I walked more slowly as I neared them, the female nibbling at a shrub as the male stood erect, staring in my direction. I was certain they would dash, but they did not. I walked toward the male and delicately touched his nose, moving so slow as though I were detached from myself. I could not believe this was happening. The female turned and walked nearer to me, nuzzling my hand as if I might have some food for her. I very slowly opened my hand to show that I held nothing, and then I reached out and gently stroked her neck. There were broken and faded antlers lying in the snow. The scene was reminiscent of the magical fairy tales Pa would tell me when I was a young girl. I sensed a charmed tranquility and euphoria flow through my veins, a sensation unfamiliar. *Where was I?*

On queue with my query, an abrupt darkness enveloped us, and the snow came heavier, biting into my face. I heard my name, "Ann. Ann?" coming from a distance, as if veiled. The deer dashed, and I turned to find the house, to see who was calling my name. The snow was so heavy I could barely see the house, and then I heard my name called more sharply, "Ann," and saw Peter through the stinging snow. It was as if a dark force had ripped me from a reverie, frightened the animals and darkened the skies. The old beech trees, with their formidable forms, came alive, as if ogres and the slight white birch appeared to move amongst them. I fought my way through the blinding snow, once running into the arms of a white pine, and struggled to free myself. Suddenly I was upon the back door, but there was no one there. No one. And the falling snow came to an abrupt end.

I trembled, but it was not the air's chill that shook me. I

found Mum and told her what happened, the magical feeling, the deer as tame as a young lamb. Mum told me that Peter had not returned from town, and she became angered and chastised me to speak no more of what I had just told her.

"I am certain it was a hallucination, Ann, caused by the blinding cold, or it may be your pregnancy, but women nearby have been hanged for making such claims. This never happened. Say no more!" she said curtly, and walked away. Such shortness was uncommon from Mum. Was her anger from fear? From wherever it came, it frightened me, and I spoke no more of what I had seen.

Chapter 15

Ann

The midwife was here with me in the bedroom upstairs. It was the end of February, and a chill remained in the air. The pain had been strong and regular for fifteen hours, and there was still no baby. The agony would come in waves, such excruciating pressure, and then exhaustion. Would this not end? Mum kept a cool cloth to wipe my face and neck, and Prudence, the midwife, said it would be soon, but her worried brow said otherwise. I caught Mum's glance toward Prudence, a glance full of anxiety.

"My dear child," said Mum. "When your baby is in your arms, this time will all be but a memory."

She wiped my brow with a damp cloth; and her touch, with the coolness of the cloth, soothed me within and heartened my body to relax. Yet my agony continued for another hour, with Mum leaving the room at intervals to let Peter, who waited downstairs, know of my condition. Mum looked worried, as my exhaustion was overtaking my strength, then Prudence said I needed to relax between the spasms, as she would reach to turn the baby. Mum gave me a bit of Peter's Scotch malt whisky, and as Prudence struggled to move the infant, I cried out in my suffering. "Now," she said suddenly. "Push now." I did so, with great effort, and the pressure continued and then again subsided. When it rolled back over me, she instructed again to push hard. With that effort, I felt a sudden relief from the pressure and my muscles relaxed.

"Oh, dear Ann, it is a baby girl. A beautiful baby girl," shared my overjoyed Mum. But it was mere moments before her expression changed to distress. Prudence was quiet, and an alarm overcame me when I did not hear the baby.

"Mum?"

She came toward me and took my face in her hands. "I am sorry. She is gone, dear." Mum was sobbing softly now and she gathered my hands, as I felt my body tightening again. "What is this? This pain?" I asked with apprehension.

"That is your afterbirth, Ann," responded Prudence. "Do not worry. I will take care of that. You need not be afraid, but remain still a bit more. This is natural and you should rest."

I could see the wrapped infant across the room, wrapped tightly in the linen, silent. My heart ached as I thought of Peter. Oh, Peter, how could this happen? Rose, I will name her Rose. Sweet Rose, who would never wander the woods with me. Thoughts and visions consumed me, and then were gone. With quickness, my eyelids were heavy and sleep released me from my sorrow.

When I awoke, Peter was sitting in the chair by the side of my bed. At first I was not aware of where I was, then I remembered, and saw that the wrapped bundle was no longer in the room. Peter took my hand, but he had no words, only a long silence. "I love you, Ann," he finally whispered. "We shall with certainty have another. I am confident God will bless us."

With those words, I felt the tears finally come, quietly, down my cheeks, and then there was no stopping them. Peter had continued talking, but I heard nothing. My loss filled me, and Peter took his handkerchief and wiped my face, softly kissed me on the cheek and then the forehead. Yet the tears would not stop. The tears took me into a brief sleep, and when I awoke, Peter was still sitting next to me.

"Peter, I called her Rose. I am certain she is with my pa. Little Rose is with Pa, isn't she?"

"I am certain, and Rose is a fitting name." Peter paused and then continued. "We cannot bury her on the property, as it is not our own. I will make arrangements with the cemetery, but with the priest not in town, we cannot baptize her."

"Oh, dear," I answered anxiously. "I had not remembered there is no church. She will not be promised to the Lord." And my tears began creeping from my eyes yet again.

"Ann, I believe that God took our Rose because he wanted her. We will pray for her soul."

I squeezed his hand, and Mum came into the room with a cup of hot coffee, urging me to drink. The three of us sat in silence for a time, and then Peter exited to go make the arrangements.

In spite of the sadness, Mum made every effort to smile.

"Prudence shared with me, dear, that the baby's cord had knotted and the knot likely tightened through your long birthing. She said it was not uncommon and that your next birthing will, assuredly, be quicker. She told me your job is to rest, eat, and rebuild your strength. She will come see you tomorrow."

Mum sat with me as I drifted off to sleep, numb to all around me. I was alone in the room when I awoke with a start. Did I hear a baby cry? I was certain I heard the cry of an infant, yet stillness wrapped me as visions of dark clouds gathered on the ceiling above me.

The next day there was a burial at the cemetery, but Mum insisted I must remain abed. Mum and Peter attended, and planned to take me as soon as I could go. Peter had arranged for John Clarke, the Baptist minister, to say a few words as Rose was interred. Obbah sat with me in the room upstairs, the room with an empty cradle, and I slept, and woke filled with emptiness, and then slept again. Sleep was my escape. When Peter and Mum returned, they told me there would be a stone with Rose's name when Peter arranged its placement.

Over the next few months, I felt as in a fog, and the days slowed as if, at times, they would never end. I worked in the garden and tried to reread the books that Peter had brought home, but my mind preferred to wander. Often I would meander through the trees in the forest, seeking the deer that had once befriended me, but finding myself wrapped in emptiness. My body fulfilled its duties and my tasks were quietly complete, but through the summer, a heavy sadness hung over me. There were times I wanted to die, along with my Rose, but I knew deep down that was selfish and a sin. My Peter and my mum loved me and would be heartbroken, so I moved through my days with hopes I would see sunlight again. My sadness brought with it illness, and I struggled to get through the humid summer. I refused to go upstairs, to the room where I had birthed Rose, the room that was to be her nursery. When I was in town with Mum or with Miles, I would walk over to the cemetery to visit the grave, sometimes leaving a flower from my garden by the small stone embellished with her name.

Mum oft became impatient with my melancholy, but she kept me moving toward the light, guiding me to a future she knew would come; and by fall I was again with child. Peter was overjoyed. I was more cautious, wary, but over time I found hope that there would be the arrival of the pitter-patter of small feet in the nursery upstairs.

Peter did not travel during this year but, instead, worked with diligence on growing his apothecary, teaching James about the medicines and herbs, and the expert use of the stone mortar and pestle for preparation of salves. He showed James how to grind the chalk, used by many for stomach ailments. They would grind burdock, mixing it with salt, to be used as poultices. James learned proper measurements and use of the scales. Peter demonstrated a bloodletting and the use of the proper knives and scalpels, but he was not ready to allow James to perform these procedures, which Peter himself did sparingly. By virtue of acquisition of the storefront left vacant next door, Peter expanded his space, including a large storeroom. In May, Mum had planted many of Peter's seeds in a portion of their garden, herbs he could use at the shop. My husband never swayed from relentlessly expanding his business, and was cheered by the reliance of local settlers on his products and guidance.

After Miles informed Peter of Mingoe's absence, Peter had engaged the services of a gentleman befriended at our parish meetings, John Elten, to find and seize Mingoe, including a power of attorney to collect a debt due him. Peter was busy developing relationships with the leaders of Newport and the growing Rhode Island colony, including Roger Williams, founder of Newport. During this year, he purchased a small plot of land just west of Newport that would support his request for freeman status. He had invested in the shipbuilding ventures in the Newport Bay, with hopes of having his own ship one day. This was a grand year for Peter, while I struggled to merely move through each day, praying my faith would one day bring joy and comfort.

Our family relied heavily on Miles at the house to keep

things running; but Peter, when he was home, had been harsher with Obbah and Zebediah. He instructed Miles to ensure punishment was exacted for slackness and poor work. Obbah was told to make sure that I did not exert myself, and to perform all tasks for Mum and me. Peter frowned on my working in the garden, but I tried to explain that the garden was a solace to me, and he acquiesced.

When winter came, it was not as brutal as our first one in Newport. The darkness at times impacted the mood in the house, and I was grateful to see signs of spring in late March. By spring I was full of child, and spent much of my time doing stitch work in the sitting room, or, on a warm day, I would take a chair outside and work in the sunlight.

I was contented each day to feel the unborn child moving in my womb, and Prudence would help me soon with my birthing. Yet, Peter had arranged for a physician to attend the birth.

It was early April when the spasms came in the middle of the night. Miles was sent to fetch both Prudence and the physician. Prudence returned with him, and the physician said he would arrive shortly. However, my dear Prudence brought forth a baby girl, before the physician arrived. She was a beautiful girl, in spite of Peter's prayers for a son. The morning sun was struggling through the trees and peeking into the window. As the first birdsong welcomed morning, Mum placed the swathed baby in my arms. I looked into her eyes as she stared at me, gazing into my own face and whimpering. "She will want to nurse shortly, ma'am," Prudence added as she gathered the linens.

Mum beamed at the sight of me with her grandchild, and placed her hand on my arm, reassuring me that all was well with the world. "I will go tell Peter. I will tell him he can come up to see you shortly. You spend a few moments with your daughter first." She smiled back at me as she left.

The infant was so tiny, yet she was mine, a beautiful

little girl. I prayed Peter would not be too disappointed that it was not the son he wished for. The baby's perfect head was rosy with health and covered with fuzz, pale yellow hair barely covering her precious head. And her toes and fingers were so tiny. I raised her to my breast as she struggled, and, with some help from Prudence, she began nursing. At that moment, I knew my life was forever changed.

It was later, likely only minutes, that I remember being awakened by Peter. I had dozed off as the infant nursed and slept intermittently. Briefly disoriented, I covered myself and, wrapping the infant, handed her to Peter. Pride filled his eyes.

"A sweet daughter. God has blessed us, as you said He would. What shall we call her?"

"I believe she will be Mary. Mary Grace Tallman." Peter took my hand, smiling at me and looking back at Mary. He held her so gently, as if she would break. This so endeared him to me that my heart swelled, and he then returned her to my arms. We were a family. The physician walked in the door, gladdened that all had gone well, and he took Mary Grace, placing her in her cradle, and examined her, finding her well.

Chapter 16

Ann

Contemplating his mercantile successes, Peter decided to invest, along with his friend Sam Allen, in one of the ships being built in the harbor. When their ship was first launched, Peter was eager to travel again. The slave trade in Rhode Island was lucrative, but Peter chose not to distract himself with new ventures, especially one that involved the complication of living beings, before he packed and sailed away,

***

"Mum, who is this Mr. Elten you speak so often of?" It had been six months since Mary's birth, and Mum appeared smitten with this gentleman she had met.

"He is a man I met at our parish meeting at the Lawtons' home. We have enjoyed each other's company, and he is a very kind man. His wife died three years ago. Peter and Robert have done business with him, and Peter has great respect for him. You must meet him, when we next go to communion."

"I must," I responded as we gathered the last of the season's crops.

"Mum, I did not expect that Peter would be gone so much. He was gone last summer; now he has been gone since June of this year, and I do not even know if he will be home before the winter comes again. I do not know what I would do without you here."

"You cannot count on my being here, Ann. You well know that Peter must travel for his trading, as did your father. Remember, Peter stayed home after you lost Rose." Mum paused with these words. "Peter does seem to spend little time at home when he is not sailing. I believe he has great ambitions, which is not bad. Be patient, Ann."

Our baskets and bowls were full, and we had more than enough squash and berries to preserve for winter. At Peter's request, I made greater use of Obbah in the house and with lifting. Mary brought me much joy, and she loved it when I carried her with me into the woods as we explored the plants, birds and small animals living in God's forest.

As I carried some of the baskets back into the house, Mum caught up with me, carrying a whimpering Mary, ready for a nap.

Miles and Zebediah had finished building the cottage next to the barn. Mingoe was still missing. The cottage was not fancy, but it was larger and sturdier than most slave shelters. It had quarters within for Miles, which was the central part of the home, with rooms in the back to accommodate Zebediah and more. Peter had purchased a small piece of land near Portsmouth and, with his properties, had hopes to receive his freeman status soon. The apothecary thrived in town, and Peter had made some trades with the local Indian tribes. His contributions had only enhanced his status on the island. Though I had not yet adjusted to the brutal winters, our life here was good and the people kind.

It was a chilly day in October when I dressed Mary in her finest dress, as our Reverend Blackstone was coming to say communion at the Lawtons' home, and Mum was dressed and waiting for us. Peter was still abroad, and Miles had brought the buggy to the door. The trip was, as usual, short, and the crowd large today. Miles had dressed in his best attire, as we had invited him to attend the service with us.

"Well, Elizabeth, how delightful you look today," said a charming gentleman near the door as we entered.

"Mr. Elten, this is my daughter, Ann Tallman, and my granddaughter, Mary," she said, looking back at me with a twinkle in her eye. "Mr. Elten."

"I am pleased to make your acquaintance, Mr. Elten. Mum has spoken much of you. She says that you live near the Massachusetts colony, but I pray that in your travels you can visit with us."

"Yes, why do you not come to dinner this evening, after our communion here," Mum offered.

"Well, that is most generous of you both. I do not see why I cannot do so. I can stay the night in Newport with my friend and I will ride on home tomorrow."

Mr. Elten sat with us at the services. Afterwards, Mary and I visited with my friends and their young children as I watched Mary's delight at being around others her age.

When we left, Mr. Elten rode his horse alongside us as Miles guided the buggy home. Obbah had chickens roasting in the oven, and Mum helped her prepare vegetables for a proper dinner. Mr. Elten was quite impressed with Peter's library, saying that such luxuries were rare and precious in the colonies, considered sinfully excessive by some. I could see that Mr. Elten was entirely smitten with Mum. Mum was yet a beautiful woman whose self-confidence gave her an elegance frowned upon in the Puritan community. One could see that this only heightened Mr. Elten's interest, and before he departed that evening, he had invited Mum to visit him at his home in the future.

"Is not he a charming man?" Mum asked after Mr. Elten left.

"Yes, much so. You and he seem quite affable companions," I added. I was gladdened that Mum may have found love again, but, in my selfishness, dreaded the thought she may leave us. With Peter gone so much, her presence was my godsend. I did find Obbah's company pleasing, but Peter frowned upon such familiarity with the slaves.

The difference in the mood of our home when Peter was gone as opposed to his presence was striking. I had heard through my friends that the issues of slavery were controversial within our colony, and though I relied upon having Obbah at my side to help, I would at times pray for her freedom. She was a young woman, and I am certain she would wish for her own life with a family and the love of a man such as Zebediah. I did not see her as property, as did my husband. Zebediah was older than she, but it was clear that he likely loved her. I had witnessed flirtations at the barn as I worked my gardens. There had been one day Zebediah had asked my permission to cut a few of my fragrant garden flowers, and the next day I saw them arranged in a small crock in the kitchen, where I am certain that Obbah had placed them. My heart chuckled, and I was thankful that Peter was not here at the time.

It was not long after this happened that Mum and Mr. Elten were married and Mum moved north to Robert's home. They chose to reside at Robert's home as he was often at sea. I was beside myself in my suddenly empty house that once seemed so small. It was not truly empty, with little Mary and Obbah there to help. I missed my mum's company, though we visited often and still saw each other when the parish met. At times, the parish would meet at Robert's home, and on those occasions Mary would be delighted to see her grandmother and Mr. Elten. With Peter's absence, Miles would be certain that I had everything I needed, and encouraged me to visit my friends in town or took me to visit Mum. I learned to spin the wools and cotton in fabrics that I used for clothing; and, when Robert returned from his trip to Europe, he brought some yardages from which he allowed me to choose those Mum and I might use. I stitched an elegant dress in deep-red brocade and two nice shirts of heavy cotton for Peter. I passed much of my time alone at the house, embellishing with embroidery and grogram the little muslin dresses I stitched for Mary.

With Peter still at sea, I decided to join the sewing circle at Mum's house in January. Robert's house was on the other side of Newport, just off the road to Portsmouth. Winter was before us, so I gathered some wools and muslin for lining and asked Miles to take me to Robert's house, where Mum had a regular group of friends over to sew. Miles said he would do some needed repairs in Robert's barn while he waited for me. As Miles walked toward the barn to yoke the mare and buggy, I remembered that Robert had again returned to sea and I had seen little of him in Rhode Island, though I heard he oft visited New Amsterdam and had visited with Jeremy in Barbados. I imagine he was not happy to learn Peter had been collecting monies from our friend.

When I arrived at Mum's, there was a group of six women gathered in her sitting room, including two young women I had not met.

"Ann, this is Mary Clarke from town," said Mum, "and this is our newest young lady, Martha Wilbor, from Portsmouth. Martha is just learning how to stitch and weave cloth, and she is expecting her first baby in the spring."

I greeted each woman separately, and then said my greetings to the women I knew in Mum's group of friends. "I am joyous to be with you all, since it is so quiet at my house," I said, and I winked at Mum.

"Yes," said Mum. "I look forward to seeing that sweet little granddaughter soon."

"Well, I've barely caught my breath, and my husband is yet at sea." I smiled at Martha. "Let us get busy. Little Mary every week outgrows her clothes, so I know what I need to work on."

Mum served tea as we gathered our fabrics, shears and needles.

"Aye, Ann. My husband says he sees your husband, Peter, at the White Horse often when he is not sailing," said Mary. "I guess they both have a fondness for the whiskey. I have seen him at your apothecary; he is a fine-looking man, Miss Ann. Did you hear the news about Samuel Gorton, from Warwick?" Mary addressed the group. "He declared himself president of Rhode Island, and I heard yesterday that my husband's uncle, John Clarke from Providence, is sailing to England about the colony's charter with the king, to set things straight."

"Oh my, you would think our fighting with the Indian tribes would be enough without fighting with each other. With Newport growing, and Portsmouth too, it is eternally about who has the power, is it not?" asked Mum.

"Aye," said Elizabeth Lawton. "Yet it is good the towns are growing. I pray we can get an Anglican priest to join the new settlers in Newport, and maybe a church. Forgive me, dear Martha; I think you are a Puritan. But we are sorely missing a church in Rhode Island for our own sacraments."

"That is a fact, Mrs. Lawton. But I forgive you your wicked ways." Martha smiled at Elizabeth, accentuating her teasing words. "That is the grandness of our Rhode Island, is it not? We all have free conscience of our own souls. Thank you, Lord, for the bravery of Anne Hutchinson and for Roger Williams."

"Did you know that Master Williams lived in the woods for months after Plymouth Colony had banished him? Before they came to arrest him?"

I later learned, from Peter, that Roger Williams had hunted for food in the wild, and with the help of the Narragansett tribe, he survived to come to the Isle of Rhodes and lead our community of freethinkers.

"His wife and young children must have been terrified of what might have become of him," I responded.

Mum brought some blueberry scones from the kitchen, tempting us to put down our stitchery.

"I heard that the council in Newport is debating the abolishment of slavery in our colony," said Martha. "There is word that we may be required to give them freedom. We have no slaves, only one servant; but many of my acquaintances have slaves. I cannot believe this will happen. Look at the flourishing slave trade at the docks!"

My heart leapt at hearing this news, but I knew that Peter would not take to this kindly. I knew that such debates and proclamations did not happen quickly in the colonies, so I had no intention of raising Obbah's hopes.

"Yes," said Mum. "Such news does not surprise me, considering the freedom in this community. But I saw many slaves freed in Barbados, and often their freedom on the island resulted in great struggle for both them and the community. Many became beggars. They need the structure of their work, as do we, oft for their own protection and survival. I pray the colony makes the right decisions."

We spent the balance of the afternoon visiting and gossiping, getting little stitching done. But it was a good time, and I was sad to leave. Miles and I rode through Newport, on Thames Street, where Peter's shop sat between the silversmith's shop and a boardinghouse. As we left town, the sun was shining but the winter chill remained. At home, Mary was playing in the dining room, and Obbah was preparing dinner. It was a grand day, and I felt nary a worry in the world.

***

It was not quite two years later when Mum came to see me at the house. I asked Obbah to fix some coffee, and we sat at the dining table.

"Ann." Mum paused as if looking for her words. "Robert is moving to New Amsterdam, and John and I have decided we are going with him. He has asked for Hannah's hand in marriage, so he will establish a home there, as well as a new trading market." We sat in stillness.

"It is with such a heavy heart I leave you, and Mary and Peter," Mum said, in a whisper.

"Mum, I do not know what to say," I stammered, feeling short of breath. "We have forever been together."

"I know, and I cannot tell you how dearly I will miss you. But you are stronger than you believe, Ann. Ye at times have relied too much on me, yet you have managed this home, and your servants. You bravely faced tragedy, and God rewarded you with joy. I will see you again. You and Peter will have a grand life here in Newport. He will soon be a freeman and, I am certain, hold positions in the town and the colony. I have seen you well manage Peter's temper and his overbearing ways. You are Ann Hill Tallman. You are a strong and graceful woman. Do not forget that, Ann."

My mind wandered briefly, upon hearing Mum's words, with visions of my dream of Pa on that beach with me so long ago. I remembered Pa's warning, still vague. I was so fearful, but now Mum told me I was brave. For a moment,

I felt alone, but the moment passed as my mind returned to Mum talking about packing up my brother's house.

As the afternoon sun passed over the trees and lit the windows, we visited, sharing coffee and plans. I hugged Mum tightly when she left, and then walked out to her buggy with her and hugged her again, reluctant to let go. I stood in front of my home, watching her buggy travel down the road, away from me. The constant role model in my life, the loving support I reached for. Gone.

***

It was the year of our Lord 1653 when Peter prepared to sail again, in June. As he prepared for his departure, I discovered I was with child, again. Peter was excited to hear this news and, as before, promised to be home before winter set in. He vowed he would let Miles know that he needed to look after the household essentials, and asked me if I wanted for more help in the house.

"No, Peter. Obbah has been a blessing, and I would not know what to do with more servants."

"Well, dear one, get used to it. When I build our own home you will certainly have need of more help. Shall I bring you some new fabrics from France and London?"

"I can plainly use some rich fabrics, and I am certain you will bring some sugar if you go to the islands. Obbah and I can use some sugar."

By the end of the week the house was again quiet, and Obbah broke the news to me that she too was with child, Zebediah's child.

Chapter 17

Peter

It was the year 1653, and I had again left my young wife and daughter alone, in Newport; but the sea drew me like a bewitching siren. Our friends, the Lawtons, had promised to look after my family and help where they could, and I knew that I could trust Miles to provide for their needs. I had promised Ann I would be home before the harshness of winter. Leaving my beautiful Ann behind was hard, but she could not make such voyages and I needed her to oversee the home. On this trip I wished to see my father, but that would remain God's will and the chance of *Vater*'s arrival in Amsterdam while I was there.

My ship was built well, and I relished the journey. It was not long after our departure, maybe one week, when the ship rolled mightily with a vicious storm. For the first time in all my years at sea, I feared for our lives, for my ship. The Atlantic's fierce waves crashed over the starboard deck. We pulled down the sails to protect them, and I feared the worst in the darkened skies enclosing us. We were not yet close to the islands of the Azores, and there was no shelter to be found. As the winds raged, my skipper and I struggled to control the ship. The holds were full of lumber, tobacco and molasses, and I prayed the ship was not too heavy for this battle with the sea. There were countless prayers to God over the three days as we were tossed about like a child's toy. But, at last, with the loss of but one man overboard, we arrived on the other side to sun-filled skies and calmer seas, or I would not be telling this tale. It was almost two weeks more before we passed the Azores, but we did not stop and sailed on another fifteen days to Amsterdam.

My crew took care of the moving and unloading as I signed a contract for the lumber. My father and brother Stephan greeted me as they walked down to the docks. It had been so many years since I had embraced them both. I told them of my home in Rhode Island and of beautiful Ann and our daughter, Mary. Father looked older, and Stephan shared his stories of his exploits in Hamburg.

"Brother, you must make a voyage to Hamburg and meet my family," said Stephan, embracing me.

"*Ja*, Stephan has a grand home in the city, and achieved great success in the government of Hamburg. I am so proud." *Vater* put his arm around Stephan's shoulder, then promptly added, "Peter, you look weary from such a long journey. We are staying with Edmund, your cousin. I beg you to join us."

"I have some business here in Amsterdam, but let me first wash up and we shall get something to eat. The dinner fare on the ship is not up to my standards," I teased. "What do you think of my ship?"

"That is your ship?" queried Stephan, not hiding his surprise. "I thought you had but contracted passage, as before."

"Nay. That is my ship. I am in passage much of the year trading between Europe, the West Indies and the colonies.

Shipbuilding is a vast industry in Rhode Island, and I contracted this beauty for myself, along with my friend Sam, Samuel Allen."

My father gazed back at the ship and seemed impressed, but said nothing. We would put to sea in two days for England, where I had contracted to purchase some fabrics and precise orders from the more wealthy of Newport. I spent my days in Amsterdam at the comfortable accommodations at Edmund's home, visiting with my family, including my youngest brother, Johannes, who lived at the edge of the city. They were astounded at the religious freedom I described in my new home, not comprehending how such openness of conscience could be permitted while the empires of Europe struggled, often viciously, for religious power.

The time in Amsterdam was too short, as I knew not when I would see my family again; and soon I was back on the sea traveling to England. I hoped to spend almost one week in London, most of it bargaining with other traders. The needs of Newport had become evident over time, so I was looking to purchase silver ingots and a good inventory of leather for the cobbler and the saddle makers in Portsmouth and Newport. Two days after leaving Amsterdam, I was selling a large portion of my lumber while holding back a transaction for my friend Modyford in Barbados. With that done, I left the crew at the docks and traveled into London, lodging at the Anchor in Bankside, yet spending a few of my days at the notorious Devil Inn, where I could learn of more lucrative opportunities and maybe meet a pirate or two. I extended my stay, and in two more weeks I had acquired a good inventory of silver and leather, requested furniture pieces and even a carriage, as well as a plentiful selection of fabrics for trade in Newport and a few splendid colors for Ann.

With that done and planning on returning in the

morning to the docks, I walked down the street to a print shop. There I found a few books to add to my library, including some poetry for Ann and *The Child's Mirror* by Bredal and some chapbook pamphlets for little Mary. The Bredal book was Dutch, but I could read this to Mary and, in so doing, teach her some of her ancestral language. To my delight, I came across the book published by Lewes Roberts about commerce, *The Merchants Mappe of Commerce*. Another jewel! Again, I was going home with treasures. I looked forward to the day I had a grand house in Rhode Island, and I was certain to have the most enviable library to be found in the colony.

In the morning, the skies turned gray and cold and we departed England amidst a heavy fog on our long journey to Barbados. I prayed the seas would be more forgiving than they had been on our early journey. God heard my prayers, as a few small storms were but a nuisance, and as weeks passed and we neared the blue waters of the West Indies, I filled with joy to see the beaches and palms.

Modyford was fit and paid well for the balance of my lumber I had saved for him. I boasted of my prestigious apothecary in Newport and the growth of the town, including the abundance of forest that has produced some of the grandest ships now sailing the seas.

"Yes, I think I shall take a day into town with you and see your new ship, friend."

"Yes, that is a welcome plan, and we can enjoy a drink or two at the tavern before returning to your grand plantation. Let us do that with tomorrow's sunrise, if your obligations allow. I cannot grasp how your plantation has grown, and I am blessed to have you here as a friend, ensuring our trades and finding new opportunities."

"It is I who am blessed to have a friend such as you, Peter, who braves the wicked marauders of our seas to trade such goods. You said you purchased silver ingots in

England. Do you have any to sell to me? I have inquired with the silversmith in town to make some pieces for my wife and my young sister Sarah, now a young woman of marriageable age. I was plainly fortunate that I found my sweet Liza before you arrived in our isles." He winked at me. I truly had appreciated the lovely Sarah Modyford on my last trip to Barbados, and saw she was a graceful beauty, but I would not dally with Sarah or risk this valued friendship of mine. Marianne at the pub could keep my attentions here in the islands. I shared with Modyford the news of our lost infant, the arrival of sweet little Mary, and how I wished for a son, or two.

"In time, friend. In time it will come. Look at my brood, and you and Ann are yet young."

"My father expects more. He is a very demanding man, and still, as I saw him in Amsterdam two months ago, holds me up to my brothers' successes. He has no idea of the grand creation of this government and colony in Rhode Island, of my success as a vital spoke of the wheel."

"Oh, he will one day see this, and if he does not live to see this, it is his blindness. It is your success that is of value, not your father's vision. Do not be swayed by his power, but your own strengths, friend."

"Aye. You are my valued comrade, Modyford. I could speak of this to no one but you. You are like an elder brother to me, the elder I am not measured by."

"I am glad you have chosen to stay here with me, and have your skipper to rely on at the dock. And you shall eat well while you are here with us." I rose to go to the dining room, with my friend's arm on my shoulder, comforted as if I were with family.

Over the next weeks I enjoyed the company of my friend and his family, overseeing the work of the fields and warehouse with Modyford, learning more about the growing of tobacco than I needed to know, but knowing that knowledge would help me choose the best. I made one or two trips into town each week to visit Marianne, to check on the ship and loading of sugar I'd negotiated, and to make preparations for our final voyage home, via New Amsterdam. Before my ship sailed north, Modyford had loaded over two tons of tobacco on the ship. I would arrive in Newport with goods to please all and essential to many.

Chapter 18

Ann

*… the message comes as blessed words
from someone loved and with the Lord,
the words pierced me as if a sword ….*

An early February snow had fallen and Peter was not yet home. The year was now 1654, and it was said Peter's ship had been seen in the West Indies. As the skies turned darker each day, both Obbah and I grew with child. There had been only one small crisis at the shop, when James ran out of opiates, a medicine from Asia that Peter would surely purchase in Amsterdam. Peter's customers in need were not pleased with the absence of a medicine they sorely needed; but Miles assured James, who was a bit panicked, that Peter would soon return with new supplies. In the meantime, whiskey would suffice. Miles never ceased to surprise me, how efficiently he resolved problems and got things done, consistently remaining calm. I was blessed to have him, especially during Peter's long absences. I was certain that Miles would be a successful citizen of our colony upon release from his bondage.

"Obbah, what will you and Zebediah do now that this child is coming? Will you marry?" I asked one morning as I sat at the dining table and Obbah was cleaning the oven.

"Oh, ma'am." Obbah smiled at me. "I did think hard about that. Was this the man to be me husband? But, Zebediah is good to me, and a gentle man who works hard. This child is the work of your God; yet your laws do not permit us to wed." She paused a few moments. "Last month, Zebediah and I stood before God and made our promise. I am his wife before God, yet I pray that master not pull us apart."

"Oh, Obbah, Peter would never do that!" I paused, and thought to myself that maybe he would. "Let us pray that never happens. Zebediah is a good man." Yet I thought, without spoken words, that Peter sees them only as property to be traded or used. I would have to work on that, persuade him of their value to him, as a family.

"I did not know you were not allowed to wed. That is not my understanding of God's laws." I sat silently a moment. "Let us prepare a feast today, a feast of your favorite foods. I will make a tart from the berries preserved. You and Zebediah can have a wedding dinner at the cottage tonight. I am certain that Miles would allow you to use his dining table. Let us do that."

Obbah was excited and smiling, then asked, "But what about Master Tallman? He would not like that."

"Obbah, he is not here. And, besides, you sometimes eat at the cottage." I knew that Obbah was right. Peter would not approve of treating Obbah or Zebediah in any way other than slaves to do our bidding. Their personal life would be of no import to him. I pulled my silver candlesticks from the cabinet. Soon enough, Peter would be home and the work would be demanded in earnest.

We spent the day cooking chicken with dried spices, turnips with ginger sauce, corn bread and a loaf of steamed brown bread—one for the house and one for the cottage—and I made a peach tart. I found candles for the silver candlesticks and Obbah set an elegant table at the cottage. I even let them have a bottle of Peter's good brandy from the root cellar. Miles and I ate quietly in the house, speaking of Peter's expected return.

The next morning, the skies were dark and overcast and Obbah was not there. I had encouraged her to spend the night in the cottage with her new husband, so I made a cup of coffee and looked out the window toward the forest. The trees were barren, except the firs sprinkled throughout. They were dressed in snowy frost. I felt akin to the forest. Mary had been fed and was napping so I grabbed my cloak and wandered out through the trees to listen in the quiet in the forest, a stillness different than the quiet within the house. After several steps, I thought of my mum and, at that moment, sensed that my pa was walking with me. Comfort filled me. We walked on, without words, until I came upon a rill. I could still see the house at a distance through the trees, as I did not wish to lose my bearings. I sat on a rock, feeling not alone. Pa said no words, but then I heard the whispers of how much he missed me. It was as if his warm breath could melt the snow and break the cold breezes. Again, I heard him in my head: "Ann, dear Ann, be careful of your Peter. He loves you, but he wants too much." A truth in Pa's words, words as if but a breeze, filled me as I sat listening to the water bubbling from the rill's frozen rim. "Be patient. God brings you, one day, the adoration of a good man." His presence faded away as it had on the beaches in my dreams; then I heard his sighed words, "Be brave, Ann," as I heard my own name wafting in the chilled breeze.

"But, Pa," I cried out. I heard my words echo through the trees, breaking the stillness, but he was gone. *What did he mean? This cannot be. I love my Peter; my husband and the father of my children. There can be no one else. Would some horrible tragedy befall Peter, befall us?* And then I became anxious about feeling Pa's presence, about this gift that Mum reproved, calling it wicked.

How is it that I can talk with or hear my pa? This gift is not of this world, and frightens me. I remembered how Mum's earlier warning had alarmed me. The Anglican Church believed in the presence of the dead, of communion with God; but the Puritans strictly prohibited such thoughts. This foreboding from Pa puzzled and frightened me, yet I knew well to hold these fears within.

***

Peter came home from his travels in February and remained busy in town with his shop and warehouse. As usual, the mood of the house changed, yet I was overjoyed to feel his arms around me again. The smells of a man in the house were comforting and revealed that our family was complete again. Peter played with Mary in the sitting room, delighted to see how much she had grown, and I could see the joy on his face each time she giggled.

***

On a cold morning in late February, a horse arrived leading Mingoe tied by a rope to a young man's saddle. The young man on the horse had worked for Master Elten, and, upon finding the fugitive slave, had brought him to our house, as it was near Newport. Peter was home and paid the young man a bit for his trouble, taking Mingoe out to the barn. I could hear the strikes of the horsewhip as I stood at the well out back, and then the cries of the slave rang out, echoing through the trees. This saddened my heart. As I walked into the kitchen, I saw the frightened look on Obbah's face. I gently hugged her, in spite of my knowing such contact was discouraged. We comforted each other, momentarily, through Obbah's fear and my disappointment in my husband's propensity to be so hardened. Obbah gathered some clean rags and filled a pitcher with water to take out to Zebediah, who would likely minister to Mingoe. Miles would have some whiskey at the cottage, she was certain. She set the items on the counter, and shortly after Peter returned to the house, he departed on his horse for his shop. With Peter gone, Obbah took the items out to the barn for Zebediah. It was only four days before Mingoe was gone for good. Peter sold him to traders at the docks and sent the monies to Mr. Elten, who had been promised the slave upon capture.

Peter spent more time at the tavern, befriending many of the local officials, as he knew this would advance his position in the community. The dark days of winters were a struggle for me, as I spent time restricted to the house. Peter had brought new books from London for our library and delighted little Mary with the pamphlets he read to her. He would read the Dutch storybook he brought, and showed such delight when she repeated the Dutch words. The winter allowed me time to read poetry and weave and stitch finery. I made myself an elegant dress with the forest-green silk Peter had brought me, a dress that stunningly framed my treasured ruby necklace. I would alter the bodice when my figure returned after this baby. When the weather was good, Miles would take me to the sewing circle, now at Martha's home in Portsmouth, where we would do our stitch work and gossip; I prized these times with my new friends.

A daughter arrived in March. She had bright blue eyes

like Peter's and dark curls, yet I saw Peter's disappointment in the set of his face. I said nothing, for I felt only joy. We named her Elizabeth after Mum, and were blessed. Three weeks later Obbah delivered a baby boy she named Zebediah. Peter was petulant over this course of God's plan, but I reminded him that he had gained a new slave, a male, of great value to him, hoping silently in my heart that Peter would not consider selling this child as he grew older. Peter agreed that the new child might be of value, as he reminded me how useless Mingoe had been.

Chapter 19

Ann

The next few months were demanding, with Mary, my nursing Elizabeth and Obbah nursing her infant. We managed to keep up with the children and Obbah prepared meals for the family. Peter was oft in town or at his shop, but now he stayed late in town and we saw him only early in the morning before he would depart. Obbah struggled with her chores and the care of her child while evading Peter's sharp temper. We conspired to ensure he saw the operation of the house as seamless, and I helped where I was able, as did Miles and Zebediah.

In only six weeks, and with little Elizabeth sleeping at night, I returned to my marital bed. Peter was gladdened by my return to his arms, and before Elizabeth was three months old, I knew I was yet again with child. Though Peter was spending less time at the house, he reveled in news of another little Tallman. I braced myself for the year before me, and wished for the impossible—that Mum were still here.

***

Summer was filled with blooms and birdsong. But summer was usually the time that Peter left, and I struggled with my feelings. I missed my husband's presence during his voyages, his strong arms around me at night, the sense of protection. Yet I knew well that the house and those of us living there were happier when he was gone. My divided feelings lived deep in my heart, unspoken. There was routinely the tiptoeing around so as not to disturb or anger Peter. With the two children and a third one growing within me, I dreaded his departure more than usual. Yet I reminded myself that, with the help of Miles, Obbah and I had managed in the past. Mary was almost four years old and would soon be more help with her siblings.

In July, as the garden was flourishing and the dairy cow had calved, we sat at our late dinner meal. Miles was not there and the children had been put to bed; it was just Peter and I in the candlelight on a warm night.

"I have thought long and hard about my trades this year, and I have decided to go to the West Indies and back up the coast. I will not go to Europe this year, so I plan with certainty to be home for the holiday and the winter. Will you be well with the house and keeping an eye on the shop with Miles's help?"

"Aye, Peter. With Obbah and Miles's help, we will be well. You know I will miss you, as your absence disquiets me." I paused with my words. "You are gone so much, Peter. I pray the day will come when you travel less often."

"You knew my trade when you married me; it is what I do. With my trading I will be able to provide you a grand home, and you know I have purchased land towards my freeman status. I am looking at land in Portsmouth for our family. You have some friends in Portsmouth, do you not?"

"Yes, I do. I may visit my sewing circle more often while

you are gone."

"That will be good. You need not tie yourself to this house, and when I return we need to socialize more with my acquaintances and the officials in town. I will start tomorrow, preparing the shop, contracting goods for my voyage, and plan to depart in two weeks. Ready my clothing for the journey."

When I joined Peter in bed that night, after nursing Elizabeth, he took me into his arms and held me for a long time. My longing for him grew as I lay within his embrace, absorbing the warmth of his body. His lips found mine in a binding kiss followed by tender lovemaking, more heartfelt than I remember in a long, long time. I truly loved this man, and refused to heed the gnawing and subtle fear of a growing distance between us.

***

As planned, Peter sailed in two weeks, and, again, the house was quiet. I savored spending my rare quiet moments, when not stitching, reading Peter's gems in the library.

Now that Peter was away, I could allow Mary, Elizabeth and little Zebediah to play together in the house. With all going effortlessly and free time on my hands, I asked Miles to take me to my friend Martha Wilbor's house in Portsmouth, as she had sent an invitation.

Chapter 20

Peter

I spent over four months in Barbados, including voyages to Antigua and Jamaica. I chose to stay in Elizabeth's house in the village of Christ Church while on the island, spending days between visiting my friend Thomas Modyford and my comrades at the tavern in town.

When I first arrived at the old house in the village, it smelled musty and needed repairs; the fireplace in the sitting room had loosened stones. It appeared that Jeremy had made repairs to the roof after the storm season, so I walked out to check on the barn and the horses. All looked well, and my old horse was yet there. I saddled my roan and rode out to Modyford's plantation to visit and let him know I was in town. I enjoyed a festive dinner with his family before leaving, telling Modyford I would meet him at the tavern on Thursday.

Jeremy was in the stables when I arrived at the house.

"I did not know you were here, Captain Tallman. I was worried about the absence of your roan."

"Yes, I am staying at the house. It smells musty and, I suspect, you need to repair damage from seepages. Do not be forgetful, while I am here, to pay any profits due Lizbeth. If I am not here, you may leave it on the desk in the sitting room."

"Aye," responded Jeremy as he turned to unsaddle my horse.

The tavern was busy on Thursday, but I found Modyford in the crowd. He was in a heated debate with other plantation owners at a table near the bar. As I walked over to him, Marianne walked by with a tray and I caught her eye and winked. I was happy to see she was still working at the tavern. Modyford, his friends and I drank late into the night, and before the tavern started to clear I had three new orders for lumber. After Modyford left, I climbed the stairs to Marianne's room. Her door was unlocked, so I entered and lit the candle, lying down on her bed, waiting for her to finish downstairs. Her room was small, but was filled with lace and thick, soft quilts; a silver hairbrush lay before an old, tarnished silver-etched framed mirror on her dressing table. I was clearly in a lady's room, and then my mind wandered and I thought of Ann and how she strove to decorate our home to please me. At that moment, Marianne walked into her room, leaving me a bit red-faced, as my head had been full of thoughts of Ann. Marianne stopped when she saw that her candle was burning and, looking around, she rolled her eyes at my presence.

"Oh dear, how you frightened me," she whispered. After a moment she regained her calm and remarked coquettishly, "I do not recall inviting you to my room, Monsieur Tallman. What might be the purpose of your visit?"

"I have not seen you for quite some time and thought it best we reacquaint ourselves." With a more serious tone, I inquired, "How have you been, Marianne?"

"I have been good. I am still here, working, but my

bond will be paid in but eighteen months and thenceforth I will be free. Then who shall you visit here at the tavern, Captain?"

"I am certain I will cross that bridge later. What shall you do when your bond is done?"

"I am not yet decided. I would like to open me own tavern on the island, or I might become a wife and mother and follow the same path as all the others. But that seems a hard way of living, oft having one babe after another. The Lord will let me know my destiny when the time comes."

"Well, I know your destiny this night." I smiled.

As I left in the wee hours in the morn, I laid eight pounds on the dressing table next to her hairbrush. Waking a sleeping Marianne, I whispered, "Marianne, you must put the monies on your table in a sock under your mattress and save it for the day your bondage ends." Not quite awake, she took my hand, squeezing it gently, before I shut the door, went down the stairs and mounted my mare, guiding her toward Christ Church and the old musty house.

My stay in Barbados was a good one, as I negotiated several contracts for my next trip to the islands. My time with my friend Modyford was a blessing and made me think, at times, that I should have been a plantation owner. It was a busy life, but a lucrative one. Then I remembered the citizens of Newport and Portsmouth, their gratitude of my apothecary, my ability to provide medicines absent in the past. I thought of James, who had turned out to be a great asset, as he had learned quickly the names and uses of the medicines and salves and how to advise our patrons. My thoughts reminded me that I did need to go to Europe next summer. The apothecary would need restocking, although I did get indigo and healing herbs in Antigua on this trip. I could only get the medicines from the orient through my trader in Antwerp. I pondered adding the Virginia Colony to my journeys. I was not certain of their needs, and it might behoove me to find out.

December approached, and my crew was antsy to return to sea. We readied the ship for a winter voyage to the north, ensuring we had plenty of citrus. The warm days and easygoing life on the island begged me to stay, but I knew my commitments. I mused of a respite in Virginia on our return journey, but the crew did not wish to delay our return, and we yet had a delivery in New Amsterdam, so we sailed north. The cold winds battered the ship as it blurred our path and stung our faces while we passed the bays of the Virginia Colony. It was a new year when we docked in Newport.

It was the Epiphany as we disembarked the ship and found the snow was deep. I gave instructions for unloading the ship's hold, telling the crew they could go home when finished. I fought the bitter wind from the docks and onto the main street, where I entered my shop, and, after talking with James, I considered spending the night in the back room in hopes that the blizzard would end by morning. But both James and I were eager to be home, so I helped James close the shop, gathering the receipts to review at my leisure. James offered to take me home; and, after getting his horse from the stable, I mounted the steed behind him and we persevered through the bitter cold and stinging snow.

Ann ran to hug and kiss me as I walked in the door with James.

"Oh, my dear, it has been so long, I was fearful something had happened to you and your ship. You fought this storm to get home? Look at you! You are frozen, and you too, James." Ann turned to Obbah and told her to get two blankets. "Here, give me your cloaks; they are like ice."

"James, I think you should stay here the night," I said as I handed my cloak to Ann.

"Yes, yes, James," said Ann. "You cannot go back into

this blizzard. And I am certain ye are both hungry. I will have Obbah put on a hot meal for dinner."

Little Mary came into the room and she barely recognized me. I was certain my frozen eyebrows and my long absence had made me but a stranger in my house. I picked her up to give her a kiss and she saw it was I. "Pa, Pa!" Elizabeth was crawling from the dining room; Obbah came in with the blankets and then swooped little Elizabeth into her arms and vanished. We wrapped ourselves, and James and I sat at the dining table as Obbah and Ann warmed rum and coffee and gathered a grand meal. We talked for hours, and I welcomed a soft bed at the end of the day.

***

March arrived with little sign of spring. The shop flourished, and I was speaking with a customer when Miles came into the shop and said that Prudence was with Ann and she was soon to deliver. I told Miles I would be there in short order. I finished with the customer before me, Mrs. Morrow, and then headed home.

When I arrived, it was quiet downstairs, but an infant cried upstairs. Obbah was in the kitchen with Mary and Elizabeth at the table.

I ran up the stairs two at a time. Ann's face glistened from the labored effort of bringing another life into the world, and though her hair was yet pinned, dark, damp curls framed her face. She appeared as a Madonna, angelic yet alluring. The infant she held was squirming as Ann looked up at me, smiling.

"Peter, I must nurse him," she said as she unlaced her blouse, modestly covered her bosom and slipped the baby beneath. "He is anxious. Aye." She beamed. "You have a son."

I sat in the chair near the bed as Prudence gathered and stacked the linens, lifted a pot and excused herself from the room.

"Mrs. Tallman, I will be back in a bit. I will let you visit with your husband."

I turned back to Ann. "Dear Peter," she said, "you have quite the proud smile on your face. A brother for the girls. It is Peter, is it not? Our son, Peter Tallman?"

"Yes, Peter Stephan it shall be. Our family is growing. I believe I must get our new home built. This one is becoming tiny for such a grand family." We sat in silence for a while, and then Ann took the infant from the cover, swaddled him and handed him to me. I was filled with joy. "Bless the Lord. I think we must find a way to send a message to your mum. I will see to it on the next ship to New Amsterdam."

I looked at the healthy baby boy in my arms. His eyes found mine and then grew heavy with sleep. When I looked up at Ann, she had fallen into sleep, and the sun's rays suddenly shone brightly through the window, announcing spring.

***

Over the next three years, I traveled often through the trade triangles to build my wealth, to grow my apothecary. James had become my trusted apprentice and dispensed cures and herbs expertly when I was absent. My friendships with the elite of Newport expanded, and having my beautiful wife Ann on my arm was a great advantage. Little Mary grew and, though she was but a girl, I considered getting her into the school that had opened in Newport. Thanks to Ann and to the pamphlets and books I had brought home, Mary demonstrated a fondness for reading and learning.

As time passed, I found the business dealings of many local citizens dubious. It was on more than one occasion that I found myself in the courts to collect debts. First, Rutgert Jansen had defaulted his indebtedness to me, and then others had done the same. I spent too much of my own time pursuing these debtors. Between this and my interpreting, I found myself oft in court. It was in 1658 that I attended Master Jan Denman in a court matter, interpreting his Dutch in court on the foolish matter of complaints of the noise from his tavern. Denman lost his license to serve beer, and after that occasion, the courts would oft contract with me for interpreting litigation, in both German and Dutch, on matters regarding foreign traders and sailors.

To add to my troubles, another trader had the audacity to sue me for nonpayment of tobacco for a trade of Spanish wine and stockings. The rogue had been paid in full with tobacco from the Indies, though I paid him only in value of the goods I had received. I protested such trickery loudly through a letter to the court; however, the court ruled against me. I had paid this huckster what he was owed and was riled that the courts could not see through the swindler, forcing me to pay more.

The sea brought me escape from such petty troubles and an excitement away from my ordinary life. I relished the time I spent on the oceans and in foreign lands. The reward from my long absences from home was the mercantile growth I brought to Rhode Island, in Newport, Portsmouth and Warwick, as well as the growth in my own stature. I was grateful for my life and longed for the day when my father, in Hamburg, would acknowledge the breadth of my success.

Chapter 21

Ann

My heart was full and my days were busy with toddling Peter and little Elizabeth, as well as Mary, the ever-helpful big sister. I was daily grateful for summer, and Mary and Elizabeth were in the garden with me on a beautiful July day. In spite of Peter's protests, I continued to find great peace working in my garden and letting the little ones run in the sunshine.

The year was 1658, and Peter, who was purchasing land throughout the island, purchased acreage in Portsmouth from Richard and Mary Morris. He had negotiated a good price for a piece of land he coveted; yet he came home quite peeved in the course of the sale.

"I have found the land for our home, but in the course of this transaction, I find I must get the signature of Morris's wife. I cannot believe such a thing. Women cannot be deeded property, and the fact that Richard cannot sell this property on his own signature is an abomination."

"Did Mrs. Morris sign the deed documents?"

"Not yet. Richard said he would get her signature and

have the deed to me tomorrow, and the transaction will be filed. When a man cannot transact his own business is a sad day. Our laws have gone awry."

"I am happy, dear, that you have found the suitable site for our home. I cannot wait to see this place."

Peter stewed the rest of the evening but had the deed signed by all parties and filed the following day. After that, he purchased a piece of adjoining land from William Wilbor, a relative of my friend Martha. I was grateful that soon we would have our own home, on our own land.

Peter was busy with the apothecary and the construction of the house in Portsmouth. He said it was to be grand, and he had promised to take Mary and me to see it one day soon. He had taken me in the carriage to Portsmouth shortly after the purchases to see the land and what he described as the view from our home. The site was a wooded hill just east of the town and there was, indeed, a blessed view of the Sakonnet River through the trees. It was a tranquil place, yet filled with abundant birdsong amongst the trees and the sound of a rill somewhere nearby. It was a place where one might have a conversation with God or, as I suddenly recalled, an encounter with one's dead father. It had been a long time since I had sat with my pa in God's forest; and, as I stood there next to Peter on that day, I recalled the unthinkable consolation Pa's spirit had shared with me just a few winters before. It was true that Peter could be harsh, but he provided for us and held his goals in gravitas. I adored this man.

Because of the house, Peter chose not to travel this summer. He desperately needed supplies for the shop and he had contracts to meet in Barbados, so he negotiated a commitment from a trusted fellow trader to captain the ship. The merchant, along with his own goods, agreed to sail to Barbados with Peter's contracted goods for his friend Modyford, as well as others, and to negotiate the purchase of enumerated medicines and herbs in Amsterdam and Antwerp. The ship had left only last week, and I was gladdened that Peter had stayed.

On this day, little Zeb was running through the garden with Elizabeth, chasing after kittens living in the barn. Their giggles were like echoed harmony, and little Mary sat near me but kept her eye on the young ones. She had grown into such a dear helper. Miles spent most days in Portsmouth and would soon be staying there every day, once the new barns were built. Peter had contracted two slaves from a slave trader at the dock, but Zebediah stayed at our Newport home and provided help and transport for us in the new closed carriage Peter had purchased from a trader recently returned from London. Though I knew these were mere business decisions for Peter, I was secretly happy that Zebediah was able to stay near his Obbah and his young son.

When Peter heard of the town's debates on restricting slavery, he was enraged. He considered his slaves his legal property. I later heard that the new law before the council would not abolish slavery, but require citizens of Rhode Island to give them their freedom after ten years. This appeased Peter little. But the law failed to find consensus, so Peter's only concern was the eventual release of Miles's bondage and indenturing another.

My thoughts returned to the garden as I saw Mary run toward the woods. The babes had wandered into the trees, and she went to retrieve them. As Mary guided Zeb and Elizabeth back toward me, I gathered the bucket of vegetables and we headed to the house, where Obbah would be starting dinner.

Zebediah walked from the house, where he was repairing a cupboard in the kitchen.

"I'll take Zeb with me to the barn. We brush the horses, yes, little man." Zebediah picked up his son. Elizabeth started to whimper at the loss of her playmate. I smiled at Zebediah and picked up Elizabeth with my free hand as we headed inside.

I found Obbah sitting at the table, sobbing, as Peter sat playing on the floor.

"Mary, take Elizabeth and Peter upstairs. Put Peter down for a nap and you can play with your sister before dinner." I sat down next to Obbah. "Obbah, what is wrong?"

Through her sobs, she spoke. "Master … he is gonna sell Zebediah … after … the house is done."

Her words shocked me. Why would Peter do such a thing? We would need Zebediah's help at the estate in Portsmouth.

"Why? Do you know why, Obbah?" I asked.

"'Cause he's getting too old … Zebediah said Miles told him this, that Master wants to keep the young men in Portsmouth." Her crying grew softer as she calmed herself. Even then, her tears still trickled down her cheeks, and I handed her my linen kerchief.

Within my thoughts, I was livid. I knew Peter was the head of this house, but he had said nothing to me of this. How could he do this? He knew that was Zebediah's son living under our roof. Zebediah worked hard for us, and he was a kind and gentle man, yet strong. What can I do? I knew my anger would not sway Peter, but only swell his ire. I must help them stay together. The house was to be finished before the year ended, so I would find some persuasion. I could not delay.

Peter came home late for dinner that night. The children had been fed, but I waited for Peter to come home so I could eat dinner with him. We sat in the candlelight at the table. I could see that Peter was tired.

"I went up to Portsmouth today to oversee the house. It is coming together well. I believe next week I shall take you to see it. I think we may move in November."

I smiled. "I cannot wait to see the house. Were you busy at the shop today?"

"Yes, each day is busy. I cannot complain about that, but I should have gone to Amsterdam this summer for more stock, yet I want to be certain the house is done to my liking. I do pray Captain Brownard gets back soon with the purchases I contracted. The stock is low in the storeroom and will soon be so in the warehouse."

"You know, Obbah and I manage well here at the house, maybe you could take Zebediah up to Portsmouth to work on the house with Miles. He is such a hard worker, and so strong. Obbah and I can manage the buggy when needed."

"I have the two young slaves working. I contracted them for as long as needed. Zebediah is older. I would be better with the two young, healthy slaves working on the house than with Zebediah."

"Are they reliable? Or looking for freedom, like Mingoe?" I paused, letting doubt creep in. "Zebediah is steadfast. I imagine he could teach the others things they do not know."

"Perhaps." He sat in silence for a time.

"I do not like you and the children here alone. Maybe when we need some help to finish I will send Miles for him. Such things are not your worry. Besides, who would care for the animals?" He paused, searching for a new topic, I am certain. "We have been invited to a formal dinner on Sunday at the Sherman estate."

I said no more. I had placed the thought in his head.

"Wear your best dress," Peter added. "Phillip and his wife live on a grand estate in Portsmouth. There will be many important officials at the dinner, so you should plan on our being gone for much of the day."

"I shall be ready."

When Sunday came, Peter told me to dress early and that he would take me by the house to see it before dinner at the Sherman home. I nursed little Peter, leaving the children with Obbah, and then dressed for the event. I chose the velvet-trimmed blue brocade gown and my indigo-blue cape. I fastened my ruby necklace at my nape and carried my dress gloves to put on later. I could see by Peter's smile, when I stepped into the sitting room, that he approved. We departed, with a picnic that Obbah had packed, as the sun rose toward its peak. Though the road was bumpy, the beautiful countryside made the trip seem short.

Peter guided the buggy up a trail to the hilltop, where I could see the roof of the house sitting on the downslope beyond the trees. Peter had cut down just enough trees so that the vista of the river was stunning. There were two large barns near the woods on the west side of the house. I had not even seen the inside of the house, but I was in love with this place. I imagined my gardens nearer the barn. Peter showed me the beginnings of the well that was being dug near the house and told me that the second barn annexed the servant quarters. He pointed out the two chimneys and said there would be a fireplace in our bedroom. I could not believe that we would live in such a splendid place.

We were hungry, so before entering the home, I placed a blanket for our seating and spread out our picnic by the steps to our front door, facing the river. I put out some fresh cornbread and blueberry jam, and there was a bit of cheese from the root cellar, a light lunch for we would dine at the party. I soaked in the serenity and beauty of the trees and the meadow down the hillside toward the river, as I sat on the blanket, careful not to muss my dress. Oh, how I wished Mum could see this place.

"Well, dear Ann, is it grand enough for you?"

"Peter, this is beyond anything that I could have dreamed. I can see our children running through the grasses and the trees. I think I shall never want to leave such a tranquil and heavenly place."

"Wait until you see the inside. Of course, it is not quite finished and there is no furniture, but you will see how grand it is. There are four bedrooms on the second floor, plus the maid's room. And, I have told you about the library. It is my favorite room."

After we finished eating, Peter took my hand to help me up, as I was again with child. I packed up the basket and set it on the step. We walked in the front door and I was taken aback immediately with the grandeur of the stairway. It was curved and exquisite, with a chandelier suspended and candelabras on the walls. I suddenly thought of poor Obbah and all of the extra work she and I would have in this house. The kitchen and eating area was long and narrow, as at our current home, but there were two windows along the length of the outside wall, with a large brick oven. Our bedroom was on the lower floor, next to the library. The rooms upstairs were simple, but I was awed by the view of the river all the way across to Little Compton, an area disputed amongst the Plymouth Colony, Rhode Island and the Sakonnet tribe. I could not help but think of how brave, or perhaps foolish, the English were who had settled there.

As I turned from the window to return downstairs, I found Peter standing behind me. I walked into him and he took me in his arms and kissed me long and hard, stirring in both of us a desire that overtook me, as Peter's hands found their way to unlace my bodice and bare my shoulder. The weight of Peter's passion had me pressed against the window frame, my knees weakened by the hunger of our kisses. Suddenly, Peter's fingers tightened on my arms as he pushed himself back, resisting our desires.

"We must go. Sherman and his guests are expecting us," he said sternly, while adjusting his jacket. "Your hair is mussed." After a moment of awkwardness, we descended the stairs as I struggled to lace and tie my dress.

"Is there a root cellar?" I asked, carrying the lunch basket as we walked toward the buggy.

"No. No, there is not," he responded, pausing in thought. "I should think we can put that to the side of the house near the south chimney. I will have Miles add that to his list of tasks." Once in the buggy, I pinned my hair as best I could as we jostled down the path toward the road.

The dinner at the Shermans' mansion was, indeed, quite formal. Sarah, Phillip Sherman's wife, was delightful, and the meal she served was savory, with many courses. I would need to ask for some of her kitchen's recipes. We stayed well after sunset, and Peter spent much of the evening sharing his stories with the influential men of Aquidneck Island. He appeared in his element, while I was dreaming of spending my days with the children on the shores of the Sakonnet. I was excited for the future.

Chapter 22

Ann

We moved into the Portsmouth house just after Peter received his coveted freeman status, in November. Though the house in Newport had not been our own, I was saddened to leave. I had come to crave the silence and serenity in the heavy forest that I first feared behind the house. Obbah had squealed with excitement upon seeing our new home, with its large kitchen and her room upstairs. I was so glad that Peter was not home when Obbah arrived, for she would not have shown such emotion in his presence; but her delight made me happy, as did the children running up the stairs to explore.

Annie was born in December. She arrived in our new home, with the doctor present. I missed Prudence and her loving tenderness during the birthing process, but Peter had insisted the physician be present. It was fortunate that my labor was short, and Annie came into our family as a healthy hazel-eyed girl, with Peter's blond curls. Obbah helped as best she could, but her days were full of the children and caring for the house. I spent much time alone with sweet Annie, in confinement, but was thankful my friend Martha came to visit and laugh with me two or three times each week. As much as I loved my Peter, I dreaded the day I would return to my marriage bed, as it often predicted the arrival of another pregnancy.

After our relocation to Portsmouth, Peter purchased new furnishings for the house, including a splendid desk for his library. When we arrived at the house, Peter and Miles ensured we had bed frames for our bedding, including some built-in trundles for the children upstairs, and a large wooden table in the kitchen. There was a grand dining room in this house for formal occasions, but it was not yet furnished. As Annie slept on a schedule and I felt stronger, I started making drapes for the windows, and I made some lace curtains for the bedrooms upstairs to allow in the summer breezes, and brocade drapes over the lace for warmth in the winter. I surely missed Mum being here to help with the sewing. Infrequently a letter would arrive from New Amsterdam.

Peter planned to sail to England and France for the coming summer and said he would return with fine furnishings for the sitting room and some Persian rugs. Such things were less important for me, as it was the outdoors here in Portsmouth that I savored so much. When Zebediah had come to Portsmouth to help with the finishing of the house, I had asked him to work up a tract between the house and the barn for a nice garden. I had harvested the last of my fall greens and turnips, and the persistent winter storms delayed spring planting. As the cold days shrouded us in the house, Peter would spend more time at the tavern in Portsmouth and in Newport, and he was oft ill-tempered in his drunkenness when arriving home. I endeavored to shelter the children from Peter's anger; in spite of Peter's mischief, the children and I began to feel at home in Portsmouth.

When March came, I worked readying the soil for spring gardening. Zebediah was still here, and Peter had purchased one of the male slaves who had worked on the house, a young man named Ibrahim. I was unsure of Zebediah's future, but believed in my heart that my words last year had persuaded Peter of Zebediah's value. Elizabeth and Zeb were playful companions, and Mary helped keep an eye on them and little Peter, who was now toddling about the farm, exploring. Life was good during this time.

Peter relied heavily on James to run the shop, for Peter had a great need to be in the midst of all that was happening in Newport, both at the apothecary and in politics. Sometimes I resented his long absences, both at home and at sea, but family filled my days.

When the little ones were napping, I would take time to teach Obbah some tailoring skills and Mary some embroider stitches. My friend Martha visited and we worked on our sewing and caught up on the gossip. I often had little news to offer, now that Mum was gone and Peter shared so little. When Miles would take his meals in the house, he would tell stories of what he heard at the local Portsmouth and Newport taverns.

Soon enough, Peter was sailing to foreign shores again. Zebediah helped at times in the house with heavy work or repairs. I wondered, on some days, if I did need another servant in the house, but there was no good reason. I could manage my own home and my children. Zebediah would oft help Obbah with some of the drudgery, such as forming our candles from the animal fats or the beeswax Peter brought from his shop, and Zebediah would help Obbah gather wood ash for making soap, though I suspect he seized this time to be near his sweetheart. The laws regarding any restrictions on slavery were seldom enforced, as the slave trade in Newport continued to prosper. I knew that we were lucky that Zebediah was not sold, and little

Zeb was old enough to help with chores in the barn. When I was able, I would gift Obbah with some fabric or a toy for Zeb, and she never failed to share her pleasure. It would be the coming year when Peter would be obligated to release Miles's bond, but I knew he did not want to do so. Peter relied heavily on Miles, but Peter would give him a bit of monies and likely grant him a small bit of land, as is the custom.

In spite of Martha's weekly visits, a sense of loneliness overtook me while Peter was gone. It was not only Peter's absence, as his absences were frequent; but a weight sat in my chest: the loss of my mum's nearness, the loss of dear sweet Rose, and the loss of my youth and joyful memories of Barbados. I had an ache for the sweet fragrance of mangoes, of the juices running down my arms. I yearned for the bright hues that clad the homes in the parishes of the island and the women themselves, the long days of a brazen sun across the calm turquoise waters, with my shoes off and my toes in the sand. Oh, how I missed my mum. I thought early on that I would visit Mum in New Amsterdam, but it had not happened. Mum's husband, John, had died this past year, and my brother Robert had married his Hannah. I knew that Robert itched to move to Virginia, and I believed that now that he was married, he might do so.

One early September evening, as Obbah put the children down to bed, I walked down the steps from the front porch toward the river, feeling the breeze on my face. The sun had set and the half-moon glowed as if with intent to light my way, as moonlight bounced back from the mirrored river. I stared at the stars, increasing in number as I searched the sky for answers. I longed for the moon over Barbados before grasping that this was, indeed, the same moon. And this was the same moon shining above Mum in New Amsterdam and upon my Peter somewhere at sea.

The same moon shone brilliant, connecting us all at once. I knew at that moment it was time to visit Mum.

It was early September when I asked Miles to purchase my passage on a ship to New Amsterdam, and a return ship as well, if he could do so. I knew well that Peter might be livid that I would travel without his permission and on my own. I would take Annie with me, as she was still nursing; Obbah would care for the others in my absence. I would not be gone for more than two weeks, and sailing to New Amsterdam was not a hardship. Miles warned me that I should not go alone. He said I would need help and he was concerned for my safety. Traveling with the baby, I was certain that Miles was right.

I spoke to Martha of my situation and my desire to visit my mum. My sweet friend said that her husband's sister Lydia, who was a cheerful, unwed young woman of some means, would surely go with me. I had met Lydia, and Martha was certain that Lydia would be a suitable and eager traveling companion. I gave Miles the monies for our passage, and the deed was done.

The following week, Lydia and I, with the baby, boarded the Dutch ship captained by Arent van Curler for our journey to New Amsterdam. Captain van Curler was gracious, and assured us the trip would be uneventful. During our voyage, he engaged in conversation with me regarding the growth of the colonies and the religious philosophy of Rhode Island. I was astounded by his discussion of such things with a woman. He seemed to esteem me as if I were a man, which both startled me and endeared him to me. He spoke of our friend Pieter Stuyvesant and we spoke of Anne Hutchinson's terrible demise in New Amsterdam. He shared that he had married a widow a few years before, and had no children of his own. I found him charming, more so than the men I had met in Rhode Island.

Fortunately, I had brought two hammocks, and a crewmember had hung these for Lydia and me; therefore, we slept well; even the baby slept soundly in her basket with the calming sway of the sea. The sun was not yet high when we docked in New Amsterdam. It did not take me long to find someone who, for a few pence, would take us to Robert's home, not far from the docks.

Lydia was a miracle on this trip, as she had a fondness for children and insisted on caring for Annie during our voyage. We found Robert's house to be small and quaint; and as we arrived, Mum came running out the door, both laughing and crying at the sight of us.

"Oh, my dear. I pray this is a good visit and no peril has befallen you," Mum said as a plain-clothed young woman walked out behind her.

"Oh, Mum," I said as I hugged her long. "There is no peril. I missed you so. Your missives were not enough." I put my hand on Lydia's shoulder. "This is Lydia Wilbor, a friend from Portsmouth."

"Welcome, Lydia. I am grateful for your traveling with my daughter," said Mum, as she took Lydia's hand in hers for a moment. Turning back to me, she introduced my new sister-in-law.

"And this is Hannah, Robert's wife. They have been married but a year, and now Robert is again at sea." She turned toward the house. "Let us go inside and put your belongings away, then let me see that new grandchild." Hannah graciously gathered my parcel as I held onto Annie, tucked into her sleeping basket.

The house was charming inside and I could see Mum's handiwork throughout. I handed Annie to Mum as she asked about Mary and the other children. A young girl of about thirteen or fourteen, with long red curls and an Irish accent, served us tea as we sat and visited.

"This is Maureen. John indentured her at a young age,

when she arrived at the docks alone, her father lost at sea on the voyage. She is a blessing to us and is like family. Right, Hannah?" Mum winked at Maureen, who smiled in return.

"Yes, ma'am."

"Hannah still calls me ma'am," added Mum, smiling at Hannah. "I cannot get her to call me Mum. And I encourage her to wear a bit of color. See, I have embroidered her apron with reds and greens."

Hannah was quiet, quite pretty with her fair complexion and braids the color of white corn, and exuded a serene nature. I could see why my brother had been smitten. Mum glowed with cheerfulness, in spite of her loss now of two husbands.

"Robert has sailed to Virginia to barter a trading arrangement, soliciting partners. He wants us to sail there next spring, for he has purchased land near Jamestown and is yet looking for a cabin or house on prime land for us. If he cannot find that, he says he will start building on the land he now owns. He is well. And Peter?"

"Peter is good; he too is at sea, journeying to England and to Barbados. How I wish you could visit our new home, Mum. It is indeed a splendid mansion on a hill by the river. You would find it blissful. Peter is now a freeman, and plans on running for office next year." I paused and grew more serious. "Sometimes I feel he only comes home to beget me with child again."

The room was silent, and my face reddened when I realized I had said that, aloud, in front of Lydia and Hannah.

"Please, forgive my frankness," I added to Lydia and Hannah.

"Do not worry," said Mum. "We all feel that way at times. I knew that Peter was ambitious, so this does not surprise me. I am certain he is more than pleased he has a son." Mum smiled, knowingly. "His ship has stopped here at times. I have heard he spends some time at the tavern, and he did stop by the house once when John was still alive. I am glad, and surprised, he permitted you to travel."

I paused for a moment. "Mum, I did not tell him that I was traveling. He has been gone for weeks and will likely not be home until the end of the year, so I made the decision on my own."

"Oh my, he will not be happy about that. Yet I am proud of my resilient daughter. God has given us the strength and wisdom to birth, rear and bury our children and to conduct the affairs of a family; He knows our métier. I suspect you can handle Peter's outrage, which will likely be flamboyant."

I took Mum's hand and squeezed it tightly, touched by her belief in me, and I smiled at her encouragement. As I did so, I noticed that Lydia and Hannah had expressions of reverence and their eyes were wide, as they had listened to our conversation.

"Oh, please do not follow in my rebellious ways, ladies. I am not a standard to mimic. Though I love my husband dearly, I do find I am embracing a newfound independence. The future will determine if my choices are bravery or folly."

We stayed in New Amsterdam for ten days, with Mum, Lydia and Hannah fussing over Annie. I could see that Hannah would be a devoted mother, and prayed that she and Robert would be so blessed; an unnecessary prayer, as Mum shared with me, in confidence, that Hannah believed she might be with child. With everyone doting on Annie and surrounded by loved ones, the rhythm of my breath eased and I found my soul again. Spending hours doing stitch work with Mum took me back to our charmed days in Barbados, and Mum was impressed with my work, saying it was as practiced as her own and more artistic than any she had seen.

"I believe you could make a little money of your own if the tailor sent some work to you," said Mum.

"I truly have no need for extra money. Peter provides well, and I am certain he would not approve of my doing work for others."

"But you do have the talent. Just remember that. One never knows what hardships God may bestow, so be strong, as I see you are." After a silence, Mum continued, "Ann, you have not had any visions in the woods again, have you? I have worried about such. You know, there are times I feel that your pa is with me, as if he is watching over us. Be careful, Ann, near the Puritans, for they believe such visions and ghosts are wicked and warrant severe penance."

"No, Mum, I have been too busy for such things. I am planted quite firm on earth and immersed in laundry and gardens these days," I assured Mum, keeping my conversations with Pa to myself.

When the time came for our parting, I hugged Mum with all my heart. She was wise and loving, and I did not know when the fates would bring us together again, especially in light of knowing she was moving farther away.

Lydia and I rode in the buggy that Mum had arranged with a neighbor to take us to the docks. This ship on which Miles had arranged passage was larger than Captain van Curler's vessel. For almost two days it rained, until we arrived in Newport, where I commissioned a buggy to Portsmouth, first dropping Lydia at the home of her parents and then taking me on to my home on the hill. Obbah was delighted to see me and took sweet Annie as the man from the dock unloaded my parcel and handed it to Zebediah. It felt good to be home, as Mary and Elizabeth came running, followed by little Peter behind them. Winter would be coming soon enough, and, in spite of our difficulties, I would look forward to Peter's return before spring.

Chapter 23

Peter

It was the year of the Lord 1660, and it has been yet another fruitful year for me in Rhode Island. Upon visiting my father and uncle in Amsterdam, I shared the news of my trading successes and the blessed details of my growing family. As well, I told them of the lands I had purchased, including my trading relationships with the Indians, the community's reliance on my apothecary, and my path to become an official in the colony's government. I believed I saw a hint of pride on *Vater's* face; however, he did not neglect to remind me of my brother's position in Hamburg. On parting, he hugged me and said he would pray for success in my election. *It was never enough*, I thought.

I sailed to London, and was now sailing toward Barbados and then to Virginia, where I would sell the balance of my lumber and rum, my ship's hull filled with tobacco, coffee and sugar. I had medicines and small goods I had purchased in Amsterdam and in London stored in my fore cabin. As I was preparing to leave London, I negotiated a bond for a young man to replace Miles, whose contract I would release upon my return home. I had promised Miles a small acreage of land I had early purchased in Newport, and I was saddened for the loss of his service. The young man, of only seventeen years, whom I am bringing to Portsmouth is called Thomas, a strapping young man who, given some guidance, should be useful to my family.

The sea was unkind on this voyage home, throwing the ship from side to side, and on board were four unfortunate families, fearful for their lives in our rough passage toward the Indies. My ship neared the Azores, controlled by Portugal, and I ordered the crew to bring the ship into port at the bay near Mount Brasil, into the town called Angra, for sheltering. We spent four days at the Portuguese settlement, within its forted walls, and before we set sail again, we ate heartily from the local offerings on the island and restocked our food supply with crates of bananas, oranges and liqueur.

As we enjoyed the delights on the isle of Terceira, I was anxious to return to the sea. The call of the seas after the last perilous voyage, after last defying my own demise, is akin to a woman's forgotten agony of childbirth as she longs for another babe. So to the sea we returned. The waters remained rough, though we circumvented savage storms on our long journey from Angra to the docks of Barbados. Upon arrival, Thomas and I, with the crew, unloaded our goods, selling some at the docks and arranging transport for the lumber to plantations such as Modyford's. Thomas and I stayed at the old house in the orchards, and as I negotiated future sales throughout the island, I had Thomas make repairs to the house and barn. I considered selling the property. After a couple of weeks we sailed on to Virginia and then home to Newport.

Once we arrived on home shores, I spent the day ensuring our goods were stored and working with James to restore our necessities on the apothecary shelves. I sold the sugar before we had finished unloading, and my profit for this voyage had been better than any before. Thomas proved to be a hard worker, and before the day was over Miles arrived with the cart for our transport and the loading of a few goods, including the sugar and rum, I had purchased for the house.

"Miles, this is Thomas Durfee of Yorkshire. Good news, as I can release your bond, aye, Miles? I am certain Thomas will be in need of some guidance, so I pray you stay long enough to do so."

"G'day, Miles. I know I have much to learn and am grateful to God to be on land again." Young Thomas did appear ashen from our long and perilous journey.

"Well, let us get these parcels and this table in the cart and be on our way. It is much too cold to delay. I have a wife I have not seen for half a year." Thomas and I lifted a serving buffet into the cart, tied it down, and Miles guided the horses, with care of our load, out of town on the road to Portsmouth. A light snow had begun to fall when we arrived at the house.

Ann came out to the porch as I grabbed the parcels and instructed Miles and Thomas to put the serving table in the dining room. She walked to me and took me into her arms as I tried to return her embrace with my hands full of satchels.

"I thought you might never come home. It has been so long, Peter."

Dropping my parcels to the ground, I kissed her long right there in front of the house.

"Let us go show the boys where we want the new table I brought from France," I said, and we walked into the house. I laid the parcels in the sitting room and, taking Ann's hand in mine, we went to the formal dining room.

"Yes, there, between the two windows." I said, looking

at Ann.

"Yes, that is good. It fits well there."

"Ann, this is Thomas. Thomas Durfee from England. He will replace our Miles." Turning to Thomas, I added, "This is my wife, mistress of my home." Ann nodded in his direction.

"Obbah is feeding the children, but let me tell her you are here and we will put on a fine dinner. Miles and Thomas, can you join us?"

"Aye, excellent," I responded, before Miles or Thomas had a chance to respond. "We are all hungry, and weary from such a long voyage. Let us all meet in the kitchen after I settle and catch up on my receipts from James. I do need to clean up, and, Ann, I have brought you the most expensive fabric from France, in the parcels."

As Thomas and Miles left for the barn, I led Ann into the sitting room to show her the treasures I had brought for her. Her face lit as a young child with a new toy. I watched her pull each yardage from the sack, and I yearned to take her in my arms and have my way. But the sun was yet shining as it neared the horizon, and dinner was yet to be served. I would wait, in spite of the wisps of her dark locks about the graceful curve of her fair neck seducing me. I kissed her gently on those lips and went upstairs to wash and change my clothes. Ann said she would bring me a pitcher of fresh water.

When she came in the room and set the pitcher beside the basin, I could wait no longer. I pulled Ann into my arms and drew the pins from her hair and unlaced her dress. She did not resist, but instead kissed me with her own brazen desires. Her unleashed passion oft surprised me; it aroused my appetite for this unfettered young lass. We were once again merged as man and wife in a most hasty and feverish way. I was home.

***

It was not long after my return when I found my associations with the gentry of Newport and Portsmouth had proven to be worthy of my time invested. I was elected to the Court of Commissioners in Warwick and would now serve in the government of our great colony. Later in that year I was to be appointed general solicitor. I could not be more grateful for God's blessings and the fruition of my ambitions; if only I could have shared this news with my father, who never ceased measuring me. In addition to providing the settlers of the island with their only apothecary, I had, since my arrival in Newport, continued to serve as their invaluable interpreter in the court and at the docks. I had a beautiful wife, a family and a grand home on a hill in Portsmouth. There was little more for which I could ask.

My friends at the White Horse in Newport were, without exception, eager to share a pint of ale at the tavern. A celebration was warranted. On this night at the welcoming of a new year, my old friend John Smith, who had once been president of the colony, and my new friend Frances Brayton were present, and we drank heartily and laughed, celebrating our good fortune. By the time I arrived home, I was heartened that my mare knew the way. Ann greeted me at the front door and took my cloak, and I remember little else from that night except that I slept well and long into the following day.

***

As the snows continued to fall in this long winter, I made a courageous purchase of land from my friend Wamsutta of the Wampanoag tribe. Wamsutta was an old Indian man, a chief in his tribe. He was stooped from the will of his old bones, but he still braided his long gray hair, and though he conversed seldom, he expressed great conviction when he spoke. The English had dubbed him with the name Alexander, and his younger brother they called Philip. Philip had been the bane of the Plymouth Colony. My friends Thomas Olney, William Staples and I exchanged monies with Wamsutta and the deal was done; however, the Plymouth Court declared our purchase a violation of their laws and, after a second violation, imprisoned Wamsutta, frail with age and hardship. In our attempts to aid our imprisoned associate, the tribes repaid our monies and we released our record of purchase, returning the land back to the tribes. But it was too late for my friend Wamsutta. Upon our release of the land, Plymouth released Wamsutta from his imprisonment, yet my friend died only days after his regained freedom. Our land acquisition would have been a coup for the colony; but, instead, it hastened the death of Wamsutta and had truly increased the tensions between our Rhode Island and the loosely bound colonies to the north.

Chapter 24

Ann

It was in the year of our Lord 1661 when Susanna was born in the heavy days of August; she came early and was tiny. I feared she may not thrive, but she nursed well and gained her strength, and a fiery temper, as she was her father's daughter.

Peter did not travel to Europe that year, but he did sail to Barbados and Virginia in the summer. He was gone when Susanna was born, and Thomas had gone for the midwife, a middle-aged woman called Emily who lived in Portsmouth. She was kind enough to stay with me for three days after Susanna's birth, since we were concerned about Susanna's health. Susanna grew into a hearty baby, and when Peter returned from the islands, he was gone from the house often.

The months after Peter's return had been difficult, as he became more overwhelmed with responsibilities and too much ale, increasing his impatience with the demands of others, including his family. One week, he had reproved and then struck Zebediah when Peter's horse had not been readied timely for Peter's departure into Newport. I witnessed this through the window as I watched Peter leave, and this vision renewed my fears that he may sell Zebediah, which would devastate Obbah and little Zeb. Miles had well trained Thomas, the new bonded servant; and Thomas, though quieter than Miles, had learned his duties quickly and managed the estate faithfully. Thomas was more soft-spoken with the slaves, which I am certain did not please Peter.

He came home late one night in December when snow had lightly covered the hills. As was more frequent, Peter was heavy with the scent of ale and scarcely able to walk. After I took his cloak, he asked where the children were. I told him Obbah had put them to bed hours ago. He became furious they were not there to greet him. He opened the front door and yelled at Thomas, who had come to take his horse to the barn.

"What think you are?" he yelled, becoming more incoherent. "You think ye are a slave? That is slave's work." He slammed the door. As he turned to face me, the back of his hand smote my cheek and I fell against the harsh timbers of the wall. I was stunned, my cheek stinging more from humiliation than the back of his hand.

"Get the children," he bellowed. The noise had awakened Obbah and she came timidly down the stairs.

"You wench," he said to Obbah. "Get the children. Why are they not here to greet me?" Obbah turned to go back upstairs to the children's rooms.

I was frightened. I did not want the children to see this, yet I feared his reaction to my spoken words.

"Peter, Peter," I spoke in almost a whisper, as I rose from the floor and strove to keep my voice from cracking and revealing my fear. "The children wanted to stay up to see you. It was I who told them it was late. Please forgive me." I backed away from him.

Anger yet contorted his face, but I could see his senses fading and his knees failing him. "Can I help you?" I asked, keeping some distance between us. "Obbah is getting the children."

Peter stumbled, toward me, and as he neared the floor, I took his arm. Obbah was at the top of the stairs, Mary and Elizabeth standing behind her in their nightclothes, their eyes wide and confused at the sight before them. I signaled for Obbah to come help me.

"Let us try to get him to bed, Obbah." She took Peter's other arm and we helped him toward the bedroom. The fight had left him and I praised God for that. After I lay him on the bed, we took off his boots and left him there as we both went to calm the girls, still standing atop the stairs, sleepy and frightened.

As Obbah put the girls back to bed, I heard a light knock at the front door. It was Thomas.

"Are you all right, ma'am?" he asked, as he had clearly heard the commotion on his way to the barn. "Do you need any help?"

"No, no, Thomas. We are fine."

He saw the swelled redness of my cheek, and as he departed he said, "Ma'am, you should hold a bit of snow on you own face." He bent down and gathered some snow, patting it to hold it together. He handed it to me. "It will help. I am sorry if I angered Master Peter." Thomas paused, and quietly said, "G'night."

"Goodnight," I responded, in a whisper I felt certain he did not hear. I looked in the mirror in the dining room and, upon seeing my swollen face, briefly held the snow up to my cheek. The melting snow dripped down my neck and onto my bodice, and, full of sadness, I blew out the candles, readied myself for bed, and lay next to my husband, the father of my children, this man I scarcely knew. I realized that he would return tomorrow as the charming Peter who had once stolen my heart. Yet I did not know how long he would stay.

***

In January it was the Epiphany, and I had invited Reverend Blackstone to our home for the sacraments, passing the word through our Anglican friends about the services at our home. I had avoided conversation with Peter since the scene in early winter. After the skirmish, I had stayed in the house, reading and playing with the children, not wanting anyone to see the bruises on my face. It had been difficult hiding that from Obbah and the children, yet I persevered as though all was right. The religious holiday had been quiet, but Peter had suggested we host the sacrament services for Epiphany. Peter was proud that we were hosting the event, and he ensured that Thomas had cleaned the barn and had the house and fields readied. Obbah and I had baked all of Friday and Saturday for the guests.

Reverend Blackstone arrived early at the house and Obbah served him a cup of our Jamaican coffee, for which he was grateful. Soon there would be buggies lining up in front of the house, and Thomas had ensured that Zebediah, Zeb, who was now eight, and Ibrahim were ready to offer any help. Obbah and I had brought all of the chairs from the house into our front sitting room.

"Reverend Blackstone, I am so pleased that you are here this week. You know well how eager we are to have our own church in Rhode Island, and I am assured you will be influential in that as well." I passed him a plate of blueberry scones; he smiled and took one. "So, please tell me, why is it you ride the white bull, Reverend?"

"Dear Mrs. Tallman, I am too old to ride that bull, who is as well too old now to be ridden. I came here today on my fair horse Bonny. I am fond of that bull and trained him early to be saddled; he could take me far, and it was a pleasant ride. I had hoped to bring my wife, Sarah, with me today, but she is at home in Rehoboth with our young son. We are all blessed, are we not?"

"Yes, friend. My two oldest daughters will sit upon the sacrament this day. Yet I am blessed with those, likewise, who are yet too young. Oh, here is Peter. I will take leave to greet our guests." Peter sat down near the reverend to visit.

The Lawtons were coming in the front door, and I ran to embrace them. I had not seen them for a lengthy spell, as Thomas Lawton had been ill. As the buggies continued to arrive, I greeted and escorted our guests into the sitting room. Thomas appeared to have things under control with the horses, and Obbah had the dining room arranged with the china, provisions and the vase of flowers from my garden that I had arranged. Mary and my Elizabeth sat with me through the service, and we thoroughly enjoyed the company of our friends. Reverend Blackstone had need to leave early for yet another service before traveling home, and he promised, God willing, to return to Portsmouth in about six weeks.

I tightly hugged the reverend as he left. I did not know how much longer he could do this, as he was aging and oft limped on his right leg, and I was thankful he no longer rode his grand old bull. Mary ran to hug him, and we walked back into the house. It was approaching sunset before we said goodbye to our last guests, and I could see that Peter was content to have hosted the popular event. He had been instrumental in starting a fund for a future church on the island, but our numbers were yet too small to support the completion of such an endeavor.

After the children were fed, I took a book from the library and was reading when Peter came and sat next to me.

"I have decided to run for the office of deputy to the General Assembly. My name is on the ballot, and, when elected, I wish you might attend the event with me. I am grateful for the gathering today here at the house; your efforts here are valued." He paused, seeming awkward. "You have been absent from our bed, and I have missed you. I know you were, at times, present in person, but your heart has been clearly absent. Will you please join me this night? My arms long to embrace you and I yearn to run my fingers through your hair and kiss those sweet lips I remember used to tremble at my touch."

I longed to hear his kind words, yet in my heart I knew what answer he expected. I was torn, uncertain of the true nature of my own feelings. My heart felt heavy and cautious, like a bird sitting haltingly in a cage with an open door, but I put down the book as he took my hand. We joined that night, as husband and wife, in a gentle and quiet manner that lacked Peter's usual brusque ways. The passion was absent. It was a search for love perchance lost that fueled our intimacy. Peter told me he loved me; his words rang hollow and my heart felt empty when I drifted to sleep. Joseph was born in September.

Chapter 25

Thomas

Zebediah pitched the old hay into the barrow as I brushed my mare, Betsy. With the rhythm of my wrist's movement, my thoughts traveled back to the year of our Lord 1660, the year when my pa died in an accident at the coalfields near Newcastle. I did not see it, but was told by others that Pa had slipped on the loose coal, down a slope, bringing with him an avalanche of rock that crushed him. I had only recently started working with him, having turned seventeen and well past any schooling I would be offered. Pa had been my only parent after losing my mother to a fever when I was but thirteen. Ma had come from Scotland, from a village near the port of Inverness, and she had brought with her a three-string fedyl, an instrument the English called a fiddle. I remember hearing Ma's sweet music throughout my youth. I was her only child, and she would spend hours teaching me to read and write, reading the books she brought from her home in the Gaelic lands.

When I was nine, she taught me to play her fedyl and I learned Irish and Scottish tunes such as "Tullochgorum." I fondly recalled the music that, at times, brought Pa to doing a jig, but he was firm that I needed to learn a skill, a working skill. After Ma died, Pa would take me to the coalfields when I was not in school, and at sixteen I was working there each day for a pittance. With Pa gone, our house was no longer home to me. The empty house and the hard labor at the coalfield encouraged my journey to London in search of a better life. I had not been there long before I took a job at the docks, and it was there I met Captain Tallman as he negotiated trades and commanded the loading of his ship. I overheard him ask the old dockhand if he knew of any young lads wanting an indentured position for travel to the new world, so I approached the captain.

"Captain, sir, tell me what this new world is like. I am no stranger to hard work and would be gladly bonded for such a chance. If you may, sir, what is this place you speak of?"

The captain looked eager at hearing my words. "You are young, boy. But that is not bad, as I can see you have a strong back. This place where I live is called Rhode Island. It is beset on the shoreline with many rivers and bays. I have a shop in the town of Newport and an estate in Portsmouth. There are animals to care for and transportation for my family, and you would oversee the slaves, which now number three. Four if you count the child, who can do meager chores. Can you do this? I will bond you for seven years, at which time you are free to go as you wish. Aye?"

I eagerly took this agreement, shaking his hand and being bonded to Captain Tallman. Shortly thereafter, I traveled with him to the isles of the West Indies and then on north to Rhode Island. I had ne'er before been on the sea, and I found it at once frightening and exhilarating.

Seafaring took some adjustment, and, though the sway of the sea troubled my gut, I was awed at the vastness of this world beyond England, especially the enchanting isle of Barbados.

Then I was here at the Tallman residence, with quarters more sufficient than anything I had in England, though I was filled with a gnawing emptiness without family. I had never experienced being around slaves, but the slaves I oversaw were good people, especially Zebediah. Zebediah was older than Ibrahim and adored his young son, Zeb. I could see that my master treated them with some contempt, and I felt it was not warranted, but knew well my expectations. I quickly learned my duties, with the assistance of Zebediah and Miles, before he left for Newport and his own freedom. I sometimes saw Miles in the town when my chores took me there, and over time, we were to become fast friends.

The work was not hard, and Zebediah and Ibrahim effortlessly cared for the animals and milked the cows. I brushed the horses daily and oversaw the birthing of foals and calves. There was a natural cadence to the work, and I felt blessed to be here rather than the brutal coal mines.

I would oft take the milk to Obbah in the kitchen at the main house, and Mrs. Tallman told me that I was welcome to join the family for dinner. I did so seldom, but when I did I was treated like family.

There were many children running around the house and the gardens. Mrs. Tallman did not appear of an age where she could have so many children. I thought that Captain Tallman might have been married to another before the missus. She was at all times kind, so on the night last winter when the captain came home late, as a drunkard and screaming, I was horrified to see, through the window, when he slapped Mrs. Tallman to the floor. I could hear the children crying. I wanted to barge through the door and strike my master, but I knew with certainty that would make matters worse for all.

The next day I saw the bruises on Mrs. Tallman's face, yet she maintained a sweet spirit and evaded looking me in the eye. I think she had not iced her face with the snow I had given her on that terrible night. I prayed this was not a normal occurrence in my master's home, and I noted that Master Tallman frequently did not return home until the late hours, and oft in a foul mood. I decided to work hard and mind my business, praying for the day of my own independence.

I found the winters hard, but the springtime was as green as England and filled with sunshine. As spring blossomed, it became apparent that Mrs. Tallman was yet again with child. I worked hard to care for the family's needs, while running the captain's errands between Portsmouth and Newport. He apparently was a man of great position, as I heard from Miles that he was elected as a deputy to the colony's General Assembly.

On a sunny day in early fall, Obbah came running to find Zebediah and me in the barn. Master had been gone to sea for more than a month. Obbah said I must go get Emily; the missus was in her labor and needed help.

"Hurry, hurry."

When I pulled the wagon up to the house, Emily got out and went up the steps to the front door. She came back out in just minutes to share that we had not made it in time, but the baby was strong.

"Please wait a bit. I am going to minister to the baby and Mrs. Tallman, but if you can take me back home in one hour, that will be good." She turned to go back in the house, and then yelled out, "It is a loud baby boy this time."

The captain was on his voyage to Amsterdam and then the colonies, and he was not expected to return until well into the winter. Mrs. Tallman invited me to join the family at mealtime several days each week. She said the children would benefit from a man in the house and she would enjoy the company. It was hard to refuse such a request, and the foods prepared by Obbah and Mrs. Tallman were delightfully tasty.

"Thomas, tell me about where you come from. Does your family miss you?" Mrs. Tallman asked me at dinner one evening.

"I am from a small village near Newcastle, ma'am, but my family is gone. My mum died from typhus when I was young. I was seventeen when my pa died in an accident and your husband was looking for an indenture. I volunteered with eagerness for a new adventure."

"My mum and pa were from England as well, the port of Bristol, they told me; but I was born in Barbados. I have never seen England."

"Oh, but I did think Barbados beautiful when I traveled back with the captain. Are your ma and pa gone to heaven too?"

"No, only my pa," she answered. "My mum traveled here with me, but she now lives in the Virginia Colony with my brother and her new husband, Captain Hudson."

"Ah, you are fortunate to yet have your mother." I heard an infant crying upstairs.

"That is but baby Joseph. He is quite the demanding son, like his father. The baby is good and full, and will sleep shortly, I pray." She smiled, such a fetching smile, and handed me a plate of roasted beets. "Thomas, what is that music I sometimes hear, out in the barn? Is that you? For I have not heard it before."

"Yes, ma'am. I play the fedyl, some Welsh and English ballads. And, for certain, the Scottish, like my ma. It is comforting to play, and little Zeb likes it. Maybe your Mary would like to learn to play. She has come out and danced a bit with Zeb and Elizabeth as I played."

"That would be so generous." She turned to Mary. "Mary, would you like to learn to play the fedyl? It is like a guitar. I believe."

"It is normally played with a stringed bow instead of the fingers, though I use both," Thomas added.

"Yes, Mum," answered Mary politely, but I saw a sparkle in her eye, which told me she would be excited to learn.

The infant upstairs was now screaming, so Mrs. Tallman excused herself from the table. Obbah and Elizabeth came in and sat down with little Mary and me as we finished our meal.

"Do you like living in the barn?" asked Elizabeth, looking at me with a bit of mischief in her eye.

"Well, Miss Elizabeth, I do like living in the barn. I have a soft bed where I lay my head and I have friends to talk with and animals that revere me. For what more could I ask?"

Elizabeth pondered my response for a moment or two, and Obbah was smiling.

"I do not know," Elizabeth answered, her face revealing more wonder than mischief.

As fall passed and winter came, I enjoyed many such meals with the Tallman family, noticing how much more at ease Mrs. Tallman, as well as Obbah, was when her husband was gone to sea. Upon learning that I could read, Mrs. Tallman would sometimes lend me a book or two from her library, and I would read and oft reread by the candlelight in my room at night. Before Captain Tallman returned, Mary was able to play a tune or two on my fedyl, much to the delight of her brothers and sisters.

Chapter 26

Peter

This voyage felt longer than my voyages of the past. I felt, at times, that I spent much of my life on the oceans; yet, why do I complain? I loved the danger, the vastness of the horizon beyond the waves and the breadth of the skies, especially the night skies. Though my home sat in Rhode Island, the sea filled my soul, replenished my manhood. I would never want to choose between the two.

I relished my new positions in the government of Rhode Island, my goal that now awarded me the power I had long sought. I was grateful. Yet the sea whispered to me, as a lover, calling with the sound of each wave breaking upon the shore. There was a part of me, my heart, that yearned to be here; mastering the might of the sea made me even more powerful. It was akin to a man's craving of a woman's warm embrace, at times just beyond his reach. My responsibilities, I feared, might overcome my seafaring. I could, with ease, contract others to conduct my trade and mercantile matters. Yet, standing near the prow of my ship, nearing the coast of France, I knew in my heart that I would guarantee my power, my position, allowing my warranted freedom to sail the seas.

I visited with my brother in Amsterdam as I conducted my trades of lumber and rum for herbs and medicines. *Vater* was ill and could not make the journey. I shared with Johannes the news of my family and my election to offices in the colonies, as well as the success of my trades, but I was not certain any of this news would be revealed to my father. If so, it would surely be diminished. Perhaps I would write a letter to *Vater* when I arrived home. I had been delinquent in such communications, but now had cause to boast.

After spending almost two months in Amsterdam, Antwerp and London, I sailed for Barbados. The ship was yet half filled with lumber for the plantations, and I was anxious to visit with my friend Modyford. I could stay at the old house, but truly preferred the camaraderie at the tavern. For all my eagerness to see the beaches of Barbados again, the seas raged against me, leaving us to seek respite in the Portuguese isles for almost a week. As we departed the port of Ponta Delgada, I remembered the words of Lewes Roberts, "When God leads, no harm comes." With God's help amidst winter seas, it was almost November before we arrived in the Barbados port, and the crew and I spent another day unloading the lumber I would sell Modyford and two more plantation contracts I had secured on my last voyage.

I washed and fell into the bed in my room across from the tavern, sleep pulling me in a black darkness without dreams. When I walked into the tavern the following day, some of my old friends were there. A new barmaid caught my eye, and I learned later she was called Helene. Marianne had been gone on my last visits here, and I assumed that she had paid full her indenture. I did miss her and would ask after her, but for the evening I would find my way around this Helene, a buxom young woman with long copper curls tied back in a green ribbon. I was certain that she had caught more than mine own eye.

"Yes, I will have a rye." Giving her a wink, I added, "Captain Tallman of the Rhode Isles, formerly of the isle here. And you, you must be the daughter of Zeus, the cause of the Trojan War, with your beauty." She nodded in my direction, with just the hint of a smile, and I winked as she turned toward the bar.

I spent two days at Modyford's place, where he told me that Marianne had married a strapping young dockworker by the name of Edward. I was bewildered that she had not aimed higher, for she was a shrewd wench. Modyford was aging; I saw an absence of the old enthusiasm for working his land. After our visit, I returned to the docks in town, where I negotiated the sale of the balance of my bounty and engaged in writing new contracts for my next voyage. As I walked down toward the docks one foggy morning, I saw a woman, familiar. As she neared, I saw it was Marianne, walking toward me. She had not seen me, but I saw that she was with child and a young lad at her side. She looked up as we neared each other and appeared startled to see me.

"G'day, dear friend. It has been a long time since I have seen you."

"Yes," she replied, somewhat reserved, twisting the curl of her hair. "As you can see, I have married. He is a fine man who works at the docks. And you, are you well?" she asked, avoiding my gaze.

"I am quite well. You know that I relish being in the islands," I said, awkward at the absence of our usual flirtatious banter. "And your young man here? Is this your nephew, your brother?"

"Nay. This is my son. Nathaniel." She paused for a moment and turned to her young son. "Nathaniel, this is an old friend, Captain Tallman." The young boy held out his hand in greeting, and I noted the firm handshake for such a young lad.

"I am going to the docks to ensure my rum and sugar are loaded properly on my ship. I wish you well, Marianne, and you too, Nathaniel," I said as I smiled at the boy.

I finished my work on the ship and returned to town for a meal and a drink at the tavern. A couple of my old friends were there, as well as a group of younger fellows from Antwerp. The new barmaid, her bosom peeking amply above the laced velvet bodice, took my order.

"I will have a brandy, dear. You are new here, are you not?"

"Yes, sir."

"You are a pretty thing. And what might be your name?" I asked.

"Helene, sir. My name is Helene. Let me get your brandy." And she walked away. There was no play in her eyes. It could be I was losing my charm; but I think, instead, it was the girl's prudishness. Yet, I still had my saucy Joan at the tavern in New Amsterdam. She is getting older, but she knows how to please a man. I may need to stop in New Amsterdam more often. And then thoughts of Ann were fleeting, unexpectedly, through my mind. Ann was yet a beautiful woman, in spite of birthing the children, but the change in her was baffling. I had, with frustration, observed a growing independence and disinterest. She was no longer the sweet, naïve girl I remember from Barbados. My musings rumbled in my stomach and constricted my chest. Ann seemed to need me less and less and our words, even our coupling, had grown stilted.

I recalled when, just two years before, Ann had sailed to New Amsterdam, without my permission, to visit with her mother. The audacity of making such a decision and traveling as a lone woman on a ship was unforgivable. I am not certain that my admonishment or my temporary withdrawal of her funds had impressed upon her the embarrassment she had brought upon me. Ann seemed, of late, a stranger to me.

My reverie vanished as Helene placed my brandy before me and served my friends' ales, but I had lost interest in pursuit. I shared my trade routes with the new sailors from Antwerp, speaking in Dutch, which made them more comfortable in conversation. I queried them on their trade sources in Antwerp and discovered two fresh sources for new medicines coming west from Asia.

Before I left for the evening, George shared with me how much he missed Marianne, knowing that I remembered her. He shared that she had married a reliable young man, a supervisor at the docks. He added that he had some good rum he could sell me, so I added a few casks to my inventory.

I spent a day ensuring all goods were loaded properly in the hull of the ship, and we headed north the following morning. I planned on a short stop in Virginia and maybe two or three days in New Amsterdam on my way home toward another cold winter.

Chapter 27

Ann

Winter came hard and early the past year, and Peter had been to sea since summer. I had marveled at the colors of autumn, the brilliant reds and oranges of the maples, as if a wonderland; but autumn was brought to an abrupt end by the assault of biting, windswept snows in October. Over time I had come to rely more and more on Thomas, who had grown from a lad of seventeen to a fine young man. He had taken on the tasks at our home and kept close tabs on Peter's shop in Newport, ensuring that James had whatever he needed from the warehouse. Zebediah and Ibrahim worked well with Thomas, whose hunting skills kept my family well-fed with wild game in the winter. He was a godsend.

Things had been peaceful at home and I filled with anxiety at Peter's return, chastising my own self at these sinful thoughts. I celebrated Epiphany with a fine meal with family and friends, a meal of roasted venison, beets and corn I had preserved from my garden, and wine, and I had made blueberry pies. The snow continued to fall, and I invited Zebediah and Ibrahim into the kitchen to eat with Obbah. Thomas joined the older children and myself in the dining room and the Wilbors stopped by to join us. We feasted merrily as cold winds blew outside. Thomas entertained the children with games and tales of his life in Yorkshire. The only thing that would have made this evening better would be my mum sitting at the table with us.

I did not know when or if I would see my mum again. Peter had been furious about my travel to New Amsterdam to visit her. About once a year, Robert would travel over to Portsmouth to visit when he sailed into Newport, and he had visited during this holiday, catching me up on the news. Robert shared that Captain Hudson, Mum's new husband, was a kind man who could make Mum laugh as Pa had. We smiled in memory of those joyful times long gone, and then a knock at the entrance into the sitting room interrupted our reveries.

"Ma'am, I am sorry to disturb you, but I am afraid that little Zebediah is dreadfully ill," said Thomas. It was the day after Epiphany. "I need to get him to a doctor. Who may treat the slaves?"

"Oh, dear, Thomas," I fretted, trying to think who might help. "The weather is so dreadful. Can you get to Newport? James might help, or tell you who can help." Then I remembered Emily, my new midwife. She had much medical knowledge. "No, with this snow, leave him here and go fetch Emily. Obbah and I will tend to Zeb while you are gone. Tell Emily she may stay the night until the weather clears."

Obbah was beside herself with worry, walking about the kitchen. Before Thomas left, he brought little Zeb, so feverish, from the barn and placed him in the bed in Obbah's room upstairs. We told the other children to stay away, being concerned with contagion. Maybe we should have left him in the barn quarters, but, even though the barn was heated well, I could not do so with Zeb being so feverish. Zebediah paced the floor in the kitchen downstairs.

When Emily arrived, she examined Zeb and said he had the measles, a common, yet at times deadly, ailment throughout the colony. She recommended a poultice for the rash, drink, and wet rags to his body to keep his temperature cooled. She said there was little else we could do, but that it was more likely than not he would be well in a few days or a week. She advised we move him back to the quarters in the barn so as not to spread this amongst the children, but added that it may have already happened if there had been contact before his symptoms arose. Emily wanted to brave the weather to return home, and told Thomas he needed to get the poultice in Newport. I embraced Emily as she left with Thomas. Obbah and I gathered clean linens and a pail of cold water, and we wrapped Zeb in blankets so Zebediah could carry him out to their quarters. Zebediah and Obbah would take turns tending to Zeb, and Thomas, after taking Emily home, was going through the snow to the shop to get the poultice. I gathered the linens from Obbah's bed to launder.

Zeb's fever broke after two long nights, but then Elizabeth and young Peter came down with the rash. We went through the same process, and I was thankful for the poultice James had provided. Thomas was a blessing in keeping the well children occupied and creating games that would keep them from touching each other. He and Obbah would take over for me when they could so I was able to sleep. Peter arrived home as January ended and the snow had melted away, when Elizabeth was well enough to eat and her brother was back at play.

Peter was in a sour mood when he arrived home, and his mood only worsened when he heard of the illness throughout the house.

"The damned slaves. You are not to have them in the house, except Obbah. You are too lenient with them, Ann," he reproved me sharply. "And what is Thomas doing here playing with the children? Those are not his duties," he said as he looked toward Thomas in the sitting room reading a tale to the young ones.

Peter's eyes were angry, so I gathered the children to send them upstairs with Obbah.

"Master, forgive me," said Thomas. "I was only aiming to assist the women dealing with the illness in the house. I will make my way out to the barn and check on Zebediah and Ibrahim. Do you need any errands run in Newport, sir?"

"Tomorrow," barked Peter.

I was impressed with Thomas's demeanor in response to Peter's anger. Thomas was always polite, revealing no fear of Peter's ire. I stood watching the exchange, admiring Thomas's confidence as he held his head tall and walked from the house.

After Obbah settled the children upstairs, she prepared a hot meal and wordlessly served Peter and me as we sat in the dining room. We all returned to our other roles, the people we were when Peter was home. Obbah carried food out to the barn for Thomas, Ibrahim, and her little Zeb and his Pa. After his long voyage, Peter retired to our bedroom after dinner.

I helped Obbah ready the children for bed, kissed each of them goodnight and put on my cloak. I walked out into the night, down the hill toward the river, the soil yet damp from the recent melting snows. The air was chilled and the moon was full, reflecting a luminescent glow off the river. I sensed Pa's comforting presence, as if he were walking beside me. I missed both Mum and Pa.

As I neared the river and heard the water lapping onto

the shore, my eyes fell upon a figure sitting on the large rocks. I had a strange sensation of feeling both startled yet calmed at the same moment, so I stopped in my footsteps and stood quietly. *Was it Pa?* The figure called to me in a soft voice.

"Ma'am. Mrs. Tallman, it is just I." I recognized Thomas's voice. "I do not want to frighten you."

I walked toward him and sat on a rock nearby.

"Mrs. Tallman. I am sorry if I have caused you any distress. I seem to easily anger your husband."

"No, Thomas. It is not you who angers him, and it is probably not I either. He is a changed man. He is full of unhappiness, and I do not know how to mend it. Peter has everything he ever wanted … sons, a family, a grand house, great position; the success he craves. Yet all of this seems to have robbed me of the man I married."

"I am sorry, ma'am. I do wish I could help, but I seem to disquiet him."

"Rest assured, Thomas, it is not you. It seems resentment and powers have corrupted him. I love him yet, but it is hard when he is not the same man I knew."

We sat silent in the darkness for a time.

"You know, Thomas, my pa died when I was young in Barbados, but I often sense he is by my side, like this night. Do you ever have such feelings?" I startled myself in asking such a personal question of Thomas, a young unmarried man who worked for my husband.

"Yes, ma'am," he answered in a soft voice. "I do at sudden times sense my father with me, guiding me; and there is, as well, my mother's laughter and music I oft find lifting my spirits. It makes me strong and gives me comfort."

I thought long of Thomas's words. It makes him strong. That is what Pa had done for me, all these years. His presence had made me stronger than the little girl I once was.

I rose to climb the hill back to the house. "Thank you, Thomas," I whispered. "G'night." As I walked away, I was overwhelmed with a sense of wonder at the moon and stars that sparkled in the sky through the trees and behind the house, as if lighting my way. As if God were lighting my way.

Chapter 28

Ann

The children were growing and were well, and Joseph was now walking. Spring was in full blossom, and I found happiness working in my garden as the children ran free in the yard, chasing the chickens and exploring the edge of the woods. The government had ordered Peter to erect a fence between our own property and that of our neighbor, Lot Strange, who had filed a complaint. The Strange family was Puritan and had never been friendly toward our family. I am certain there was too much joviality and music and dance on our land for their liking; however, Mistress Strange and I exchanged pleasantries when we met in town or on the road.

My fortune included my many friends in Portsmouth, including the Wilbor family and the Cooke family, with by dearest friends Martha Wilbor and Mary Cooke, and now Lydia. I hosted the sewing circle at our home every two or three months, which permitted me to catch up on stitching as well as the gossip. Most of the ladies were careful to avoid sharing rumors, in my presence, of Peter's shenanigans in Newport, but I knew well that his reputation for flirtations and propensity for lawsuits were known throughout the colony.

I had tried to speak with Peter on two occasions over the winter about his drinking too much and how it had changed him. To Peter, my words were but a dagger in my hand. He resisted and diminished me; and the second time I raised the topic, he almost smote me again as he came toward me with a raised hand. I backed up quickly enough.

"I will say no more. It is only that I love you, Peter." He turned and walked away, speaking to me not once for weeks afterwards. His late nights and his drinking did not abate. As a routine, when Peter was home, we stepped gingerly about our days, but Peter was demanding when home. It was fortunate that he was home little, but busily away with his duties at the courthouse and visiting his apothecary, planning his next voyage to England and Amsterdam, and stirring up conflict at the White Horse tavern.

In May he asked me to attend an event in Newport, a formal event of the commissioners and colony officials, to include an official from England. The process to declare Rhode Island a colony of its own was in play, and Peter wanted to impress his colleagues. I dressed in a mauve gown and, of course, wore the necklace Peter had given me so many years ago. I pulled my hair atop my head, in curls, with a silver comb Peter had brought from France the same year he had returned with our Thomas.

As I climbed into our buggy, Thomas was holding the reins of the horse and turned to smile at me in greeting.

"What was that at the house, with Thomas?" Peter snarled as we rode the familiar road to Newport. I suspected he referred to Thomas's smile. "What is going on with Thomas? I think you and he spend generous time together. Are you cuckolding me?"

His words seized my breath. I was stunned, and grasped for my composure.

"Peter, what a cruel thing to say! Of course I am not. Thomas helps out with things at the house, as did Miles. There is nothing untoward, and I am hurt that you would think this."

"I will keep my eye on him. And I have heard Mary is playing his fiddle and you have permitted him to instruct her. No more of that. What Mary and the children need, they can learn at school, and not from a pauper off the streets of London."

"Aye." There was no need to argue with him, as it was futile. Mary would be distraught.

The dinner was delightful, as was the conversation with Peter's friends and their wives. As I spoke with Jeremy Clarke and his wife, I glanced to the side and saw Peter cozying up to a servant in the hallway, in view of myself as well as some of the guests. I was shocked that he would behave so despicably in my presence as well as in the presence of his esteemed colleagues. I pretended through the evening that I had seen nothing, but inside, I felt lost. Doubts and fears for my future, my family, bounced intermittently throughout my head as I struggled to converse lucidly with the event's guests. This man, Peter, the father of my children, had gone to sea year after year. My heart withered as I questioned the true love of my life, the Peter I met so long ago at the marketplace in sunny Barbados.

Our ride home was quiet. It was dark, with a new moon, and Peter forced the horse a bit too fast. I was afraid that he might topple the buggy on a curve, but I said nothing. I had come to know him well enough to know that any complaint would only enrage him.

I withdrew to quietness over the next week, spending time sewing in the sitting room when Peter was home. This was not hard, as Peter usually was gone, and by the first day of July he had sailed for Amsterdam. This meant that for the next few months we could live with ease at the house. We could laugh and dance, and little Zeb could spend time with his mother, and I even permitted my Mary to play a bit of music with Thomas. The stiffness throughout the house waned, and a welcomed benevolence returned, but I knew that this could not go on.

One morning at the breakfast table, after the children had run upstairs, Thomas revealed to me that before Peter had sailed, he had come to the barn and admonished him.

"I do not want to tell you this, ma'am; but Captain Tallman said I needed to stay away from you and the children. I probably should not be eating at the house any longer. I have yet more than three years on my indenture, and I want to earn my freedom and a bit of land."

"Thomas, I am sorry to hear these words. You have to do what will work for you. You are forever welcome in the house and at meals, but I will understand your decision. As I have shared before, I do not know how to fix this problem. My husband emerges more and more lost in his unhappiness."

"I do not mean to worry you. You are a kind lady, but I think I should focus on my chores in the barn and managing the staff. I might spend more time at the apothecary when the captain is gone, learning the skills that James has mastered. It will do me well to learn this. I will take you and the children where you need to go. Please know that I am at your service and I appreciate your kindness, but I do not want to anger my master."

"I am sorry, Thomas. You are a good man and are not deserving of such treatment."

"Nor are you, ma'am," whispered Thomas as he rose to leave the table.

***

I kept myself and the children busy through the summer and fall. I spent much time stitching and in the garden, and we had a grand crop for preserving for the winter. I saw Thomas working through the day, and he would hitch the horse to the buggy when I wanted to go to town. Often I would go alone, as I had managed to learn the intricacies of guiding the horse and controlling the buggy. After we moved to Portsmouth, Miles had taught me to ride a horse. I seldom did so, but knew that I could do so should there be such a need.

At times in the evenings, when the fireflies were twinkling, I would hear Thomas playing his music in the barn. Sometimes it was a sad melody, and at other times it was joyful and I could hear the laughter of Obbah and Zebediah and their son as they danced to a tune. I wanted to be a part of that, but Thomas and I, in our own words said and unsaid, had come to this agreement to distance ourselves. Peter's jealousy was unreasonable, but neither of us had any desire to give him cause for his suspicions and anger.

At sewing circle I would sometimes hear rumors, stories of husbands gone astray, but my friends were careful to never mention Peter. I saw the look in their eyes; at times it was sympathy. I wanted no sympathy. I had made my own choices, and though Peter was no longer the man I married, he was, before God, my husband. I had become strong enough to stand my ground, with both integrity and with affection. I knew how the sea called him, as much as, if not more than, the influence he wielded in our community. Sometimes, at night, alone, I would agonize of a day where he might step beyond what I could forgive. *What would I choose then?* But by each dawn, my hope would return that my Peter, playful and caring Peter, would come back to me.

There was a pleasant evening as the sun was setting, in early November, when Mary, now ten, and I had walked down to the river. As we climbed back up the hill, I could hear the joyful notes of Thomas's fedyl and Obbah's laughter coming from the barn.

"Mary, what do you say? Shall we join them?"

Mary hesitated. She knew well her father's feelings about cavorting with the slaves; yet she revered Thomas and Obbah as well. She looked at me with her mischievous grin. "Yes, Mum. Let us go dance too."

We walked into the barn, standing and watching for a few minutes. Thomas saw us when he looked up from his fedyl, and he smiled. First Mary joined in, dancing about with little Zeb. Thomas began playing his familiar tune, "The Fairy Dance," and after a few moments I joined them; and, for an hour or so, I forgot all my troubles.

Chapter 29

Thomas

The year of our Lord 1663 was a difficult one. My master had made, without cause, unfair accusations and slighted greatly my reputation and that of his wife. I worked hard for Captain Tallman and denied him no request. I knew that he wanted me to be firmer with his slaves, but there was little need for such. Their work was reliably done in a fine manner, and willingly. There was no cause for harshness.

Through late summer and autumn I had spent much time in Newport, at Captain Tallman's shop. I would make certain that James had received goods he needed from the warehouse, as was my charge. But I stayed longer, and James would show me how he mixed the poultices and salves and share what herbs were good for fever or fainting spells, or the other ailments his customers revealed to him. I learned much at the apothecary, and over these weeks James and I forged a friendship that would last long. He shared with me that the captain was a difficult and demanding boss, but his responsibilities kept him otherwise occupied and, for a decent recompense, the captain truly relied upon James. In spite of my interest in the dispensing of medicines, I checked with Mrs. Tallman each morning and made certain to be home well before sunset in case she had any chores.

My heart leapt with an infrequent joy on the evening in late autumn when Mary and Mrs. Tallman walked into the barn as I played my fedyl and the rest were dancing, even little Zeb. Each time I saw her, she looked beautiful, elegant as she stood next to her daughter on this evening, as if two vaporous angels had lit the dreary barn. Little Mary loved the music she had learned to play on my fedyl, and it was not long before she joined in the merrymaking and dancing. There was no denying any longer that my heart had opened to loving this woman who stood across the barn floor. The last rays of the sun illuminated her silhouette from behind, and my heart filled in a way unfamiliar to me.

Though adoration filled my head, I was ashamed of myself for loving this woman, the wife of another; the wife of a man who had first saved me from the London docks but now accused me of impinging on his own territory, of acting dishonorably. In spite of a blossoming in my heart, I knew it was a secret I must keep. Yet, standing there, Ann was striking, and I had seen, with clarity, the generosity in her heart.

Captain Tallman came home in December. As I had noticed over the years, the mood of the house changed yet again. There was less laughter, both in the house and in the barn. The captain did not seem pleased that I had spent so much time at the apothecary, but said little about it. I kept to my chores and limited my contact with James at the shop, not wanting to jeopardize his position. James had worked at the apothecary for many years, and now had a young wife, Ava, a quiet young woman with yellow hair and a slight accent similar to the captain's.

My master was curt in his orders to me and avoided my presence when he was home. In spite of his clear distrust of me, he revealed one day that he had a mistress in New Amsterdam. He spoke salaciously of her, with details of how she pleased him. I only listened, puzzled and disgusted by his revelation. *Why did he share this? Was he hoping I would tell Mrs. Tallman? Was he trying to anger me?* I believed there might have been a treacherous side to this Captain Tallman, and resolved to be cautious.

It was not long after the captain's revelation that he confirmed my suspicions of his character. He came one day to the barn and ordered Zebediah to pack his belongings and those of his son, Zeb. Zebediah looked at me, confused, but did as he was told.

"What is it, Captain? Are you taking them away for a chore?" This did not make sense, both of them leaving with all of their belongings.

"That is not your concern, Thomas," he responded crisply. "You will have the help you need here."

Though the community had debated banning slavery, it yet flourished in Newport. Few citizens had released their slaves, and there was ample trading at the docks.

"Come," Master yelled at Zebediah.

"Master, can we say g'bye to Obbah? Please, sir?" asked Zebediah.

"Get in the cart, both of you," barked the captain.

Ibrahim and I stared at what was happening. I had little doubt they would not return, and my heart broke for the pain that would ensue. My heart sank for Zebediah and his son, for Obbah, and for Mrs. Tallman. The missus would be shattered. I knew that she loved them all, as family.

"Return to your chores, both of you," he yelled at us. "You will have a strong, young back to help you by evening."

Ibrahim and I returned to the barn. The hay needed pitching before feeding time, and I asked Ibrahim to finish that task. I sat for a spell on a hay bale near the door. I could only think of Obbah, in the house, unknowing of what was happening, and tears crept down my cheeks. *Should I tell the missus? Obbah?* I did not want to be the one to give them this dreadful news, yet I was not certain it was good to have the news come from the master. I took my cup and walked to the well near the house.

I filled the cup and sat on a stone nearby, drinking the water and composing my thoughts. Then the anger crept in. I was furious the captain was doing this. Doubts set in. Maybe he was not selling them; maybe they would come home. I did not believe this, but I could neither believe that this man, the father of these beautiful children in his own house, could take Zebediah away from Obbah, take her baby from her. Surely, he could not do this. But I had seen malevolence in his eyes before, and what I saw today was bitter determination.

I walked into the kitchen and saw Mrs. Tallman preparing food. Obbah was not there; likely she was upstairs with the children.

"Ma'am. I believe I have some terrible news." I paused, the words caught in my throat, and I swallowed hard to release them.

"What is it, Thomas?" She brushed the loose curls from her face, leaving white meal in her hair. Her expression gained concern as I struggled to speak.

"I am afraid the master may be selling Zebediah and Zeb. He took them and their belongings to Newport."

She stood there, looking at me. I think she was unsure of what she heard.

Then, softly, she said, "No." She stood in silence yet again.

"No, this cannot be true. Is it?" She looked at me, her green eyes pleading, pleading for me to tell her I was probably mistaken.

"Ma'am, it is possible I am wrong. But I believe I am right. The captain said he would bring a young slave home by this evening."

The missus let out a cry, a deep cry that she quickly softened so Obbah would not hear.

"No, no, no." She began crying and, before I knew it, she was weeping in my arms, begging for the comfort of an embrace, an embrace I could not withhold. I held her tightly, trying to give relief where none could be had.

We stood in this embrace for quite some time, until Mrs. Tallman's tears waned. She squeezed my arms, standing back and looking into my eyes.

"You may be wrong. I pray?" She was searching for hope, as I had done.

"The fear may be unfounded." I could not deny her the hope she craved. Tears still crept down her face, and, without thinking, I leaned forward and kissed the tears on her cheek. Neither of us was surprised by my boldness. She did not resist, and again she held me tight.

At last she stepped away, trying to compose herself.

"Thomas, we will not tell Obbah, not yet. Let us see what happens this evening. I will confront Peter when he gets home. I have to believe we have misunderstood something. He cannot have done something so cruel."

I nodded. I knew that she did not believe the words she had said, but I agreed it was best to wait. Before I left the house, she took my hand, and, in a gesture more intimate than any I had known, she put my hand to her lips and kissed it softly; and with that, she walked away to her chores, and I left for the barn.

Chapter 30

Ann

The night was chilled when Peter returned home with a new slave, Gabriel. Thomas had come to me in the afternoon, telling me of Peter's actions, how he ordered Zebediah to pack all of his and Zeb's belongings. I had said nothing to Obbah, for I prayed we were wrong. Yet, as I looked out the window, in the moonlight, I could see Peter taking a tall man to the barn. It was not Zebediah; this figure was slighter and taller than Zebediah. The children were fed and I instructed Obbah to ready them for bed upstairs; I was ready to confront my husband when he came in the front door. I was finished being fearful. I was finished obliging his bad behavior.

"What have you done, Peter?" I asked as he removed his cloak.

"As if it is your concern," he growled. "You do not conduct the business in this house. I have traded for a new slave to work the property. His name is Gabriel, and he has a good back. You have done nothing but spoil these slaves. The price I paid for Gabriel was Zebediah and his spawn."

I saw the revenge and hate in Peter's eyes as he said these words to me. He knew well how this would distress me, how it would devastate Obbah.

Peter was looking for an argument. The hate he felt within himself was purposefully being inflicted upon me.

"Yes, Peter, who is going to tell Obbah? Who is going to tell her that her son is gone, maybe forever? There is no certainty that the traders will keep Zeb with his pa. Do you have no heart? You, Peter, are not the man I married," I said, and with those words I walked away. I took my woolen cloak from the hook near the door, exited from the kitchen and walked toward the woods. The moonlight lit my way, yet the tears blurred my sight and left my footing uncertain. Losing my balance, I tumbled next to a fir tree, and I did not get up. I sat in the night's chill on the damp, rotting leaves and wept silent tears.

I wept for Obbah, and for Zeb and his father. I wept for the loss of my marriage; and, sadly, I wept for the man in my house who was empty and had lost his way. I wept for Peter.

I sat there for a long while as I watched the candles in the house be extinguished, one by one. I would tell Obbah in the morning. I am certain that Peter said nothing, for Obbah was beneath him.

As I watched the house grow dark and the stars shine bright, I rose and made my way to the barn. The moon was high in the sky and I saw a dim light in Thomas's room. I knocked softly. When he opened the door, his face revealed surprise to see me standing there.

"Ma'am, are you all right? I have shown the new slave to his quarters. Master will be angry to find you here," he whispered, as if warning me of something I did not know.

"He sold Zebediah and his son. He sold them to traders and their futures are surely uncertain. I have not yet told Obbah."

Thomas looked muddled and saddened, his doleful eyes yet confused by my presence.

"Thomas, you are my friend. My husband, I fear, is a madman. He has broken my heart and I am lost." I sounded like an ungodly beggar, but I did not care.

"Missus, I want to comfort you; yet I fear, should he find you here, it will justify his accusations and enrage him." He paused. "I fear the master may harm you and he may send me away. I cannot take advantage of your sadness. You are dear to me, but I will not risk your safety nor benefit from your sorrow, your tears."

"You are right, Thomas. But I am done. I will have to find my own way, I am certain. But, now, just hold me a moment. I pray my rebellious ways will not harm us, but it is your comfort I crave."

Thomas blew out the candle by his chair, but the moonlight dimly lit his face. As he came toward me, reaching for me, I placed my hands up and held his face, looked into his eyes. There was a defiant courage deep inside that rose up, and I kissed Thomas with an intimacy I had not felt for many years. It was a long and tender kiss, returned in kind. Thomas pulled me closer and kissed me with a sudden hunger that startled us both. I pulled back.

"Forgive me. Ye are the wife of my master. I should not have taken such liberty."

I took his hand. "I am your friend," I said, but my heart knew. I was more than his friend. I rested my head on his shoulder, and Thomas held me in his arms. It was a safe place. I sensed he did not want to let go, but I moved away to return to the house before my absence or whereabouts were questioned, before my longing for sweet Thomas overwhelmed me.

"Thomas, it is Ann. Call me Ann. I will see you tomorrow, for whatever it brings. The days before me, before all of us, will be hard," I whispered as I walked out the door.

I slipped carefully, in the darkness, back along the edge of the woods where I had wept earlier. I did not join Peter in our room that night. I climbed the stairs and lay in the small bed with Elizabeth, but I slept little that night.

***

Arising early, before the sun was up, I filled the pot with water from the well. I started a fire to warm water for coffee and to prepare the porridge for breakfast. Then I went back up the stairs to Obbah's room. I knocked on her door. She was dressing as I sat on her bed, but she saw the expression on my face. She saw the misery in my eyes, in the furrow of my brow. I told her what Peter had done; Zebediah and Zeb were gone.

She fell into a heap on the floor, sobbing into the skirt of her dress.

"Obbah, I cannot tell you how sorry I am. Never! Never will I forgive Peter for this. His heart has hardened and I no longer know this man." I put my hand on her shoulder, yet she continued sobbing. There was no easing her pain. "I will do whatever I can do discreetly to find out what happens to them, Obbah. I love them too."

I rose to leave.

"Obbah, I will prepare the breakfast and get the children dressed."

As I went to the children's room, Obbah ran past me, down the stairs and out the door. She was still barefoot, and it was cold outside. I had no doubt she was running to the barn, to the slave quarters, full of hope that I was mistaken. My heart broke for her.

As the children ate, Peter joined them for some coffee and porridge. He was quiet, but before he left, he asked why Obbah was not serving breakfast.

"She is looking for her husband, for her son." I looked at him squarely in the eyes; he could not hold my gaze.

"That is not her husband. They are but slaves. Foolish girl," he said as he rose to leave. "You tell her to get back to work."

Thomas had his horse readied out front, and Peter rode off without another word, toward town and his business of the day, as if nothing had happened. But everything had changed. Everything.

Chapter 31

Ann

The dilemmas of the previous day played over and over within my head, and my heart was heavy. As I was praying it might be but a dream, I remembered that my sewing circle was that day. The event was scheduled at my house, and I could not reschedule so late without causing hardship, as well as revealing tribulations of some kind at our home. Obbah and I would have to pull it together.

"Obbah, go out and ask Thomas to come to the house," I said as she came in the back door. She was still crying, but I needed Thomas.

"Yes, ma'am."

Before she walked out of the door, I walked over and took her in my arms. I held her as the children sat at the table with their bowls of porridge; Susanna was fussing, and Mary and Elizabeth looked confused. I did not care. I held Obbah tight and did not let go.

"Now, Obbah, go get Thomas."

I picked up Susanna and tried to get her to eat some porridge.

"Mummy," said Elizabeth, "what is wrong? Is Obbah sad?"

"Children, Obbah is sad, so we will all be kind to her today. Little Zeb and Zebediah had to go away, and she misses them terribly. We will all try to help her." I sat Susanna back in her chair and she began banging her spoon on the table. "You may give Obbah many hugs and be sweet, but, for now, I want you to say nothing about this, to no one." Thomas walked in the door with Obbah. Obbah took over the meal at the table, and out of the side of my eye I saw Mary get up, walk to Obbah and hug her tightly. Obbah took Mary's sweet head and held it tight to her bosom. The sight was heartbreaking, and my eyes met the despair in Thomas's eyes.

I walked quietly out the back door with Thomas.

"Thomas, I want you to take your horse into town, into Newport. I am not certain where Peter went today. I think he may have gone to Warwick; keep an eye out for him. Go to the slave trader at the docks and see what you can discreetly discover. Where are they? Where might they go?"

"I will leave now. I will do my best, ma'am."

"Be safe, Thomas."

I prepared the sitting room for my friends coming to sew. Obbah, once settling the children, mixed and baked currant scones and pulled the good china for the coffee. I helped her with the scones, yet her mind was clearly elsewhere. I knew well she had fears for her own future, as did I.

Martha arrived early with Lydia. She saw Obbah's swollen eyes and asked if I was well. She went on to reveal that she had heard, from her husband, about Peter trading his slaves down at the docks.

"All will be good. I will do whatever I can to help Obbah." I would have revealed more to my friend Martha, but with Lydia there and Elizabeth Lawton and others coming to the door, I did not want to provide gossip. The knowing look on Martha's face made me grateful for my dear friend, yet I knew in my heart that the stories about town would come soon enough. I saw a new young woman at our meeting. She introduced herself to me as Ava, the wife of James at our apothecary. She was very quiet, shy I believe, and looked familiar to me. My eyes returned to her oft during the afternoon, and I recalled the oil painting I had placed in the old desk at our house in Newport, the painting of a young girl with ice blue eyes. I came to suspect Ava was this young girl, and had my mind not been occupied elsewhere, I would have been more curious.

We spent an ordinary afternoon sewing, gossiping about the rumors in Newport and Portsmouth, and enjoying the treats Obbah served. Now and then, when Obbah walked in, I saw nothing but the sadness on her face as she poured coffee for my friends. Absent her serving tea and scones, she spent most of her time that afternoon upstairs with the children.

Thomas returned from Newport before my friends had left the house. I was anxious to speak with him; and as the buggies pulled away, Obbah brought the children downstairs to take them outside for some fresh air and play. As they left, Thomas came into the kitchen.

"I found them. Master's mare was at the apothecary, but I saw Zebediah and his boy at the docks. The trader had them both unloading goods from the ships recently arrived. They had not been sold and are, yet, together."

"Good, good. But what is to come is my worry."

"I have a friend at the dock, someone I can trust. I asked him to keep an eye on them and tell me if they are sold, where they might go. He said he would do his best."

"Good. I suppose that is the best we can do now. We will rely on news from your friend, and we shall pray. I pray that God looks after them."

"Yes, ma'am." He smiled at me, with a knowing look that he should not call me Ann, and he turned to go back to his chores at the barn. As he opened the back door, he turned back toward me. "Are you going to be well? When Master gets home?"

"Yes, Thomas. I will be fine; but Peter may not." I winked at him to soothe his worries.

***

Peter did not get home that evening until very late, and I had already gone to bed. I returned to our marriage bed, a place I had no desire to be, but I knew full well that I was yet Peter's wife. When I awoke in the morning, Peter was dressing.

I brought a basin of fresh water from the well, and as I brushed out my hair and pinned my linen caul, I turned to Peter, who was about to leave.

"Peter, I plead that you make this thing you have done right. I miss the man who, for all our days together, protected the honor and happiness of his family. Where has he gone? The slaves are fearful of you, the children are fearful of you, but know that I am no longer afraid." With my words yet sitting in the air, I stood to face him. "I know you flirt with other women, openly, and I have accepted that the sea is your true love. In spite of this, I am yet your wife and the mother of your children."

Peter seemed at a loss for words, startled by my outspokenness, but I knew he would find his voice. I just prayed it would not be cruel. Stillness hung in the room, but my resolve remained firm.

"You betray me at every turn, Ann. Against my wishes, you spoil these slaves. They are not your family; I am. And you shame me by cavorting with this servant, and before then you sail as a free woman on a Dutch ship to New

Amsterdam." He turned to leave. "I should let them all go … Ibrahim, Gabriel and Obbah; and then you can live like a pauper woman, as when I found you."

His words were hurtful, but I knew that was his intent.

"Peter, Mum and I were not paupers when you met us. We were content and respected. Content, as I have not been for years now. You may hurt me, but you cannot take my soul, my will, from me."

He stormed out, not even stopping in the kitchen for breakfast, not able to look Obbah in the eye. He was walking toward the barn, surely angry that his horse was not readied for his departure.

Chapter 31

Peter

"Thomas!" I yelled as I walked into the barn. He was saddling my horse. "Why is my horse not readied?"

"I am sorry, Master. It is yet early and I was showing Gabriel how to milk these cows before saddling your horse."

I grabbed the reins from the hook and walked out to mount my horse. "You can go into the apothecary today, early, and pick up some crates of herbs, medicines and rum I contracted to a doctor In Hartford. James has the directions. The doctor will pay you in shillings, and you are to bring the payment to me upon your return." I left for the courthouse in Warwick.

The wind was strong, with a chill in the air, holding spring in abeyance. I pulled my cloak and woolen scarf tight, unable to rid my mind of this servant Thomas and my wife's betrayal. Ann was my wife, the prized bride on my arm; and I could find no solace in my power and success in this mutiny within my own home. I could find no escape from my thoughts. I had to get rid of Thomas, to humiliate and belittle him before all and before Ann. I had a plan. I would break him, and Ann would know her place. I still could not fathom that Ann's mother had sued me for items and monies due her, after all that I had done for the Hill family. I had every right, as Ann's husband, to sell the land in Barbados. The court deemed I must split the monies and, at times such as these, I felt my position and power in Newport were for naught. I belonged on the sea, where I mastered my own fate.

The proceedings in Warwick took much of my day, and the sun was creeping below the horizon when I stopped at the tavern in Portsmouth. My mind was yet full of distress with my fretful thoughts, and I craved a drink to numb the pain. I saw Lot Strange on the far side of the pub, swigging a pint of ale, alone. I did not need that nuisance. One of the Smith brothers was sitting at the bar and I joined him. I had drunk a whiskey and a couple of ales when Lot walked past me.

"Aye, Tallman. When are you getting that fence erected at your property's edge?"

"When I damned well have a mind to, neighbor," I responded. This night, I had no patience for Lot's foolishness.

"You may be an official of the court, Tallman, but the judge deemed you shall get it done. And I shall see to it."

I felt the heat of my blood rise to my head, and I grabbed the clay jug on the bar near me and threw it at Lot, just missing his head. The bit of ale yet in the jug sprayed his clothes and splattered over the wooden floor. I had hoped he would dare strike at me, but he only smirked and turned on his heel to leave. I ordered another whiskey as the barmaid wiped up the floor and gathered the broken shards. Jeremiah, the barkeep, frowned at me. My friend had left the tavern, so I ordered another whiskey. After a few hours more passed, I paid my tab, mounted my mare and relied on her to find the way home.

The house was quiet as I stumbled in the door, yet I saw Ann sitting in the kitchen. I said nothing and, barely getting my boots off, fell into bed.

In the morning Ann was up and in the kitchen, but I saw that she had slept in our bed; her dressing gown lay beside me. I remembered that Thomas had gone to Connecticut, and prayed that one of the miserable slaves would be smart enough to have my horse readied.

Obbah was preparing the table for the children when I walked into the kitchen. She set a bowl of porridge in front of me and brought me a pot of coffee.

"Ann, what is it you are doing on this day?"

"I am stitching some cotton dresses and shirts for the children and I may go into town, to the tailor," she responded, with little attentiveness.

"Thomas is not here to hitch the buggy, so tell Obbah to direct Ibrahim to do so." After eating, I pulled on my boots, grabbed my cloak and, in parting, said, "I will be home for dinner this night. Obbah can prepare one of the chickens." I paused, then turned back and, holding both of Ann's shoulders, leaned in to kiss her. She turned her cheek to receive my kiss and walked away. "I will be at the shop," I said tersely, my jaw clenched, and I walked out.

The smell of spring was in the air as I rode to Newport. There were blossoms on the trees and a temperate breeze. I removed my cloak. My apothecary's presence was revered on the island, and I could rely on it to make a profit. Yet, with all of my success, my agonies weighed heavy on my spirit. This woman, my wife, had deceived me; yet I was certain that the evil was Thomas. Thomas had emboldened her, and violated his trust with me. I could not let his deceit destroy me, this mere wisp of a man, but a child. He was worse than a slave, less than the runaway Mingoe.

My thoughts and resentments swirled in my mind and,

after an untold time and with a startled suddenness, I became aware that my horse was at a standstill. My mare stood at the side of the roadway, unmoored, as was I. *How long had I been here, just sitting here? I must get my mind back; dear God, I beseech You to grant me direction.* I pulled the reins and guided my horse back to the road and toward Newport. I could not fail now, not when my father had yet to learn that his youngest son had success sufficient to embody the family name. This day before me appeared to be long and uncertain, my mind in chaos.

For the first time in many days, maybe weeks, I arrived home before the sun set and for the dinner meal. I sat with Ann and the older children, acting as though our lives were customary.

"Has Thomas returned?" I asked Ann.

"No. I have not seen him."

On the following day, upon arriving home, I asked Ann the same question.

"Yes. I saw him at the barn with Gabriel this afternoon. Did he not take your horse when you arrived?"

"No, it was Ibrahim."

"Your son Peter will start school in the fall. I spoke with the schoolmaster, and there is room for him, as well as Mary," Ann said, her goal appearing to be to change the topic of conversation. Elizabeth, though older than Peter, had not yet started attending the schoolhouse, but Ann knew it was important to me for Peter to start his education.

With no response to Ann and with my mind elsewhere, I walked to the barn to find Thomas. He and Gabriel were feeding the mares.

"Thomas, where are the monies from the medicines you delivered?" I asked.

He grabbed his saddle pack from the wall hook and pulled the monies out, handing it to me.

I counted it. "Where is the rest of it?" I asked.

"Master, that is the full payment. Doctor Easton said that was the agreed amount."

"Nay. This is short two pounds. Are you now stealing money from me? Are the affections of my wife not enough?" I asked, glaring at this scoundrel. I had him now. Out of the corner of my eye, I could see Gabriel backing up and watching us. "Be certain that theft will be punished severely by the judge, as well as by me."

"Master, I have taken nothing from your payment." He reached into his sack and pulled out a paper, a receipt, and handed it to me. "Here is the ticket that the physician wrote showing our exchange. This one is for you. I asked the good doctor, as well, for a copy for meself."

I looked carefully at the paper he handed me, matching the amounts listed with the monies he had given me. The scoundrel had outwitted me. With the monies and the receipt, I walked back to the house.

***

Early in the morning, I left the house, readied for a day at the courthouse in Portsmouth. Thomas stood there, in front of the porch, with my bridled horse readied for me.

"Master Tallman, I am leaving my indentured station. I strongly believe there lacks significant trust between us, yet I am aware that I am indebted to you. I will pay you the full penalty of abandoning my indenture, but I will be gone away from here today. And be assured, Captain Tallman, that your jealousies rely upon your own false terrors." Thomas handed me the reins as I stood there, words failing me. This course of events had taken me by surprise. He would pay dearly for this betrayal, but I felt comfort that he would no longer be here at the house, here with my Ann.

"You are correct, servant; you will pay dearly," I said, and I rode off.

Chapter 32

Ann

I overheard the last words between my husband and Thomas on this morning, Peter's words, "You will pay dearly ...." I knew then that the conflict with my husband had escalated. I would leave Thomas be for now, and I spent the morning helping Obbah with the children.

As the children sat at the kitchen table for lunch, Thomas knocked at the back door and came in.

"Ma'am, I must speak to you," he whispered, and he stepped back outside as I followed him. "I have told your husband I am leaving. I fear your husband is putting me in such danger that could result in my imprisonment. I will square my debts with your husband, be assured, but you must know that should you need help or protection, I will be in Portsmouth," he whispered. He handed me a tome.

"Here is the Marlowe book you lent to me; I have marked a page for you. Ibrahim knows that, for now, he is to be overseeing the chores and Gabriel."

I took the book from his hand, and I felt a tear creeping down my cheek and onto my collar. I wanted to embrace him, but chose not to do so as Thomas entered the kitchen and said goodbye to the children, kissing Mary, Peter and Elizabeth on the head. I felt Obbah's warm hand reach for mine.

"If I get any word on Zebediah and your son, Obbah, I will get that information to you, somehow," he said to Obbah as he walked out the door.

I felt my life was collapsing around me. A chill ran through my spine and my mouth dried.

"Why is Thomas leaving, Mummy?" asked Mary, then Elizabeth piped in with the same question.

"Thomas wants to better himself, but I am hopeful that we will see him again. I do not believe that he is going far. We will pray for him. And for Zebediah."

I walked into the sitting room and sat down. *What is happening? Thomas, now gone, had been a constant rock; Obbah's family has been ripped from her; Peter is drinking and losing his mind. What am I to do? How can I be the pillar in this crumbling home?* I felt another tear drop to my chin; and, as I looked out the window, I saw Thomas walking toward the road with a satchel and his rifle over his shoulder and his fedyl in hand. Suddenly I thought of Pa and how much I wished he were here. He would put his arm around my shoulder and bring me solace. Pa's warmth was like sunshine. Oh, how I missed him; how I needed him right now.

I felt the book in my lap, the book Thomas had handed to me. There was a slip of paper in the pages. I sat back into the chair and opened the book to the marked page. The slip of paper fell to the floor. The page was a love poem, a poem by Christopher Marlowe. I read the familiar words, slowly, word by word, taking on new meaning as I heard my heart pound greatly in my ears.

The Passionate Shepherd To His Love
by *Christopher Marlowe*

Come live with me, and be my love;
And we will all the pleasures prove
That hills and valleys, dales and fields,
Woods, or steepy mountain yields.

And we will sit upon the rocks,
Seeing the shepherds feed their flocks
By shallow rivers, to whose falls
Melodious birds sing madrigals.

And I will make thee beds of roses,
And a thousand fragrant posies,
A cap of flowers, and a kirtle
Embroidered all with leaves of myrtle;

A gown made of the finest wool,
Which from our pretty lambs we pull;
Fair lined slippers for the cold,
With buckles of the purest gold;

A belt of straw and ivy buds,
With coral clasps and amber studs;
And if these pleasures may thee move,
Come live with me, and be my love.

The shepherd swains shall dance and sing
For thy delight each May-morning:
If these delights thy mind may move,
Then live with me, and be my love.

Oh, my breath was held in my chest as if I were submerged under water. The familiar words sounded different now. A love song, an invitation that was personal. I could not deny that such feelings for Thomas had grown within me in recent weeks, through a friendship begun years ago. Yet, in spite of the avowed words, I knew that Thomas would do nothing to betray me or even his jealous master. Peter was driving us both away, and perchance driving me into another's arms.

I was yet the mistress of the Tallman home, the mother of our children. I did not know how to save us. I bent down and lifted the paper that had drifted to the floor. "*My dear Ann, you are one of a thousand stars. You are the one I will, for all my days, carry in my heart.*"

I read it again, and again, then folded it and put it in the pocket of my dress, beneath my pinafore.

"Obbah," I called. "Go tell Ibrahim to ready the buggy for me."

***

I guided the buggy down the main street in Newport, toward the cemetery. I had picked some flowers before I left home. It was too early in spring for flowers from my garden, but I had found some early wildflowers, some purple violas and some Queen Anne's lace. I walked through the gate and toward Rose's grave. Rose ... my firstborn, sweet baby girl in heaven with Pa. As I walked toward the familiar headstone, I saw a man sitting on a gravestone near Rose's grave. He looked familiar; it was Pa. But it could not be Pa, for Pa was dead and I was surely awake. The man had a worried brow; and when I gazed down to weave my way through the random headstones and looked up again, Pa was gone.

Normally such a vision would have startled me, but Pa's

aura of presence seemed more natural as years passed. When I reached Rose's grave, I felt a swift warmth and comfort, as if wrapped in a worn blanket. I laid the flowers before Rose's stone and, spreading a cloth, sat down to be near Rose, near Pa, to search for my way. I had known from the moment I asked Ibrahim to bring the buggy that it was here, in the cemetery, where I could freely search my soul and discern my strength.

I had not sat there long, revived by the sea breeze, before the tears began to fall. Before God, I was Peter's wife, but I could not find my way. *My heart is now conflicted, yet I have not betrayed my jealous husband. Or have I?* The tears stopped, but my eyes were now swollen. I sat in silence, in stillness, when a dove flew near and lit on a headstone. I sat still, watching the dove and searching my heart. And then I prayed.

Oh, Unmanifested One, I come as Your child. Grant that You may illumine my vision, may Your light shine on my heart so that I know my way. In my darkness, my pain and sorrow, may I find the radiance of Thy face shining with peace and love. Bathe my soul in humility so that my heart opens to Your wisdom. I beseech You, Father, for I cannot find my way.

I looked up at the dove nearby. The answers to my questions did not embrace me, yet a strength dwelled in me, dwelled firmly as if lighting a path through hardship. As the dove flew off, an immense capacity filled me, a knowledge that I could face any hardships, those now before me and those yet to come. I sensed there would be angels to protect me, as I was certain to come face-to-face with distress and with my eyes wide open.

I sat there, in the breeze, my own woman. I loved my husband, but his faithfulness was lacking. I knew in my heart that I had come to love Thomas, a kind man who was my true friend—a true friend filled with kindness for my children, bestowing more love than their own father. I would not turn my back on a true friend in lieu of a feared husband. I would not be weak and bend to Peter's demands. I would be faithful to my God, come hell or heaven, and I would be true to my own soul, God's creation, and true to those who loved me.

Chapter 33

Thomas

Leaving my indenture at the Tallman farm had been one of the bravest things I had ever done, risking imprisonment, walking away from the woman that I had come to love. But the decision, I knew, was to save my hide from a worse fate, from the jealous Captain Tallman. I was fortunate to have found work at the blacksmith's. Matthew Grinnell was a good man, an English immigrant who had been here in Portsmouth for many years. He had purchased land in Portsmouth and wild land across the bay. He procured his land from the Indians, and he had built the blacksmith shop early in Portsmouth. He said he needed an apprentice, as he moved slower than he had when younger, and in this circumstance I was blessed to find work. He had allowed me to stay nights at the shop until I could afford my own place. Master Grinnell liked that I could start the fires early.

In April, William Wilbor, the husband of Ann's friend Martha, told me there was a small cabin at the edge of town that could be had for a good price, and I was going in the evening hours to see it. I was not able to afford purchase of land, but prayed the owner would agree to a contract. I had learned my skills quickly, and Master Grinnell was allowing me to work for a commission on some projects. I set aside a small amount of monies each week toward what I owed the captain for my bond.

In spite of my promise to repay my debt, the captain had filed a lawsuit, as he was prone to do. I was to appear in the court on my indebtedness. William had shared with me that Captain Tallman was not well liked in town for his litigious ways. He relayed to me the incident at the pub two months earlier, when the captain had thrown a jug at Lot Strange. I chuckled at the vision of such an exchange, but was saddened that Ann was yet living with such unscrupulous behavior. I worried that Tallman may yet again strike her, as I had seen before.

The day did arrive when I was able to send good news to Ann, through her friend Martha, that the physician in Connecticut, to whom I had made the captain's medicinal delivery, had purchased Zebediah and his son. I had mentioned them to the doctor in case he might know a family in Hartford who wished to purchase good help and would be willing to keep the child with his father. To my surprise, it was the physician himself who purchased them and, based on my business encounter with him, I would expect that he and his wife would treat them well. I am certain that both Ann and Obbah were delighted to hear this news, but I had not spoken to Ann since that fateful day of my departure. I prayed each night that she was well.

I found the cabin to be dreary but adequate, and I moved in May, giving me time to put aside further funds toward my debt. I spent my evenings, with the longer days of summer, working on cleaning out and repairing the cabin. Martha had made some curtains for my windows, and, in spite of my status, a friendship grew between the

Wilbor family and myself. I built a table and picked up a couple of chairs. William and Martha found some bedding for me, and I crafted a frame and headboard so I could live somewhat civilized in the woods. I was using a horse and a cart the blacksmith had provided for my benefit, as well as his when he sent me on errands. I looked forward to getting my own horse before the summer was done. I was happy here, though alone. I had my fedyl and my hunting rifle I had bartered for last year in Newport for hunting. My cooking skills were meager but sufficient; and every now and then Martha would bring me fresh-baked bread, and vegetables from her gardens.

I imagined Martha shared information of my well-being with Ann, though we did not speak of it. Martha would have told me if Ann were in trouble or unwell, and I was gladdened there was no such news. I stayed away from the tavern for fear of coming across Captain Tallman and the probability of an unfortunate scene such as the tale I'd heard of Master Strange.

Martha invited me for dinner at her home one evening in late May. I was looking forward to a good meal, unlike my paltry feasts at home. Martha's table held an array of roasted pork and turkey, spinach, turnips, tomatoes and a magnificent pastry filled with berries unknown to me. We washed it down with a good ale William had brewed himself.

"What will you do, Thomas, about Tallman's charges against you?" asked William.

"I am hopeful that the court will require only payment of my debt, and not time jailed. I anticipate that I can meet the debt when I am required to do so."

"That is fortunate, Thomas," added Martha. "I do pray the judge will be lenient. You know that Captain Tallman has positions within the government, yet many know of his difficult demeanor. Peter's absence may mitigate your litigation. You know that he sails for Amsterdam next week."

I saw that William gave Martha a look that she should not interfere with the Tallman matters; however, both suspected I had feelings for Ann, and Martha knew well how miserable Ann was in her marriage. I said nothing in response to this exchange. William and I drank another ale, and William's oldest daughter played the piano as I played my fedyl, and the Wilbor children danced about the sitting room, squealing with glee as their parents put aside their Puritan rules for an evening of joy.

Chapter 33

Ann

Peter was in Newport, working with James to restock the shop from the warehouse and to gather records, as well as define needs, before he set sail for the Old World, and the West Indies and New Amsterdam on the way home. Obbah and I had done the laundry, and I packed Peter's clothing into his bags.

Since the departure of Thomas, the household was more chaotic. We had clear need for more help. Ibrahim tried his best to keep everything running smoothly, but he had never been trained in the wisdom and traits demonstrated by Miles and Thomas. There had been some spats between Ibrahim and Peter, and I was grateful that Peter had not resorted to the switch.

I sensed Peter was nervous about his voyage. The tension between he and I had been waxing; Peter continued to harbor jealousy with regards to Thomas, as evidenced by his dour mood and derogatory remarks about his servant. All of this, along with his conflicts with Lot Strange and others, seemed to heighten his suspicions and aggravate his ill temper.

I had considered leaving for Virginia to stay with Mum, but I knew this would likely be a hardship on my brother and his family. Peter would certainly not allow the children to stay with me if I left, so I was yet indecisive about my future.

With his ship scheduled to depart early the next morn, Peter did not return home until a late hour, after the family had eaten. I knew that he would leave for the docks and his ship in the wee hours of the following day. I had gone to bed before Peter arrived home. He had been drinking but stayed sober.

"Have you packed my bags?" he asked loudly.

"Yes, they are packed with your clothing and bedding. Obbah has parceled some dried meats for your travels as well."

He lay in bed beside me, smelling of whiskey-scented sweat. He moved toward me and kissed me. I returned the gesture, impassive, and moved away.

"You will not refuse your husband before his voyage," he sneered. With that said, he grabbed my gown and ripped it free at the shoulder as his weight bore down on me, as he fumbled with the hem of my gown, and he with a hostile suddenness penetrated my being, my very essence. The swiftness of his act took away my breath and, through tears, I protested, quietly and ineffectively resisting his strength and zealous determination. He had his way and, hastily done, rolled away and said nothing.

I lay there, fearful to move in my heartbreak. Dazed in disbelief of his callousness. He had not been drunken enough for me to forgive such malice. I waited long before rising, suspecting that he might be yet awake, stewing in his discontent. When I heard his deep breathing, I rose and replaced my torn gown with my muslin liner. I went upstairs and sat in the chair in the room where the girls were sleeping. I sat there for the longest time, listening to their peaceful breaths, their sweet forms bathed in the moonlight glowing through the window.

I did not know how I could stay, but these were my children. I loved them dearly and could not leave them; and if I took them, I would struggle to support them, as well as lose them in the end to Peter's demands. *How can a union born of two free spirits in love turn so bitter, even dangerous?* Only four years earlier, Mary Dyer of Newport had been hanged in the nearby Bay Colony merely for being a Quaker. Sweet Mary, who had once visited Mum's sewing circle, a young wife and mother who dared to preach. I had never thought my very own life might be at risk in my own home, not from the Indians or disease that had worried me, but by the very hand of my own husband. I felt entirely lost and alone, but, sadly, my heart was thankful that Peter would soon be at sea again.

***

Three weeks had passed since Peter's ship sailed, and my breath came easier with each passing day. The children were playing outside as I sat on the porch on a hot day in late June. This was a serene place, on the hill by the river, a place I had come to love. After the children had been fed dinner, after I had worked my garden much of the afternoon with my thoughts spinning, I told Obbah I may not be home until morning and I asked Ibrahim to saddle the mare. The sun would set in an hour, and I bravely guided my horse down the road toward Portsmouth.

Martha had told me about Thomas's new home and where he lived on the road inland at the edge of town. I had to find it before dark or I might be lost in these woods and hills. After one wrong turn that ended in a meadow, I turned around and came upon Thomas's cabin up the road.

212 • A Thousand Stars

It was small and quaint, almost invisible amongst the trees at the woods' rim, and I was heartened to see a light flickering through the window.

Before I could knock on the door, Thomas opened it. He seemed surprised to see that it was I, but his wide smile welcomed me. He embraced me and, upon entering his home, I found the room small yet inviting. There was a sitting area, a large brick fireplace that served as the oven, with the kitchen and a small table beyond. Behind the table there was a door to another room, which I believed to be his bedroom. There were windows in front and back, with the trees behind the house revealing abundant greenery but little light, reminding me of my house in Newport. I saw the curtains Martha had made and saw how they added cheerfulness.

"Would you like some coffee?" Thomas asked.

"Yes, that would be good, Thomas."

He hung a pot of water to boil in the fireplace and sat in the chair near me.

"Thomas, I find you to be the dearest friend I have, besides my Martha." I sat silently as I searched for my words. "I do not know if I can go on at home."

As my stomach churned and my words failed me, Thomas waited silently.

"My situation is grim, yet I have my children, whom I love with all of my heart. They need me. I am fraught with conflicting desires, yet I needed, more than anything, to see your heartening smile, to embrace the sweet peace I feel when I am near you."

"Ann. I have struggled with worry of you and how you might escape; how you might walk away with the freedom I have found. I pray every day for your happiness, but I know well that the captain is unpredictable. How could one find peace?"

In silence, he rose and fixed the coffee in earthen mugs,

bringing one to me. I was not accustomed to be waited on by a man. I struggled to comprehend the unfamiliar serenity that filled me when in the presence of this man. We sat in a comforting silence for some time, glancing at each other awkwardly and drinking our coffee. I knew well there were no good remedies to my questions. *Why have I come here?*

"I oft dreamt that you might escape and be here with me," whispered Thomas, breaking our silence.

"I read the poem you marked. And your note," I shared. "Oft I would go outside and gaze into the night sky, thinking of you."

Thomas came and knelt next to my chair, touching my face. "I have missed seeing your face every day since I left." He kissed me softly.

I took his hand. Filled with the reflection of adoration in his eyes, I followed him to his room. The bed was soft as I lay down next to him, and we held each other as the day's light waned. I could feel his desire. I could not bring myself to tell Thomas of what had happened with Peter before he sailed, yet the memory of it made me uncertain. Thomas held me as if he sensed my reluctance, kissing my forehead.

"It is getting dark. You stay here while I put your mare up in the barn. I will not be gone long."

I watched him leave, watched the man I knew I loved, a man who cared for me. I trusted him. I knew well that by properly stabling the horse, he was giving me the chance to compose myself, to change my mind. I knew the kindness in his heart. We both knew there was great cost for what may pass this night. But I had made that choice in the cemetery weeks earlier as I sat there with Rose, blessed by the quiet comfort. It was the day I found my bravery, or it found me.

As sunset passed to darkness, Thomas returned to the room. I could see the light of his eyes, and his eyes told me I would not leave for home this night. It was the night

Thomas and I came to know each other in the way God intended a husband and wife to know each other. As his hands found their way through my laces and beneath my chemise, my heart quivered at his tenderness and the first touch of his hand on my neck, my breast. A dim light yet shone from the sitting room, revealing the love in his eyes, as he ensued with disquieted passion. I saw how he savored every moment as night veiled our transgression. We slept intermittently as we joined our hearts and bodies again and again, as if it would be forbidden forever after this night. I filled with adoration for this man, a young man full of a patient wisdom, an old soul who showered me with a gentle presence I had not rightly experienced in all of my years.

My mind knew I had betrayed my vows, and I was no longer *"without offence,"* as the priest had long ago decreed while I stood before him in the parish of Christ Church. I had not betrayed my husband until this night. *Not until this night.*

Yet I was filled with an awareness of being where I truly belonged. Thomas and I awoke with the rise of the sun and the song of the meadowlark. I awoke to find him standing beside the bed; I was filled with a desire to pull this beautiful man back to my bosom. Thomas was muscled and strong, with waves of chestnut-colored hair, yet uncombed, and silver-gray eyes, piercing gray eyes like I had never seen. He was not as tall as Peter, but stood sturdier, a frame that betrayed his gentleness. His eyes never ceased smiling, even when his mouth did. I loved looking into those eyes. His hands were strong and calloused from his work, yet they were light in their touch, as I had learned through this night.

Thomas had to dress for work, and I needed to go home to the children and to help Obbah. Sitting at Thomas's table, drinking some leftover coffee he had warmed in the fire, I took his hand and my eyes held his eyes. "I do love you, Thomas. I know it is wrong, what we have done, yet I feel God Himself has brought me here."

"My sweet Ann." Those beloved eyes gazed at me. "I am filled with love for you. I have felt this for some time. I do not know of God's blessing, but I will pray it is so. Though I regret we have fulfilled Peter's foolish jealousy, I will fight to the death for you. Whatever you must do, I am there with you. With all of my soul I want you here with me, yet I know the price is high and I can give you little."

"Thomas, you have given me everything. It is I who must resolve my situation, but I will know you are with me. It will give me strength, every day."

Thomas watered and saddled my horse before he left. Riding toward home in the early-morning haze, I felt blessed. I recollected the meeting in the woods where the wind whispered Pa's words, words about a man who would cherish me. In his own way, Pa had told me of Thomas, shared his visions of my path to my sweet, sweet Thomas.

Chapter 34

Ann

It was late in September and I had been preserving the berries and canning vegetables from my gardens in preparation for fall and winter. I had seen Thomas in late August. It was a sultry late summer evening when I had gone to William and Martha's for dinner. They had invited Thomas, subtly colluding in our betrayal. We enjoyed conversation, food and wine.

"I had my appearance before the judge last week," said Thomas. "I am happy in its result, as the representative for Captain Tallman was somewhat disinterested in his presentation, and the judge deemed only that I must pay ten pounds to make good my bond. I can do so by the deadline," he added, glancing in my direction.

"Such good news, Thomas," said Martha. "God has smiled upon you again."

"Yes, Thomas," I said, smiling and avoiding his eyes, which I sensed were upon me.

"This interference from the crown has put a damper on our trades," said William, obviously wanting to redirect our conversation. "It is clear the king is looking to exert more control over us. Over all the colonies."

"I am grateful I am not trading, but it is certain to impact all of us," said Thomas. "I look to purchase some land next year, and I am privileged Master Grinnell is giving me much of the business coming into the shop. He has decided to work his land across the river. He wants to farm with his sons, thus spending less time over the hot fires bending the metals."

"You are right about the crown's impact, Tom. Do ye think our colony will be brutal in its defense? I fear hard times in our future," said William.

"Aye, but I pray it does not come to battle," answered Thomas.

I said nothing about plans for my future, yet uncertain, but I had written to my mum. I had not yet received a missive from Virginia, and awaited her response. She knew well the difficulties with Peter, as she had her own litigations with him.

To complicate my condition, I suspected that I was again with child; and this secret alarmed me. It could be Peter's child, but I did not believe that it was so. The timing was one reason the child I carried may be Thomas's, but I was likewise overcome with a longing for this to be his child. Either way, this would complicate my future. I had shared nothing about my suspicions with Obbah or Martha. My condition would not likely show for another month or so, and that was well before Peter would be returning.

Every shred of me wanted to take my children and join Thomas, but I knew there was no way this could be. In the eyes of the church, I belonged to Peter. Thomas could not afford a large family, and Peter would not allow it. However, these fears bounding about within my head did not calm the desires of my heart. Anxiety filled me at the thought of facing the hardships God was placing before me.

Thomas and I wanted to be together, but could afford no gossip. On one occasion in early September, after our dinner with the Wilbors, I visited Thomas at his cabin again. Thomas would not come near my home, knowing such information would surely reach Peter. Thomas wanted no part in soiling my reputation in the community. I had seen the tears held within his eyes as he fretted over our indiscretions while, all the while, I harbored my own secret. I was filled with sadness at the dilemmas and deceit.

"I have truly failed you, Ann. What position have I put you in, loving you as I have?" His hands held mine, his eyes moist, as I sat in his sitting room and he sat on the floor by me. "I do not know how to save you. I want to run away with you, but I know that you cannot."

"My love, I want nothing more than the same. But I will not leave my children. My reputation is a fleeting thing, and I have my friends; but my children need me." I wanted to tell him of the child I carried, but I was not certain whose child it was. I had not and would not share what happened when Peter forced himself on me, yet how could I explain a pregnancy that could be Peter's child. *When did I become a woman of secrets? A deceitful, wayward woman?*

When we met in early September, at his cabin, I told Thomas I did not know when we could meet again. He assured me he would wait for as long as it would take. He said he was buying a parcel of land south of town, and he hoped to build a home there, a home for us. I prayed he was right. On this visit I gave Thomas a letter I had handwritten for Obbah, a letter to Zebediah that Thomas had agreed to post to the physician in Connecticut. I was hopeful that someone there would read Obbah's words to Zebediah, as he was not literate. I kissed Thomas goodbye as if it was truly goodbye. I knew not what the future would bring, but it seemed surely left to chance.

***

In the brutal cold of February, Peter came home. He had brought gifts for the children, two new tomes for the library and bundles of leaves the English called tea. He directed Obbah on how to prepare a pot to warm us on the cold winter day. Peter seemed in a happier mood than when he had left. He embraced me warmly as if glad to see me after his long absence, but my feelings were now changed. He was my husband and the father of my children; I was his promised wife. I would fulfill my duties, but my heart was elsewhere.

He had brought from England an indentured servant, Gavin. He was an older man, older than Miles, a widower who sought a new life, but who was clearly large and strong. I was hopeful that he would be kind to our slaves and our family. We could use the help. Gabriel and Ibrahim had been lost without Thomas.

After dinner on Peter's first night home, he followed me into the bedroom and embraced me from behind as I undressed. I did not resist, especially after what had happened before. I knew my duty was to comply, to return his affection; and I did so with a hollow heart. In this act and those to come, I betrayed Peter. I betrayed my beloved Thomas, and my very own soul.

"You have gained some weight, Ann," he said as he stroked my stomach. "I see you are full of child yet again."

"Yes," was my only retort. He smiled as if proud of his achievement, believing his presence remained marked even in his absence, and he blew out the light at the bedside. For all the jealousy and false accusations of last year, he was quite certain of his manhood.

***

Peter had been home only two weeks when he filed a charge with the courts against Thomas. Thomas was charged with lewd behavior toward me. Again, I was devastated that my husband had done such a thing, still so filled with cruelty and revenge. For certain, there would now be gossip. On the other hand, I realized that I had now given him cause, though unknown to him, where before he had none. Now I was guilty. Thomas had saved enough money to pay his bondage in full, and I understood that he had submitted payment through the court to Peter's representative. Now he would be brought through the courts yet again, and I could not defend him without consequence. Two weeks later, I began to sleep upstairs in the bed for my imminent confinement, though I did not expect this baby to arrive until early April.

The next weeks passed much too slowly for my liking. The winter kept me homebound as my pregnancy progressed, and in March, Peter sailed to New Amsterdam to spend a week with his friend Pieter. Upon his return, Peter resumed his old habits of staying out late and drinking. Martha, on one of her visits, had discreetly handed me an envelope containing a message from Zebediah, which I read to Obbah. As I read the message to her, she laughed and she cried, but was grateful to hear her son was doing well and learning to read.

In late March, as I was large with child, I had Ibrahim take me to the tailor Daniel Gray in Portsmouth. As I came out of the shop, I saw Thomas walking across the street. Our eyes met. He smiled, but it was a sad smile; and I nodded. There was no way of knowing his thoughts. *Does he think this is his child? Or Peter's child?* I had no good way of telling him what I, myself, did not know. I had shared nothing, and I was filled with shame at my lack of courage to tell Thomas the truth. If I told him Peter had forced himself on me, in our bed, last year, it would have angered him. The conflict between Peter and Thomas remained so tenuous, but Peter held the power.

***

A week later, in the first week of April, the midwife was beckoned. Gavin sent Ibrahim to fetch Emily from Portsmouth, and she was not there long before I delivered a healthy baby boy. He had wisps of brown curls and I saw the silver flecks twinkling in the infant's eyes. This was Thomas's child; I had no doubt. I was almost shocked at the glee I felt in my heart for this bastard child. My heart almost burst with joy, except for the deep regret that Thomas was not here to share in the gladness.

Shortly after Emily left, Peter arrived. He was delighted that he had produced another son, yet I could see a brief suspicion in his eyes as I nursed. There was little doubt that this would all end badly, yet the joy in my heart endured. Yes, there would be strength in the face of hardships to come. I knew God would not abandon me. But little did I know, then, the price God would exact.

"Welcome, sweet Robert," I said, more to myself than to anyone in the room. As Obbah left, Mary and Elizabeth came into the room to meet their new brother. Peter said nothing.

Chapter 35

Thomas

On a sunny day in spring, I saw Ann in town. I was startled to see her with child. She was large with child. Was this my doing? I had been sorely torn between my fear of putting her in jeopardy with her husband and a joy that this may be the child to be born of my love for Ann Tallman. Or is it the captain's child? I was wracked with fear for my Ann.

When the captain returned from sea, he filed a charge of my lewd conduct with his wife. The words confused me. *What is he speaking of?* I loved this woman. My hearing before the jury was to be held in May. But, spring was beginning to bloom and I had heard from several in Portsmouth, including Martha, that Ann had had a son, another child to tie her to her miserable life at the Tallman mansion. I ached for her touch and to comfort her.

With spring, I decided to begin building a home on the land I had purchased, in the woods not too far from where I now lived. As I worked in evenings and, at times, on a forbidden Sunday, my thoughts were filled with a life where my beloved Ann and children were ever present. My physical labor distracted me from melancholy and fears for Ann's safety. I had purchased a horse in November of the prior year and no longer had to rely on the kindness of others to get to town. Master Grinnell had freed an Irish slave, Seamus, he'd owned, and had sent him to work with me at the shop. With the work coming in, I could afford to pay Seamus a meager wage as he apprenticed my work, yet the owner kindly shared this burden. With the wagon I had built, I could carry lumber and stones to my building site at my home. The work was slow, but averted my mind from Captain Tallman and my inability to help Ann without further harming her. If this new son was the captain's child, I was certain she would never leave her children. *Will I have only stolen moments with the woman I love so much?*

But my fears were unfounded; replaced by new fears. William and Martha came to my cabin one evening, before the sun had set. I knew something must be amiss for them both to come to my meager house in the evening. As I prepared coffee, William told me that Captain Tallman had filed for divorce and charged that the child, recently born in his own home, was not his child. Within me, my heart leapt. Yet I knew the seriousness of this news. Ann would be condemned; she would be tried, maybe worse.

I did not attend the hearing on the fifth day of May, but Martha told me as soon as she returned. There had been a letter writ to Captain Tallman, a letter Ann composed, telling her husband that her child, Robert, was not his but that of another man, unnamed. She was declared, by the court, an adulteress and sentenced to whippings, in both Portsmouth and Newport. On hearing this, I could no longer withhold the tears welling behind my eyes. I filled with anger; anger at the callous captain, anger at myself for causing this quandary.

Then, as we sat on the bench in my shop, Martha shared

that Ann had pled for mercy from the judge; and when he asked if she was willing to reconcile with her husband, she replied, firmly: *"I would rather cast myself on the mercy of my God if He take away my life than to return to Captain Tallman."* With these words said, the captain was granted his divorce. Again, I could not help her without further condemning her. But I, myself, was destined to go before the judge in only three days.

An immense sadness filled my core. Ann, who had stayed for her children, had lost everything. I wanted, with all my heart, to take her far away from here, but circumstance forbade any escape from the laws governing our own lives.

"Where is she?" I asked Martha.

"Thomas, I do not know," Martha sadly replied.

I prayed she would come to me, as she had done before. But I heard nothing. There was no knock at the door of my cabin, a sound my ear listened for each night as sleep abandoned me.

On the eighth day of May I went before the court, where the judge addressed my claimed lewd conduct, as charged by the captain. I asserted firmly, before the judge and the jury, that my prior master's wife was an honorable woman and that I would die before offending her. I was not to be imprisoned, but the jury ordered as my punishment that I was to whip one Benjamin Wild for theft of knives, and with that task I would be freed from my fines and charges. As strange as such a resolution appeared, I was grateful, yet felt it incomparable to the whippings Ann was doomed to endure.

It was merely days later that Martha came to me yet again, while I was at the blacksmith shop. She handed me an envelope and said it was from Ann. She said that Ann had taken her infant Robert and escaped to a home in Massachusetts. No words were spoken between the

Wilbors and me as to who fathered this child, but there was little doubt that it was known. Martha hugged me, saddened by our misfortunes, and I was grateful for the comfort of a friend. After she left, I looked at the envelope with my name written in a delicate cursive. I laid down my tools and walked to the bench, wiping my hands on a rag. I pulled the paper from the envelope; it was two pages in Ann's handwriting.

My Dearest Thomas,

I am sorrowful for the misfortunes I have brought upon us, but I do not regret my love for you. Forgive me, I beg, for my secrecy that I was with child. We have a handsome son, a son I call Robert. He has your gray eyes and, I pray, will have your divine smile. I am gone to a safe house in Massachusetts and do not know when I shall see you again. I know Obbah will take care of my children, as Peter will allow. I pray, with all of my heart, that we may be together again. I have no doubts that it is God's plan. I will have my own punishment to face when I return. But know, dear Thomas, that I will return. Our son, Robert, and I will come home.

With all the love in my heart, Ann

The pages slipped from my hand and fell to the ground. I rested my face in my hands and cried, cried as I had when, as a young child, I suffered a scolding of my Scottish mum. As ever, I could not help my beloved Ann. I had worked so hard to be worthy of such a woman, but to no avail. Now she was in hiding with our son; she had been ripped from her own children who, I was certain, missed her profoundly. *I must be strong. I must be constant and move forward; forward to the day we will be together.* I decided to hold in abeyance building my house, and save the money for Ann's passage so she could leave the Puritan colonies, where she might be in danger. She wanted to visit her Mum. I would buy her passage to Virginia and pray for her safety.

***

In August I took my saved monies and mounted my horse for a trip to Massachusetts. I left Seamus, who was trustworthy, in charge of the shop in my absence. I would find this safe house, where a John Arthur lived, where I would help Ann gain her passage to Virginia and, for the first time, meet my son. I rode from morn to dusk and, before the sun slipped to the horizon, I found the home of Master Arthur. He was at first wary of my presence, but when Ann saw that it was me, she, with her hair loosed and dressed in plain Puritan garb, ran from the home and into my arms.

"I was afraid I may never see you again," she cried joyfully. "Come, come meet your son. He is the likeness of you."

I entered the humble abode, where sat another woman. Ann introduced her to me as Mercy Tubbs. Miss Tubbs appeared older than Ann, frailer, and she too had found sanctuary in John Arthur's home. After a moment, Ann came into the main room, holding a baby who was rubbing his eyes, as he had only been awakened. He looked around and saw my strange face, whimpered momentarily, but then smiled as I reached out to take him in my arms. I could not believe that I was standing there, in that strange house, before the woman I loved, holding my own son. It was as if a dream, a wonderful dream; but the dream ended when I spoke of my reason for coming.

"I have monies here for your passage to Virginia, where you will be safe and in the care of family." I handed the pouch to Ann. "Can we quietly secure your passage on a clipper or a small caravel? I do not want the authorities to take you in this effort."

"I can arrange it," said Master Arthur.

"Yes, but let us contact Captain van Curler," said Ann. "It was his ship that took me years before to New Amsterdam, and he is a kind man. He will help me."

"Then it is done. I will find this man van Curler and make such arrangements," said Master Arthur.

I sat down in the chair and spoke to my son, playing with his hands and singing a tune as his eye followed mine. Ann prepared for me a plate of food. I relished each moment of our time together, as I did not know when I would see them again. Master Arthur invited me to spend the night at his home before I traveled back to Portsmouth.

That night I lay in the small bed beside Ann. I wanted to touch her body and please her. I wanted to be nearer to her, and knew she felt the same. But our quarters were crowded and the baby lay between us. Robert fell asleep after he nursed, and Ann and I looked long into each other's eyes before she finally blew out the candle. With Robert in his basket, I pulled Ann into my arms, held her tightly and kissed her hairline. I know Ann wanted more, as did I; but I would do no more harm. Another child now would be but a burden to Ann and a weapon to be brandished by Captain Tallman. I would await the day we could be together openly.

We knew not the future, but I would do anything for her. I could go with her to Virginia, but I had started to establish a life in Rhode Island. In spite of Tallman's power, I had many friends in Portsmouth and Newport, and I had land and an application for freeman status, knowing well that one day Ann would return to be near her children. It was only a matter of time. The hurdles before us, before Ann, were brutal, but I was to have dreams of laughter filling a home that would be ours. I would hold on to that vision.

In the morning, I readied to leave. I embraced and kissed dear Robert, placing him back in his mother's arms. Ann looked at me with those pleading eyes as I stood by my horse.

"Thomas, I will be back. I do not know when or how, but I will return and we will be together. I am selfish to ask, but I beseech you to wait for me.

"Wait, Thomas," she said, running back into the house with Robert. She returned, alone, carrying a box carved with an elaborate design. "Thomas, this box holds my treasured possessions I took when I left the house. It is my Bible, the Christopher Marlowe book with your note, my silver comb and Mum's pearls. Moreover, there are locks of hair from each of my children. You keep this for me. I do not need this in Virginia, and I know it is safe with you." She handed it to me. I knew well this box was a token, a token of her promise to return to me.

I carefully placed the wooden box in my satchel aside my saddle. "Yes, it will be waiting for you, as will I. Before God, I know we will be husband and wife. Look, look at my hands. They hold our future, dreams of our family. I will hold these in my heart until I set eyes on you again." I mounted my horse and looked down at Ann. "Peter does not decide the fate of our love; the court does not decide that; you have lain with me as my wife and are so." As I rode away, I called back to her, "We will celebrate that before God when you return. Write to me when you arrive in Virginia."

I looked back only once. Ann was yet standing there, watching me. I prayed that this Captain van Curler would get her safely to her mum. I would be ready when she returned. She was a woman worthy of a better man than I, and I pledged to myself, in memory of my father and my God, to become the man who would make her and Robert proud.

Chapter 36

Ann

Captain van Curler welcomed me on his ship, sailing out of the Boston port. Master Arthur had prudently escorted Robert and me to the dock, and I was gladdened to see Captain van Curler, who had been so kind to me in the past.

"Aye, Missus Tallman, it seems each time I see you, you are carrying a baby. And who would this be?"

"This is Robert." I looked at the captain with his gentle eyes. "This is my son, Robert Durfee." I had never before said this name, his full name, but I was filled with a sense of liberty upon hearing my own words.

The captain looked a bit puzzled, but I saw a twinkle in his eye. "Ah, there must be a story behind this one, my lady, for I know that Captain Tallman is not yet claimed by the wicked seas."

"Yes, Captain, there is a story. It is both sad and joyful. It is an unfinished tale, and I thank you with all my heart for your help. My mum will meet me in Jamestown, and I am overjoyed at seeing her again."

"We should be coming into the bay in Virginia in three, maybe four days. I shall make the journey directly to the first destination. I shall keep my eye on you, miss, for you should not be traveling alone."

We sailed for two days, and, as the sun rose high above on the third day, we arrived in Jamestown.

My brother, Robert, and Mum were there to greet me, as somehow they had word I was on Captain van Curler's ship. There were hugs, and Mum was holding and kissing the baby. Robert had fields of tobacco he was working, but it was a meager plantation, as he had only three slaves. Robert worked side by side with them, except when he was sailing for trade. His home was not fancy, and he moved the only slave in the house out to the lean-tos to allow room for the baby and me. Robert and Hannah had two young daughters, Bess and Hester, who doted over my little Robert.

Baby Robert and I settled into the home near Jamestown. I was a fugitive, yet a mother who loved and missed her children, now abandoned. I ached to be with Thomas, but I was not yet prepared for imprisonment, humiliation and the unknown in Portsmouth and Newport. I feared the humiliation I had brought upon my family. I did not know how long I would remain here in the Virginia Colony. Mum was not happy when she heard my story, or upon learning that Robert was not Peter's child. Yet when I told her of the events that had passed between Peter and me, she did not seem surprised. She knew Peter was obstinate and vengeful, and she had experienced it first-hand herself.

"You have sinned before the Lord, Ann. Your vows before God; you have broken them," she said to me. My heart broke. I was a disappointment to my cherished mum, yet I had remained strong in the conviction of my heart, of my decision to choose Thomas. As Mum chastised me, she gathered me in her arms, in a warm embrace. Her words to me over the next several weeks were sparse, but I was received by the tenderness of Robert's family.

I prayed each night for repentance, confessing my failures as a dutiful mother and wife, as had been expected of me. Yet I also prayed thanksgiving for the sweetness and love of my Thomas. Mum had never met Thomas, but I told her of his goodness. As time passed, I spent my days tending to my baby and doing stitch work with Mum. My mum was still an elegant woman though her hair had silvered with age, and the new lines on her face yet lit the smile in her eyes. As we sat together and embroidered, Mum smiled more often, and I began to feel the joys of the old days in Barbados. I had brought nothing but my clothing and the baby's needs, but Mum had fabrics and threads she shared with me.

"Ann, your embroidery has become as beautiful as art. Look at that deer and the tree you have sewn; they appear real, as if in the forest."

"Thank you, Mum. I have continued to stitch all these years my children were young." I started to cry as I mentioned my children.

"Here, here, dear. All will be good in the end, Ann. Peter will allow no harm to come to the children, and, in time, they will understand. I am certain. Obbah will let them forget you, in spite of Peter. You have told me how you and Thomas found her son, Zebediah. She will not forget."

I wiped away my tears with my sleeve and gathered my wits. "Mum, do you believe they will forgive me?"

"Yes. Some will. I cannot promise you that Peter will not turn some away from you, especially your youngest ones. But, Ann, they will be good with God, and successful. You have guided them well."

I wiped my eyes yet again and sat quietly for some

moments, then resumed my stitching. I came to know that such spells would likely come and go with so much loss.

"Mum, I did some stitch work for the tailor in Portsmouth, an elderly man who appreciated my work. Peter did not like this, but it gave me my own accomplishment, like you told me."

"When you return to your Thomas, you can do this work to help. It will be good, keeping your mind busy without worry. I want you to go sit and stitch in the tailor's shop in Portsmouth, as we did in the islands years ago. Your children will know where you are and I believe they will come, when they are old enough to do so."

I smiled. Mum could ceaselessly see the sunshine beyond the storm. It had forever been her way. I realized how much I had missed this over the years. She was adored by her granddaughters here in the house, and loved playing with little Robert. The joyfulness in this house made me want to stay forever, but I knew that was not to be.

When winter came and the Christmas holidays, we celebrated with a great feast, and Mum and Hannah made evergreen wreaths for the house. In Virginia, there were no Puritan restrictions on celebration. We joyfully blessed the gift of our Christ.

The day after our feast, I sat at Robert's small desk, with the inkwell and pen in my hand. The blank paper stared back at me, and once I made the first stroke with my pen, my heart filled the page.

> *Dear Thomas,*
> *I cannot tell you how much I wish you were here with my family and me, holding your healthy son. I relish the thought of your strong arms around me, your kisses, your kind heart. I picture you working in the brutal snows of winter in Rhode Island as I am here in the South where, though it snows*

intermittently, the days are mild. When shall we be together again? I ask you this without expectation of an answer, for I know that it is up to me to return. May the court have mercy on me, an outcast in my own community.

Have you laid eyes on my children in town? Has Martha or William seen or heard of their well-being? I cannot wait for news of them. And Obbah? At times I fret that Peter, out of his hateful revenge, will sell Obbah. I pray that is not so, and I rely on the knowing that he needs her help.

Are you well, Thomas? Often at night I walk outside along the edge of Robert's tobacco fields, near the trees, and I look up at the stars and think of our early conversation along the river. I think of how I no longer hear the notes of your fedyl. I know that God brought us together, and I believe with all of my soul that He will bless us, as He has now with our son. I will love you to the end of my days, and I pray you and I live long together. I send this to you, through the Wilbors, with all the affection that is held and bursting from my heart.

Ann

Chapter 37

Thomas

Martha brought Ann's letter to my shop. When alone, I sat and read her missive. I read it over and over, yearning for Ann to be sitting here next to me. My Ann. I thought of her words all day, and when I arrived home in the darkness of winter, I lit the candle at my table and wrote my answer.

My Dearest Ann,

Oh, how I have missed you, your touch, your smell, the harmony of our eyes gazing at each other. Melancholy consumes me. But I will not delay with news of your family, as I know your heartfelt concerns. Tallman has married, a woman named Joan, of the Briggs family. According to Martha, he was in desperate need of a mother for the children and, as you well know, would not rely on Obbah. Yet Obbah is still there. I have not seen the children, but Martha tells me they are well. She can no longer get this information directly, but has friends who share news; and you know well that Martha will not hesitate to question. The children yet ask about you, I am told, but have come to learn they are forbidden to speak of you around the captain. I am certain they yet miss you, for I know how much they love you. The courts have left me be and my debt is made good to the captain. The shop is lucrative and I have made progress adding some space to the house where I yet live. I decided to finish a small house on the land I purchased and have contracted that space for revenue. It is this work that keeps my mind busied. I will be ready for you when you come. I pray for the day. I am certain, as are you, there will be a warrant for you when you come, but rest assured, your friends yet love you and worry for your soul. You are well loved here in Portsmouth, but know that you are loved, more than all, by me. Kiss my son and tell him his father misses him dearly.

With all of my heart, which is yours forever, Thomas

Chapter 38

Peter

The wedding ceremony had been simple, as required by Joan's Puritan family. I had never believed I would be tied in this manner to the Puritans, but I had, three years ago, met Joan at one of the formal dinners in Newport. Her family was from Taunton, Massachusetts, where her father, a fellmonger, gathered hides for the tannery. The family was respected but not wealthy, as the Puritans frowned on abundance. In spite of such, Joan's father had managed to negotiate a grand contract for Joan's hand in marriage.

With my marriage bed empty, a houseful of motherless children and my need for the sea, my interval for finding a respectable wife had been narrow. For the arrangement, I had gifted property, a home and bovine for my new wife, not a young woman, in return for her promise to produce children. The marriage allowed me to return to the sea, the waves that forever called to me and never failed me.

Should my divorced wife have ever returned to the Island, I should have looked forward to the court's promise for her to be whipped and jailed. Yet I heard the scoundrel

Thomas was yet in Portsmouth; with certainty not a fellow worth the price Ann will pay for his affections.

After a month with my new bride, I sailed for London and France. My father had died after my last voyage to Amsterdam, as a letter had recently arrived from my brother Johannes informing me of this news. He had been ill when I last traveled to Amsterdam, and I had not had the opportunity to share my successes with him. I desired that my brother would share this information, but I could not be certain. I failed, over recent months, to sit and write the letter to *Vater*, and now it was too late.

My mind wandered as I looked toward the skies. I felt comforted to be at sea again. Often as I stood on deck, looking into the face of the moon, I thought of Ann and her hardships, brought on her own self. The last I had heard, she was at the house in Massachusetts, the Arthur house. I sensed my heart yet desired her, but she was unforgivably gone to me, a traitor. When Mary and Peter would ask about their mother, I knew not what to say; yet their wish for their mother tugged at my heart. *How could Ann have turned her back on them, on me? Is she looking at the same moon from afar?* Beautiful Ann; lost to me, now condemned by the court. My anger had not kept her with me, as I had believed, but driven her away. All the things I had given her, a grand home, servants, a position of class, and she chose to relinquish it all for a rogue.

My trade in Antwerp, Le Havre and London was uneventful. The seas blessed us with calm waters as we sailed to the West Indies. When I arrived at the docks and had settled in for a long-awaited stay, the tavern keeper told me that Modyford was gone. Old George told me Modyford was now the governor of Jamaica and had established new plantations there. I was surprised to hear such news, but I knew that my old friend, much like myself, had grand ambitions. I would sail on to Jamaica when I left

Barbados, but for the next few weeks, I had trade to conduct.

On my last night at the old tavern, George told me that Marianne had a houseful of children and likely missed her old days at the pub.

"She no more has that spring in her step that you once so admired," said George. "Do not think that I did not notice." His grin and twinkling eyes stared back at me.

I did not know what to say to that. He was not as clueless as I had believed, but what did this matter.

"You know that your son is now ... what? Six or seven. He looks just like you, Captain," added George.

"What do you mean? My son? I have no son here."

"Aye, Captain," laughed George. "I was certain that Nathaniel was your son. I knew your fondness for Marianne, who was sickly and, I could see, early with child when she wed Edward at the docks. Are you certain you are not his pa?" His question begged no answer. I could see in George's eyes that he reveled in alarming me with this news.

"You are mistaken. I am certain." I downed my ale and said my goodnights.

Tossing and turning through the night, I thought of what George had said. In the morning I ordered my crew to ready the ship, and by the midday sun, we were on our way to Jamaica. We docked as the sun rose the following morning. I was unfamiliar with this town, Port Royal, so I asked about for counsel on lodging and taverns. By noon I learned where Modyford resided, the locale of his plantation on the island. Having borrowed a mare at the livery, I arrived at the young plantation and dined with my friend and his wife. The Jamaican island was wild with pirates and buccaneers; and at the dinner table that night I met the notorious Henry Morgan. Morgan was no more than a pirate legitimized by the island's governor, Modyford himself; yet, I was captivated by the tales I heard as we feasted, drank and indulged in rum and tobacco.

"Tallman, how is your family? Well, I pray," said Modyford, directing the conversation to me.

"They are well," I responded, divulging nothing of my true situation. My words were not a lie. "My apothecary is thriving, and I am a member of the council in Portsmouth and Warwick, soon to be the solicitor. I should not be lollygagging on the seas, but I cannot deny myself visits to the Indies; and, of course, I must gather my medicines. I was surprised to hear that you had left Barbados and that you were now here in Jamaica, but I see that you and Elizabeth are well in your new paradise."

"Aye, friend. My comrades and I have overcome the Spaniards here and continue to retain control. We have achieved a new paradise for the king, thanks to privateers such as Henry here," he said as he raised his cup to Henry Morgan. We all joined in.

I stayed another day at Modyford's plantation. Then, with an escort of a buccaneer ship out of the port, my crew and I sailed north, toward Jamestown in the Virginia colony and New Amsterdam. I was but briefly in Jamestown, but saw Robert, Ann's brother, at the dock. He saw me, standing on the deck of my ship, but he looked hastily away and we did not acknowledge each other. I knew not how much knowledge he had of Ann's behavior. When we reached New Amsterdam, now called York, we docked for several days. I was certain I could sell some of the rum, coffee, tobacco and sugar I had in the ship's hold, and I wanted to visit my friend Pieter, as well as my wench, Joan, at the tavern.

At the tavern near the docks, the barkeep told me that my friend Pieter was no longer the governor, but a man at the bar said he could take me to his home for a fee. His farm was a sprawling acreage in a place called Haarlem. I saw that Pieter had grayed, and he shared that he had only recently returned from the Netherlands to report on his late governorship. There had been religious issues in this colony, as in others, and control of the town had been ceded to the English only last year. We enjoyed a fine meal as I shared the news of my father's death and my adventures in the Indies.

"Friend, I have heard the news of your wife Ann's sentence and your divorce. I pray you are well in spite of this hardship."

"I am well. I have wedded a young woman from Massachusetts. I think no more of Ann; she is a Judas and gone to me."

"She seemed such a sweet young woman when we met her, and so full of joy to be giving you a child. God has strange plans for all of us, does He not?"

"Yes," I answered, knowing not what else to say. I did not know if Pieter knew of Ann's being a fugitive, but I said no more.

Pieter raised his cup of wine. "May God bless you with your new family, with many happy years and many more children." He paused, and then raised his cup yet again. "And I will bless sweet Ann as well, for one day you shall wish you had done so."

I did not drink to this; I was puzzled by my friend's words. *What does he know that I do not?* One of Pieter's servants took me back to the tavern, where I found lodging and sent a missive via a boy at the dock to my wench Joan, inviting her to visit me. I spent the following day negotiating two large contracts for sugar and for tobacco at the docks, then overseeing my crew unload the sold goods. Joan came to my room late that night and we spent two lascivious days of gratification. Joan was a full-bodied woman without inhibitions who could pleasure a man in ways immeasurable. I left her three schillings on the morn before I walked to my ship, transformed and ready to go home.

Chapter 39

Ann

It was in the year 1667 when I decided it was time for me to return to my home. I had celebrated a festive holiday with my family, and little Robert was now two years old. He needed his father, as I needed Thomas. I ached with all of my being to see my own children, but was fearful that was not to be. I wondered often how they had grown, how Mary and Elizabeth were becoming young women. Martha's last letter to me had shared that Peter and his new wife had a son this past year. She told me that Peter traveled as he had before, and that his disagreeable behavior had not diminished. So many days I wanted to plead with Thomas to join me in Virginia, but that would separate me forever from the children. Fearful yet determined, I set plans for my return in motion.

Captain Hudson made arrangements for my passage on a small ship north, making certain there were familiar passengers aboard who would ensure my well-being. I had prayed daily to keep me strong, as brave as the women in Rhode Island before me.

On a night before I departed, I sat with my nieces and told them a tale, a fairy tale.

> *There once was a fair young woman who lived in the forests of the north. She was of weak spirit and unsure of herself. One snowy day, she walked deep into the forest, where she saw two deer. They did not run away, but watched her approach. The woman gently touched the head of one of the deer, and then the other. They stood in the snow as the birds alit around them and the snow fell harder. They were as one in nature within a peaceful world. A sharp noise frightened the deer and they ran away, and the young woman turned to find the ghost of her father, who comforted her. He spoke softly, assuring her that she would be safe from harm and one day be blessed with family and great love. He gently touched her hair, as she had touched the deer. It was as if a gentle breeze stroked her curls and filled her with a light that would show her the way and bravery that would forever sustain her. Suddenly the ghost vanished; the snow stopped. The young woman walked on through the trees with her head held high, filled with courage. She stood tall like trees of the forest. She stood tall and brave for as long as God would allow her to walk through this land, until the day His angels would carry her to heaven.*

When I finished, Hester had fallen asleep and Bess looked up at me in awe. I kissed Bess on her head, tucked her tightly into bed and walked out of their room, almost walking right into my mum.

"A fairy tale? I believe that is the story of a special daughter, a daughter called Ann." She smiled at me, her eyes moist. "I remember that day you told me of the deer in the woods, and I chastised you. I was fearful. But, Ann, you have a spirit about you that is gentle and unknown to me— a spirit that, at times, frightens me. Your pa had this, but I would not acknowledge it. He knew he was different and understood my trepidation. You have this gift as well. I know it is a gift, but do be careful amongst the nonbelievers." She took my hand and held it between her hands. "Forgive me, Ann, for my failure to embrace your gift over the years, for all the times I turned you away. I know my actions isolated you at times. I am so sorry, and I marvel at your courage, Ann. I do believe that our God stands with you, for He too communes with angels."

I kissed Mum and hugged her tight to me, for the first time feeling her equal. I knew not when I would see her again after next week. When the day came, we said our goodbyes, and little Robert was excited to board the ship. The voyage would be at least four days, as the ship would stop at New York City, previously New Amsterdam, but the travel was without incident. Captain Hudson had given me some monies to see me through, and I would have enough to find someone at the dock to take me to Portsmouth. I had sent a short letter to Thomas of my arrival, but was unsure if he had received it.

As the buggy arrived at the cabin, with a light snow falling, I saw smoke swirling in the air above Thomas's chimney. He was home. The house was different than the small cabin I remembered. He had added to the barn and an addition to the house, with one side stoned. I did not see his horse but was certain it was stabled in the barn.

I gathered little Robert and my parcels and, stepping up to the door, knocked firmly. No one came so I knocked again. The young man who brought me had left and I looked around, waiting for Thomas. With my arms full, I started to push the door open when I heard Thomas calling from the barn. He saw me and came running toward us, gathering us both into his arms as I dropped my satchels.

"Ann, Ann." He took Robert from my arms and leaned in, kissing me long, as Robert laughed and fussed, unsure of whom this man was and what was happening.

"Robert," I said. "This is your pa. Give him a kiss." And Robert did so, as he had learned. Thomas held him high in the air, to Robert's delight, while a dog that had followed Thomas from the barn jumped about us. Thomas placed Robert on the ground to run and explore, the dog licking his face and Robert giggling. Thomas turned back to me, taking me in his arms and kissing me yet again, with passion, and holding me tight as if he feared I might vanish before him.

"Let's go inside. It is cold and I am shivering," I said, noticing that I had arrived as the last chills of winter were begging for spring. "Who is this?" I asked as the dog followed us.

"That is Crabit. He is a water spaniel Master Grinnell gave me when his dog had a litter. Crabit's been my best friend, especially hunting quail and fowl."

Crabit followed us into the house, where I found that the sitting room appeared larger and more finished than I remembered. I could see that my Thomas had worked hard to make this a home. I saw the writing desk he had placed beneath the window in the front of the room. The kitchen had a larger table and he had hung shelving. His bedroom was unchanged, but he took me up four steps to a landing, where the stairs turned toward two large bedrooms he had added. He had built a chimney up the stone side of the house, and Thomas had a fireplace upstairs, and he showed me a small room with a window and fireplace off the first landing. He said this was my room to do with as I wished.

"You may choose any room in the house for our bedroom. This is your home."

"Oh, Thomas, you have worked so hard." Robert was

already finding his way up and down the steps. "It is grand. Our bedroom is good where it is."

"It is not as grand as you had before. I hope you like it. And the barn … I have a workshop out there, and there is another room, should we need a servant."

"Slow down, Thomas. It is wonderful. I cherish this home, for you are here."

"I now have two horses, and I traded for a small buggy on a job at the shop."

"And Crabit," I added, patting his head. "What is the meaning of his name?"

"Yes, my mama used to call me *crabit* when I was cantankerous. It is an old Scottish term."

"I am overjoyed to be here, Thomas," I said as Thomas picked up Robert, who had neared the brick oven. "We both know I will likely be jailed," I whispered, as if the baby or the dog could understand. "I know you can care for Robert, but I must make some arrangements with Martha or Lydia to watch over him, as you have work at your shop."

"Ann, I cannot bear talk of your imprisonment. It is wrong."

"My dear, do not fear, for I do not. I want to put this in the past, behind us. It needs to be finished. Then we may raise our son in peace."

"Ye are so brave. Braver than I, as God's witness." Robert came to him, begging his attention. Thomas picked him up and we all sat at the table. "My shop has been lucrative. I have my land not far from the house here, and I have applied for my freeman status. I want to be worthy of you."

"Oh, Thomas." I took his hand. "You have been my godsend. You are more than worthy of me. It is I who's been blessed."

Thomas brought some water in from the well and filled

a cup for Robert, and he heated some in a pot so we might have coffee. After he placed some cheese and bread before us, we sat in silence for a time, in front of the fire, in the comfort of each other's presence.

"I have seen Mary and Elizabeth in town. They were at the milliner's with their stepmother." He looked at me, pausing. "You know they have had a son?"

"Yes. And Mary, Elizabeth?"

"They looked well. Mary is so grown up. She is now fourteen years, is that right?"

"Yes, she is," I said, a sadness filling me.

"Mary saw me in front of my shop. When Mistress Tallman was not looking, she smiled at me. That smile warmed my heart."

"Oh, Thomas. I love you so much." I wanted little more than to see my children again, but I was certain that would have to wait. I remembered Mum's words, counseling me to work at the tailor's shop and that the children would find me.

"The warrant for my arrest will come soon enough. Let us not dwell on that now. I only pray my punishment will be quick and I do not dwell in a cell for long. I am ready. I am prepared, Thomas."

We readied a meal from dried venison, eggs and preserves Martha had brought, while Robert appeared to make himself at home. I was certain, however, that he missed the company of his cousins in Virginia, who doted on him endlessly. Tomorrow I would see about a garden for the spring, and I was truly heartened to see chickens near the barn.

I decided not to put Robert upstairs yet, as he was still young. Thomas and I moved the small bed upstairs into the new room off the landing. The fire in the fireplace was out, but the warmth remained in the room. I tucked sweet Robert into his bed with a kiss and sat with him before joining Thomas in our room.

We were as two lovers joining for the first time, awkward yet unrestrained in our desires and the joy of reunion. I was a woman truly loved and filled with happiness to be home. There was little trouble forgetting Peter and the life I had left behind, but a trace of shame forever followed me at abandoning my children. If I had returned to Peter, as the judge had offered, it would have been at Robert's expense, as well as the denial of where my heart rested.

Thomas and I slept little, yet shortly after sunrise and porridge for breakfast, Thomas left for his shop. I filled the water basin and washed, and it was then I saw Thomas had added a small dressing table for me in the bedroom. The box I had left with him, with my treasures, sat there awaiting me. I brushed and pinned my hair, and decided that Robert and I would explore the house and barn. I found the right spot for my garden and gathered the eggs from the chickens. I was home.

***

It was late in April when I heard that the constable had published the warrant for my arrest. The word was out that I was again in Rhode Island. It was only a matter of days before I was arrested and jailed. I would no longer hide, but choose to live freely. Thomas knew to take Robert to Martha; knowing what was to come, she had agreed to care for the child.

"I am ready, Thomas. I will be back," I whispered to Thomas as they took me away one early morning, as the wildflowers were blooming; I remember the warm breeze on my face. My words may have been whispered, but my resolve was firm and steady. He knew I would return, but I saw the fear in his eyes. Those beloved gray eyes were filled with pain, yet his demeanor remained steady as he comforted Robert.

My cell was dark and unclean, but I expected no more. I was taken before the judge the following day, as I was certain they were fearful of my escaping yet again. I was going nowhere. To my surprise, the judge lessened my sentence from fifteen stripes in Portsmouth followed by fifteen stripes in Newport to merely the one whipping in Newport. I was not certain if it was compassion for me or protection for Peter's reputation, as Peter was a colleague of many of these officials.

I was moved to the prison in Newport, the barren rooms built in town the year my first son, Peter, had been born. I counted my blessings as I sat in that dank cell. I was grateful it was not winter and freezing. I knew my family yet loved me, as did my friends. I knew my son, and Thomas, would be waiting for me. Clearly God had not forsaken me, for my weakened stomach revealed I might yet again be with child. These days were numbered, and I would go home stronger on the other side of this.

The whipping occurred after seven days. My eyes struggled against the bright sunlight as I was led into the town square and stripped, bound and lashed for my sins. I had looked Constable Emery straight in the eye, but I did not cry as the whip broke my skin. I thought of nothing but Thomas, of Robert and my children. I closed my eyes, for but a moment, and God's light illumined my soul and I was full of courage. And this is the story of how I came to be Ann Durfee of Rhode Island.

Part II

A life anew I found this day amidst
The rivers and the bays,
Where loss and pain swallowed me.
As God's gargoyle
Was my shield, my brilliant foil,
And with my head held high
I bravely stared into the devil's eye.
Peace glowed deep within my heart
My love and I would ne'er be torn apart.

Chapter 40

Thomas

I know that today my wife, my Ann, sits in a prison cell in Newport. The Wilbor family has welcomed me into their home, where Martha is caring for my son Robert, for I cannot bear to be at my own empty house. With my prayers that Ann will not be imprisoned long, I am torn each day between melancholy and a desire to go to the Tallman house and challenge the captain to a proper fight, shouting that he never deserved a woman as fine as Ann Tallman and that he is but a coward full of wickedness.

The court will never allow Ann to marry, but we are man and wife forever in my eyes. Of that I am certain. The silversmith in Portsmouth is a friend, and I will have him make a special ring for Ann, a symbol of our promise. As I arrive at the Wilbor home after closing the shop, leaving Seamus to finish some work, I see an unfamiliar wagon in front of the home.

"Thomas, Thomas," yells Martha, running from the house. "They have freed Ann. She is here. Miles brought her. He heard the commotion in the square, and helped her to his wagon when they freed her. Hurry."

"Praise God." I run into the house.

"My girl is cleaning her wounds. Come, come."

Miles stands in the hallway. "Miles, you are a good man, but I have known that of you since the day I met you, friend. God bless you for bringing her home." I am so grateful and excited that I hug Miles as if he were my family. My friend has brought her back to me.

"Thomas, I am dismayed by what has happened to you and to Mrs. Tallman ... to Ann," he adds, uncomfortable with calling her by the Tallman name. "You are both good citizens and kind, yet I am fearful that the captain may not be done with his harassment." I move to enter the room with Martha. "Thomas, if you and Ann need help, commendation, a friend, you send for me." Miles turns to leave.

"You are a friend, Miles. It will not be forgotten."

Ann is sitting on the bed with Martha's oldest daughter, Lenora, who is applying water and whiskey to cleanse and disinfect Ann's wounds on her back. Ann is holding her torn blouse, bloodstained, covering her unclothed bosom. My head spins with the awareness that someone had done this to her, knowing full well it was decreed to be, as did Ann. The judge could have fulfilled the original decree to stripe her in both Portsmouth and Newport, but he chose to be less harsh. Nevertheless, this was harsh.

Ann looks at me with eyes reflecting at once both humiliation and courage. *How does she do this?* She is at once a queen of delicate beauty who can simultaneously strike down an enemy warrior. I refrain from embracing her amidst Martha's and Lenora's ministrations, so I take her hands into mine.

"You are well, and safe with us. We will be home soon, with Robert. I love you so much."

I watch her wince. "Ann, I am going to bring Seamus to live there, the quarters in the barn, to help you when he is not at the shop. He can live there with us for lodging and meals for as long as he needs. I will bring a cow and goat for milk and cheese. What you need you shall have."

"Thomas, dear Thomas, slow down. We are together now. That is everything. I need no more."

"Thomas," says Martha. "Get out of here. We are going to get Ann dressed." She shoos me out of the room, seeing that my concern and worry are of no help.

I pace impatiently in the front parlor. Ann finally enters the room, yet I am still afraid to embrace her. She says she is better, but I see she moves haltingly.

"You are both staying here tonight," commands Martha. "We will check Ann's wounds tomorrow, and then you can take her home. I am selfish, for it has been a joy having your sweet boy here."

"Robert. Where is he?" Ann queries, looking about.

"He is upstairs with the other children. Thomas, go get him. Lenora and I will put food on the table." She turns toward her kitchen and turns back. "Ann, you rest here. We must get you well."

With Robert in my arms, I race down the stairs to Ann. She sits in the tall chair and takes Robert's little hands and kisses his head, over and over again. He struggles against me to be taken into his mother's arms and, as he cries, I give him to Lenora to take him back to the other children.

That night, I hold Ann's hand through the night as she tosses with her pain, unable to find comfort or sleep. The warmth of her hand gives me assurance that she is still there, with me. Seamus is already working when I arrive at the shop in the morning, and I tell him of my plans for him to move to the Durfee house. He is grateful, though he knows it will mean more work. Living at our house is a blessing in his eyes, a place where his meals will be prepared and where he is welcomed. I pay him a percentage for his work, and he will still be able to save or spend his monies as he wishes. Though he is fond of his ale, he is a good man. On Saturday I will send him to find us a dairy cow and maybe a goat. There is abundant space in the rooms I added to the barn, next to the horses.

Ann is on my mind much of the day as I stew about her well-being and Miles's words of warning, words I had put aside when first heard. What more could Tallman do to us? I bring Ann home that evening after the shop is closed, but Robert does not come with us. Martha felt it best if he stay with her until Ann can move more easily and is able to lift him. I agree. Robert has playmates at William and Martha's house, and he will be happy, and home soon enough.

I prepare a meager meal for Ann and me, and afterwards we walk outside and sit on the bench near the porch, soaking in the simplicity of the serenading yellow-throated warblers and the sea breeze rustling the trees. We gaze upon Ann's garden as we sit here, a garden unfinished and barren due to Ann's absence.

"I am saddened that I cannot give you the life you were accustomed to. I will do my best, but I can give you no mansion on a hill."

"I need no mansion on a hill. Ye are my gift."

"I am not certain of that, but I will do my best."

"Thomas," she says. "I believe I am again with child. You are to be a father again." She looks at me with those bright eyes, gleaming with a smile. This news brings tears to my eyes, seeing my sweet Ann before me, bandaged, with news such as this. I cannot contain my emotions; I cannot abate my dismay. This woman I love with all my heart has been beaten and humiliated by a brutal constable for nothing more than loving someone, and she carries my child. Would they have done this to her had they known? She never deserved this judgment and punishment.

I feel Ann touching my face, brushing my tears.

"Are you not happy about this child?"

I compose myself. "Nay, nay. I am elated." She smiles, and I continue. "I cannot fathom that you have been imprisoned and punished like this while you carry our child.

"You are the bravest woman I have ever known. Why did you not tell me? How long have you known?"

"I was not certain before they took me, but my queasiness forewarned me in Newport. It is not the time to dwell on such. Thomas, I want desperately for this judgment to be finished, to be done. We are now together."

"You are my wife, Ann Durfee. The courts be damned, damned to hell."

"Careful of such talk, Thomas. The courts have power. But, yes, I am Ann Durfee, wife of Thomas, mother of Robert. I feel blessed by God with these last sunrays of this day shining here upon us."

Taking her hand in mine, I say, "As man and wife." We sit here, our warmth merged, her hand in mine, together without conversation yet in communion, until the sun falls into the trees and filters the light toward night's darkness.

Chapter 41

Ann

Shortly after returning home, I gain my strength as my wounds heal; and William and Martha come to visit us at the house. My sweet Robert runs to me for an embrace and then to his pa, filled with giggles. My heart beats faster when I see the sweet bond between them. Thomas and Seamus had brought home a dairy cow, and Robert will now have fresh milk every day. During the summer I will tend my garden and prepare preserves for my first winter in this home. My figure begins to swell with the child to come.

While Robert is napping, I pick up my stitchery and begin sewing again, something I have not done since my time with Mum in Virginia. I began a scenic piece in Virginia, so I resume my stitches on linen panel, sitting near the window for its light. I am grateful that I had thrown all of my threads, my thimble pouch and a few fabrics in my bag when I left the house on the hill. While Robert naps, I pass each day working on the tapestry, following mornings working in the garden as my son plays. As autumn arrives, the trees turn their brilliant reds, yellows and oranges. The depth of the colors dressing the maples and birches each autumn in Rhode Island is akin to a wrapped gift, with warning of the approaching harshness of winter. My winter garden grows, full of chard, squash and pumpkins.

The mornings in the garden bring memories of my sweet maid Obbah and how we used to preserve our tomatoes and berries for winter. I make soap and candles for the house, chores that were once done by Obbah and Zebediah. Seamus helps with some of the chores when he is at the house. Though I miss Obbah's help, what I miss most is her presence, the warmth of her company, and I pray she is well. I am thankful that Seamus is here to milk the cow and care for the horses, but he is gone during the day to the shop with Thomas.

November in the year of our Lord 1667 comes, and I am full of child and the days are short as the snow begins to fall. It becomes more difficult for me to do my chores and chase Robert, but my heart is full of love for Thomas, whose heart is larger than any I have known. It is the company of others at the house that I truly miss. With my impending birthing and confinement, Thomas decides I should not be at home alone, so he and Seamus take turns staying at the house, working around the barn and helping me where they can. It is a late afternoon in early January, a cold day, and my birthing commences suddenly. I walk to the barn, stopping twice to catch my breath with pain, and call to Seamus to gather little Robert and hurry to town to get Thomas and Emily, my midwife.

As the pain strengthens and the early sunset approaches, as I pace and gather linens for Emily, all the while fearful that I may deliver my own infant, Emily arrives with Thomas. It is not long after their arrival that our second son, Richard, is born. Emily stays with me until the night is late and the infant and I sleep. Before she left, we spoke of my children at the Tallman house. She shared with me that she had seen them and they are well and growing, but she had not been called to the home for Joan Tallman's birthings. A dear friend, she held my hand and prayed with me for my happiness after so much hardship, and for my children to find their way back to me. She promised to come visit me, and then I fell asleep.

I have come to care for Emily, a plain spinster who still lives with her elderly father, her mother having died when she was but twelve. She is a Puritan, but in spite of her plainness, she exudes a beauty of one with a golden heart.

In the morning, I find Thomas sitting at the table. He has made tea from the leaves Martha had shared, and sits waiting for me, knowing I was nursing the baby. I take the cup of tea Thomas has made, and warm my hands holding the hot cup.

"Thomas, you are my gem. I am still not accustomed to you waiting on me. Look how we are blessed, happy together and two beautiful sons."

Thomas smiles, always with that twinkle in his eye. "A beautiful son," he says.

"I have a gift for you." He reaches into his pocket and takes my hand. He slips a ring onto my finger, and as I look back up at him, he returns my gaze. I never cease being surprised by the love I see in his laughing eyes.

"This is a wedding ring for my wife. It is not gold or precious gems, but it holds my promise and vow to you."

The ring hugs my finger perfectly and, looking at it, I see that the ring forms a heart of silver in the center, with delicate ridges at the edge to outline the design. It is simple but stunning.

"Thomas, it is beautiful. You never cease celebrating our union, and I never cease thanking God for blessing me with you." I look at Thomas, a sacred stillness surrounding us. "Thomas, I love you; each and every day I wake to God's sunrise, I love you."

And with those words, the heartfelt moment is broken suddenly by Robert's bouncing down the stairs and the cry of Richard from his cradle. We smile at each other, knowing fully the words in our hearts.

As I prepare Robert and Thomas a bowl of porridge, Thomas says he will go into the shop, as he and Seamus are behind in the contracted work.

"Martha has promised me she will come over later this morning. She said she would bring her youngest daughter with her," says Thomas.

He pulls on his boots and smiles back at me, and, as he leaves, says, "I will see you this evening, but it may be late. We truly must get you some help out here."

"I can manage the chores, Thomas."

"Yes, you have brownies, I see."

"What, may I ask, are brownies?"

Thomas grins. "They are elves. When I was a young lad, my mother would tell me of the Scottish brownies, little elves who would come out when no one saw, at night, and help with the work. We would imagine them sneaking about the house. I believe you need some of those."

He laughs as he walks out the door. At the end of the week, Thomas brings home a young girl of fourteen or fifteen. He shares that a customer had told him of this young girl who lost her parents in an Indian attack at their home in the wilds of Massachusetts. Thomas has no intention of indenturing her, as is the custom, just as he refuses to purchase a slave. His own indenture has soured his heart to such practices. The girl's name is Esther, and she is thin and frail, as if she has not eaten well for a long time. Her hair is long and thin, and she appears unkempt, as she wears it loose. For a girl this young, I am disheartened to see no sparkle in her eyes and no smile on her hollowed face. Though I am uncertain where I will board Esther, I am grateful for the help and pray she will be just half as good as Obbah with the children.

Thomas finds he has some extra pallets in the barn and sets one up in the second bedroom upstairs as I gather some linen and blankets for her. I move both of the boys upstairs into the room next to her.

"Esther, you and I will clean that bedding tomorrow. You can hang it on the line in the morning," I add, worried about the pallet from the barn. I decide we will work on properly furnishing the room as time passes. Esther is quiet through our dinner meal and beds early.

"Thomas, she is so young," I say to him after Esther has gone upstairs. "She is not much older than my Elizabeth."

"Yes, but she can not only help you, she needs our help. This will be a good arrangement, providing she is willing to work. She has lost her parents and a brother. She tells me she has two married sisters in London."

"We shall see. With the new baby, I can use the help with Robert and my gardening."

"You need the help. And you deserve such, Ann."

The following morning, after Thomas leaves and I sit nursing the infant, Esther cleans the utensils and pots from our morning meal. Thomas has made it clear to her that she is here to help me, but in return she has free room and board, and a "family of a kind," he told her.

"Esther, I am certain you are sorrowful, full of woe at the loss of your family."

My words send her to weeping.

"Oh, dear, dear. I am foolish to bring up this. I would hug you if I could now," I say, looking down at my hungry little Richard, oblivious to all around him. "Dry your tears. We will speak of this another time, but today we shall be busy and happy," I say, and I smile at Esther. Her tears fade and she returns to her chore, scrubbing the work counter.

When I finish nursing Richard, who is dozing, I wrap him and ask Esther to take him.

"Can you clean and dress him?" I ask, seeking to learn her abilities.

"Yes, ma'am." She carefully takes Richard in her arms. "Are his clothes in your room?"

"Yes. There is a stack of linens for swaddling on the side of my dressing table, and a can of dust to powder him."

When she is done, I see Esther sit in the chair, near the fireplace, and rock little Richard. I go into my room to finish dressing, and brush and braid my hair. My plan is to visit the tailor in Portsmouth to see if he needs any help, but I am not yet comfortable in leaving the young children with Esther. Thomas is not fond of my idea to do work for the tailor. He assures me that there was no need for me to work outside of our home, but I have not forgotten my mother's advice. No future is ever assured, she had reminded me. However, I have another motive. I know I will never see my older children if I stay, day after day, at our home in the woods. But there is ever the chance I might see them in town, or maybe the new Mrs. Tallman would stop at the tailor shop.

Today I will find time, with Esther's help, to work on my landscape embroidery. If I can finish it, I may show the tailor my finest work when I see him. I know him to be a kind man, and I am hopeful that he might allow me to do some work at home. With the sun shining bright, I sit near the window in the sitting room and work my design on the panel for much of the day. I instruct Esther what to prepare for dinner and show her the root cellar.

Through the evening, I see that Esther relishes caring for baby Richard, and she is gentle with him. As I observe her, I surmise that the heavy burden of her great losses may be comforted by the chance to tend to one so helpless. The soup she prepares is delicious, and she bakes a fresh pan of corn bread. The girl knows the workings of a kitchen, and I can see she will be a great help to me. Now I must find a way to make her feel at home within our sweet family. Esther is so young, yet those she loved and the life she knew has been seized from her reach. Suddenly, I realize that these thoughts describe my own life, and an overwhelming sadness grips me, momentarily. The remembrance of Thomas's gentle kindness brings me back to the moment. I walk into the kitchen and hug Esther. I know I've startled her, but I hold her tight, as if holding all the parts until they come back together; and after a moment, her arms reach around me and we hold each other, releasing pain and opening our hearts to what might come.

"Thank you, Mistress Durfee, for your kindness and a home." Then a slight smile lights her face through her sadness, and I see hope.

Chapter 42

Thomas

"Seamus, you need to get the shoes done for Charles Wilbor's horses. He is coming to have the two horses shoed in the morning. I am going to the tavern. Baulstone wants me to check the accounts before our taxation." I untie my mare from the post and yell back, "I will see you in the morning."

Two months after Richard was born, I entered into a contract with a friend, William Baulstone, to buy the old tavern in Portsmouth. Business at my shop has been good and has afforded me the opportunity of investment. Baulstone is to run the tavern and manage the staff, while I will take care of the accounting and inventory, an arrangement suiting our skills and schedules. Baulstone is the son of a Portsmouth founder and has connections benefitting our business.

It is early afternoon and there are few officials and farmers already at the bar. Baulstone is not there, and I nod at our barkeep Paul as I walk in. I go back to the office and gather the boxes of recent bills and receipts and set them on the desk. Just as I have pulled the papers and am in the process of recording them, my friend William Wilbor walks into the office.

"What are you doing here, friend? At this time of day?" I am certain my voice reflects genuine surprise at his presence.

"I have some bad news. Seamus told me you would be here. My friend at the hall tells me that Tallman has filed another charge against you and Ann."

Staring at my friend, I am too shocked to speak, and recall Miles's warning.

"Is there no end to the evil in that man?" I say as I place my head in my hands in disbelief. "Well, we shall fight this. Surely the court will not punish us yet again. Oh, how do I tell Ann of this?"

William sits in the chair against the wall. There are no words to say. We sit in silence for a time.

"Thomas, you have my support. I am confident that you have an abundance of support from your many customers and your friends. You have more friends than you know, Thomas."

William's words lighten my heart. We both rise and I place my hand on William's shoulder, shaking his hand.

"You are a grand friend. Please do not share this news with Ann. I will have to tell her this evening."

"'I will tell you promptly of any news I hear, including a hearing date," William leaves the tavern.

After a long afternoon finishing the paperwork for the taxman, I file it away for Baulstone's examination. I check the inventory in the stockroom and write out a list of items we need, and a note to call for replacing three empty ale barrels.

It is dusk when I arrive home, and I am not eager to share the news with Ann. In the kitchen, Ann and Esther are preparing a meal, with Robert underfoot. I grab the toddler and whirl him around until he is chuckling, and it is now I make the decision to wait until we retire for the evening to speak with Ann. Ann, Robert, Esther and I dine on a fine meal of a chicken stew and a brown bread with ale. Esther seems more comfortable with the family, even smiling at times and playing with Robert. Ann grins at me, clearly reading my mind as I watch the interplay at the table. At times I have wished I had joined Ann in Virginia and been done with Tallman's evildoing, yet I know my reasons for staying had been sensible.

"Ann, I have some bad news to share with thee," I say softly as Ann hangs her dress on the hook in our bedroom. "William came by today and told me Peter has filed a new lawsuit against you and myself, the wording similar to his prior charges."

She sits, heavily, on the bed, head in her hands. "No," is all she can muster.

I sit beside her and gather her into my arms.

"We shall be good, Ann. We have survived immeasurable hardship to be together. And we are happy, are we not?"

"Oh, Thomas, I am so happy with you and our family. You are right. And I am thankful that our Rhode Island is fairer in its laws than many. Let us keep hope, as I yet remain hopeful that I will see my children again."

I hold Ann tight, kissing her face, her hair and then her welcoming lips. This graceful woman is like an angel sent to me. Never in my dreams, sailing the wild ocean from England, during my indenture and from my humble beginnings, did I envision having a woman such as Ann. Gently, my hardened hands find their way over my love's soft skin and I once again I make her mine, all mine, through the early hours, until the baby's cries call her away. I will protect her and stand by her side in the good and the hard times to come.

***

The court date arrives on the eleventh day of May in the year 1668, and as I stand before the judge, on charges of fornication, I plead guilty to having relations with my wife. I knew the court would not consider Ann my wife, as the solicitor reiterates that we are not and cannot wed. I stand still, and the judge proceeds to sentence me to fifteen lashes or a fine of forty shillings, and then he sentences Ann, who is not present with me, to two lashes or a fine of four pounds. Though Ann's fine was greater than mine and yet her punishment less, I pay her fine as I leave the town hall. I will pay my fine within the week, and have made such promise to the court. The judge knows well that I firmly consider myself married to Ann, and I pray the court will now look the other way.

As I walk down the main street of Portsmouth, I am tempted to forbid Tallman from entrance to my tavern; yet I have no inclination to further the tension. Besides, after the prior incident I heard of at the tavern with Master Strange Lot, I suspect Tallman did most of his drinking at home or in Newport. The issue between Lot and Tallman is yet unresolved, and I believe he avoids the tavern and his archenemy, Strange, one of many enemies.

Ann has been working a few hours each week for the tailor in Portsmouth, so I enter the front door of his shop, on the opposite side of the street from my own workshop.

"Good day, Daniel. I need a word with Ann," I say, and I walk to the back room, where Ann sits near the window, sewing. She looks up at me with worry lining her expression.

"All is well, my love. The judge ordered fines for each of us and I have paid yours. I will pay mine within the week, but I made clear to the officials that, in spite of their restrictions, ye are my wife. Let us pray this is the end of it."

She smiles wide, hearing my words, and rises to embrace me. We hug long, with a knowing shared between us that our tomorrows are never promised.

Chapter 43

Peter

After a day on the road between towns and at my shop in Newport, I walk into my sitting room and pour a whiskey. I need a drink, especially after hearing the news from the court hearing today.

"Papa, you are home," declares Elizabeth, now fifteen and a tall young lady, her blue eyes striking in a delicate visage framed by flowing raven locks. "I am glad you are here. I have worked the reading lessons with my sisters today, and Peter is upstairs doing his lessons."

"Yes. You are a good teacher, Lizzie. And Mary?"

"Mary led the lessons yesterday. She is in the garden now, Papa," answers Elizabeth.

"I need to speak with Joan. Go see if your sister needs any help."

"Joan, here in the sitting room," I call into the kitchen, where Joan and Obbah are cooking and watching over the young ones. Walking back into the sitting room, I pace back and forth.

"Yes? I am glad you are home in time for supper."

"I am not certain I am in the mood for supper. I have heard the judge today sentenced Thomas and Ann for whippings or fines in lieu of the punishment for their charged fornication, yet I am told that Thomas paid the fines. I am glad to have lessened the cad's pockets of his meager funds, but there will be no deserved public shame. He has walked away again. And Ann! How can she live in sin with this cad, so despicably?"

"Peter, it is unfortunate, yet they have both been punished before. The past is behind us. We have a happy family here, do we not?" Joan pleads.

"You have no understanding. This woman has humiliated me, and you, and her children. Abandoned them!"

"Peter. That is past. Why do you care so much about the past?"

Anger welling in me, I smite Joan across the face.

"Who are you to question my feelings? Get out." I pour another glass of whiskey.

Downing the drink, I set down the empty glass with my shaking hand and walk out toward the barn, without a word said as I pass the girls in the garden, and find Gabriel brushing my horse. My servant, Gavin, is nowhere to be seen. But my fury yet fills me, and I walk on out of the barn, on through the meadow by the woods. For as much as I am proud of this place, my own land, I spend little time relishing it, while Ann used to meander through the flowers down to the river or, after working in her garden, vanish into the woods. The hill toward the river is blooming with wild flowers, cinquefoil everywhere and a few pops of red wood lilies; the river is quiet, with a gentle lapping of the water on the rocks as I near the shore.

Unending thoughts of Ann overcome my anger. Memories of our flirtatious courtship in the isles, the first time I laid eyes on her, with her smiling gaze and dark auburn-lit tresses, fill my head. Ann's unbound locks had been like polished onyx glistening with sunlight. Oh, to run my hands through her tresses again. Though she had cuckolded me, I cannot banish my desire for her, memories of her laughter, her beauty, her gentle touch, never absent when I needed it. And my dreams! Too many nights her beauty and wit visit my night visions, leaving me muddled, as if yet a schoolboy. *Why can I not get her out of my head?*

Joan is right about Ann's presence in my thoughts, sparking my temper. Though Joan has stepped in and mothered my children, though she is a good and obedient wife, she cannot replace Ann. My fury at Ann ravages my heart. Oh, the loss, the loss of the one I had so adored, as though she were my right arm, ripped from my body. My heart aches to take her in my arms, right now, right here, in spite of all she has done to me. Yet I am at once furious at my own weakness, allowing this woman to take such hold of me.

As I look about me, my mind returns to the present and the river. Dusk approaches from the sea and I see a small ship, a caravel flying a flag from Spain, coming up the river from the ocean towards Portsmouth's docks. The sails are full, and as I watch it move slowly past me and hear the breezes catching the sails, my soul is again drawn to the sea. I have not been to Barbados, to Amsterdam, for three years, but my first love calls me, and I turn to walk back up to the house, where candlelight begins to flicker in the windows.

Chapter 44

Ann

I am grateful for the recent news Thomas brought me that there will be no flogging in the town square. My mood lifts, seeing that Esther becomes more comfortable each day in our home. She and I worked together sewing some curtains and bedding for her room, and Thomas found an old dressing table that Esther and I cleaned up.

While the boys are sleeping after lunch, I take the hairbrush and comb through Esther's hair, removing stubborn tangles. With a better diet, her hair is now thicker and healthier, so I braid and pin it fashionably high. She looks fair and angelic, and I see a light in her eyes as she admires her reflection in the mirror.

"Oh, Mrs. Durfee, you must teach me how to do this. It does look so elegant, does it not?"

"Yes, you are a sweet and arresting young woman, Esther. I will show you each morning until you learn to do it yourself. See how beautiful you are?"

Esther smiles. I spend the balance of the afternoon sitting outside and doing some finish work on my embroidered panel. It is almost finished, and I am pleased with it. The tapestry is a true art piece, more so than the few small ones I display about the house. The top of the panel is a scene of the tall ships at Newport's harbor, with the intricate stitches of the masts and the sails of the ships at sea. I've used colors to enhance the buildings along the shore, and shades of blues and greens at sea, textured with blends of white and ivory and yellows to properly present the play of sunlight and shadows. The middle scene is my favorite, the portrayals of the starred yellows and deep blue skies of dusk, with a rising moon reflected in the serene Sakonnet River. In the moon I've used some of the golden thread Captain Hudson had gifted me in Virginia. This landscape is my memory of my old home, but it is, as well, the memory of the night Thomas and I had spoken quietly along the rocks by the river, revealing our vulnerabilities and a kinship that was the first spark of my future. It is where my beloved children live. The bottom scene on this piece reveals the woods of Rhode Island, with the red and orange remnants of autumn as the first snow begins dressing the trees. I am so proud of my work, and am eager to show it to Master Gray at the tailor shop.

Thomas tosses in bed during the night, and I hold him tight, knowing how the heavy work at his shop taxes his body. Finally he sleeps, and I too fall into a deep slumber.

When I wake in the early morning, I am at first unsure where I am, still partially in my dream. I had been walking in the woods, but it was the woods in the forest by my old house with Peter in Newport. The trees and the glen were familiar, even comforting. Then I saw myself, as if from afar, walking side by side with another young woman. Was it Esther? Who was it? No, no, it was Mary, my daughter Mary as a young woman, who was but a girl when I last saw her. Yet I recognized her, her eyes and her shy smile. She and I walked deeper into the woods and I saw she took my hand, as I used to do with my mum. The sense of comfort was overwhelming, flooding throughout me, and then I am suddenly fully awake, yet wishing to return to my night visions.

I tell Thomas about my dream, and he smiles.

"You know that they still love you, Ann."

I agree, with some uncertainty. I recall how I have not been to the church gatherings during recent years. I would have seen them there, but well knew my presence would have caused a disturbance, and Peter would have likely taken the family and left. Though Thomas has shared that he has seen the older girls in town on one or two occasions with Obbah, I have not seen them. *What was the message of my dream? Does Mary miss me? And Elizabeth, and Peter, and the young ones? Oh, how I miss their sweet faces.*

***

On a warm day in July, it is my day to work in the tailor shop, doing some special requests for Master Gray. After having lunch with Esther and the boys, I take the buggy Seamus had readied for me and go into town. Sitting by the window in Master Gray's shop, the meager light on this rainy day highlights my work on some smocking for Mrs. Clarke's gown. As I look up, I see three women walk by the window, and then I hear the sound of the front door opening. I stand up and, through the curtain, see a woman I have never before seen and there, with her, stand Mary and Elizabeth.

My throat dries, tears water my eyes, yet I am ecstatic, all at once. After greeting Master Gray, they walk toward me.

"Ann? Are you Ann?"

"Yes." My voice cracks as I glance over at the girls.

"I thought you should see your daughters. My name is Joan, now married to Master Tallman." She pauses. "He is at sea," she adds, as if needing to explain her presence.

"Mary." The new Mrs. Tallman puts her hand on Mary's shoulder, guiding her towards me. I can see the girls feel awkward, hesitant. "Give your mother a proper greeting." I see Elizabeth stand back, somewhat reluctant, but Mary comes to me.

"Mama." Mary puts her arms around me and hugs me so tight I can barely breathe, but I do not need breath with my daughter's arms at last embracing me. I feel as if I am amidst angels. "I have missed you so much, Mama."

"Oh, dear Mary, not as much as I have missed you. Let me look at you. Look at how you have grown into a young woman." I look over at Elizabeth.

"And you too, Elizabeth. A young lady. Come give me a hug."

Elizabeth, unsure, walks toward me and hugs me tightly, as if she does not want to let go. I have lived for this day. My children were my reason for returning to Rhode Island, and for Thomas.

I take Joan's hand.

"I cannot thank you enough for your kindness. Thank you and God be with you."

"I did bring in this gown. I hear that you do embroidery and, being unskilled at such, I thought you could add some floral to the collar."

"Yes, Mum, that is my dress, if you can embellish it," says Elizabeth with the glee I recall from her young years.

"I will have it done in a day or two."

"Will you be in the shop next week on this day?" asks Joan.

"Yes."

"Then we will pick it up on that day."

"You are so kind, Joan," I say, and tears of joy blur my eyes. I sense a veiled sadness in Joan's presence, and I know well the source. This woman's gesture today is a blessing sent of grace and God.

"Mama, you look happy," says my sweet blue-eyed Elizabeth as they leave the store.

The door closes before I can reply and before the tears stream down my cheeks, tears of sadness and, most of all, joy. I sit still by the window for a long time, astonished by the good fortune of this summer day. I cannot wait to share this news with my Thomas.

***

The following week, I sit working in the shop, anticipating the return of the new Mrs. Tallman and hoping I will see my daughters again. There is a light rain, and I have lit a candle to work by. When I hear the door open, I rise to see one of our regular customers dropping off some work. Master Gray is working at the front, and he pens the instructions for the items to be mended and sees the disappointment in my face as I return to my work. After our customer leaves, he walks over to my worktable.

"Ann, I am certain they will come again. You are a good mother. I saw how they hugged you last week."

"Yes," I reply, with hope in my voice and my heart.

It is late in the afternoon when the front door opens again.

"G'day, Obbah. Mrs. Durfee is just behind the curtain, there." He points.

I rise to see Obbah, with the biggest grin shining from her face, and the girls are with her. Obbah runs to me and hugs me so that I almost fall over. With laughter and tears all at once, the girls begin giggling to see such a greeting.

"Obbah, Obbah!" I cry. "Oh, I have missed you so. You are almost like a sister to me, sweet friend."

"Missus, you were every day good to me ... as was Thomas," she whispers. She knows well that Thomas has helped her son and Zebediah. "I asked Mrs. Tallman," she looks down, somewhat embarrassed at her words, "if I could come today and pick up the master's jacket. She let me come."

"Oh, Obbah. You look well. Are these girls minding you? And the little ones?"

"Yes, ma'am! They are good girls and help their sisters and brothers with their lessons, and at times help with the cooking. Susanna and Ann are growing, as is sweet Joseph."

"Sit down, here." I pull up a stool near me for Obbah.

"Mary, tell me about the lessons. And Peter, is he yet in school, and the boys?"

"They are, Mum. In Newport. Elizabeth and I are doing lessons in writing and reading for Ann and Susanna," says Mary.

"And Peter shares some of his lessons with us, so we use those as well," adds Elizabeth, excited to share her achievements.

"Are you still doing your stitching as I taught you?"

"Yes, Mum, but we shall never be as good as you."

I lift my landscape work from near the window. "Look at this piece I am working on. It is a panel and I am almost finished. It is complete except for the borders."

"Oh, Mama," says Elizabeth. "This is beautiful."

"Yes, ma'am. This is more pretty than anything I have ever seen. Look! Look, it is the river by the house, with the wildflowers in bloom! I cannot believe you sewed this, Missus," says Obbah.

"Where shall you hang it, Mum?" Mary asks.

"Oh, I do not know yet. Maybe here at the shop? You know I have two little boys at home. Your brothers, Robert and Richard. I cannot wait for you to meet them one day."

A gloom comes over the girls, not knowing if they can ever visit. Mary quietly glances at Elizabeth.

"Pa is away at sea for a time. Maybe one day we can go to your home, Mum, and visit." She looks pleadingly towards Obbah, then me.

"We shall see." I add quickly. "Maybe one day Joan will allow that, but I know well we are not to anger your pa." Obbah nods, looking solemn.

I show the girls my worktable and some of the things I am working on, such as Mrs. Clarke's smocked gown. We visit and laugh, the girls telling me stories of the animals at the farm and the antics of their young brothers and sisters. Mary tells me of a young man named John who her pa has introduced to her. John is the son of Richard and Susannah Price. I had spoken once to Susannah at one of the more formal dinners I attended years ago with Peter. As has forever been, Peter is in control of matters, but Mary seems quite smitten by this young man.

After some time, Master Gray walks over and hands Obbah the dress Joan had brought in for the embroidery, and Obbah remits the payment her mistress sent with her. Master Gray is such a dear man, feigning that he had misplaced the dress as a design to allow me a longer visit with my girls. I kiss the girls each goodbye, and Obbah too; not knowing when I will see any of them again.

Chapter 45

Ann

In the spring of the year of our Lord 1669, I find myself twice blessed over the past year. My beloved daughter, Mary, wedded her sweetheart, John, in May of last year. I would never have been invited to the wedding at the Tallman home, but shortly after the ceremony last spring, I arranged a lawn party to celebrate Mary and John's union. It was a charming garden dinner with friends and family, where Esther and I served roasted quail and rabbit, early summer vegetables, hasty pudding and blueberry pastries. Thomas played his fedyl, along with a friend who played his guitar, and I danced with the boys, filled with joy when Mary took the fedyl and played a piece. I danced with Thomas as his dog, Crabit, ran around us, wanting to dance. Both Elizabeth and little Peter, now thirteen, were able to get away and come to the celebration, and what a grand day it was!

The years have been good to Thomas and me. My older children stop by Master Gray's shop whenever they can and, at times when Peter is at sea, they visit at our home. I made the frightening choice years ago to return to Rhode

Island for this reason, for my children, and my dreams have come to fruition. The love of my children makes each scar yet raised down my back worth my return; the love of my children and my Thomas.

To further exult the past year, I welcomed my third son with Thomas, our little Tom, with a bit of hair the color of corn and his father's gray eyes, like his older brother Robert. Esther is still with us, a blessing I am thankful for at this time. A young man, a shipbuilder from Newport, is courting her, and I know well the day will come when she will leave us.

After the recent birth of Tom, I am no longer working at the tailor shop and have little time for stitching. I will return to my beloved pastime of sewing when time allows. When the town of Portsmouth chose to mount and hang my landscape panel in the courthouse, I was humbled and honored. The Wilbors have most certainly been instrumental in this recognition, but the overwhelming sense of acceptance into a community where I was once condemned fills my heart. My breath caught, the first time I walked into the town's hall and saw my work hanging on the wall. Oh, how I wish my mum could have been there to see it.

Peter's travails certainly add to the further acceptance of Thomas and me in Portsmouth. Peter, oft known for his argumentative temperament and litigious ways, escalated the old issue with his neighbor Lot Strange. It had been years since the court had directed Peter to build a fence along the property line between the farm and the adjacent property of Lot Strange, and periodic conflicts ensued over the years. However, this year, after the court directed Peter to erect the fence, he built such a fence through the properties and straight across the road into Newport. This act did not sit well with town officials and travelers, and caused quite a stir. In this instance, his contrariness impacted many more people than himself and, as one would expect, angered many. I know Peter well enough to know that his act was to make clear his own point; however, his decision plainly ricocheted on him and added to his woes.

The fence blocking the road came down shortly thereafter, and it was not long after this that Peter departed on a voyage to Amsterdam. I oft wonder if his new wife, Joan, feels as I had, and if she breathes such a sigh of relief when he departs for the sea. For me, now, the feeling is familiar because it means that my children from the Tallman mansion feel unhampered to come and visit me more often. I believe, in my heart, that Peter has at last resigned himself to the fact that our children yet hold a bond with me, one he can no longer control.

Thomas, on the other hand, has never disappointed me. He has no grand ambitions for power, only to do well in life, contribute to his community and care for his family and friends. He is a simple man with a kind soul like none I have seen. When Mary or Elizabeth or Peter visits, he holds these children in his heart as though they are his own. There are many days I do not feel worthy of this man, but I have never forgotten my pa's promise that such love would come to me. There have been no visions of Pa since my pleading prayers in the cemetery years before, though I am still oft amazed how the animals in the woods show no fear of me when I walk amongst the trees, hunting for blueberries. Once, a young fox walked beside me through the trees and then sniffed my hand before he ran off.

It is in this year that Thomas makes arrangements for young Zeb, Obbah's son, to travel to Portsmouth in February. He knows that Obbah will travel into town for errands and is certain he can arrange a meeting. Thomas and Zeb, now a young man, are at the blacksmith shop speaking of the process of bending the iron when they see

Obbah going into the general store. He is thankful that she is alone, and Thomas runs across the street to get her.

"Come, Obbah. Come with me for a moment."

Obbah smiles at him. "I have errands to run, Master Thomas."

"No. You must come," he says as he guides her toward his shop.

Thomas tells me later that the moment she saw Zeb, she recognized him at once. She dropped her bag and ran to embrace him.

Obbah stays over an hour at the shop, visiting with her son, who shares the difficult news of his father, Zebediah's, illness and death from a stomach ailment. Zeb still works for the physician who purchased them, and the good doctor ensured Zeb received some education. Zeb works with the doctor and assists him with procedures and preparation of medicines and salves. Later, Thomas tells me how Obbah could not stop hugging her handsome son, and Thomas, as well, for his kindness in bringing her son to her. We talk and dine with Zeb while he is here at our home; and my dear Thomas arranges to ride back to Connecticut with him to ensure his safe arrival, and to thank the physician in Hartford for his kindnesses.

At times the thought crosses my mind that I might have never found this love I have, my Thomas. If Peter had not tormented me so, I would never have left; I would have never known there was more than what I had with Peter, the adulation and first lust of a young girl.

As a woman of an age with grown children and a full life, I have come to know from where my mum's elegance came. After hardships, sorrow and joys, I have grown into it myself. It is a confidence and fullness of life that carries me, the joys made keen through the tears of loss and struggle. I am Ann Hill Tallman Durfee, with the blessings

and the scars that brought me here and the serenity that
now lifts me with each new sunrise

Chapter 47

Thomas

Over the years, my business has been successful, and I have been blessed with two more sons, William and young Benjamin. I have purchased the blacksmith shop and have made Seamus part owner. I have hired others, including the son of a Puritan from the Bay Colony and Ezekiel, a liberated slave; and now I split my time between the shop and the tavern I own with Baulstone. There is a Godly purpose in the manual labor of blacksmithing, the sweat of the fire and its warmth in the winter, the satisfaction of creating a new thing, even as small as a latch. So, in spite of having Seamus and the hired help, I spend two or three days working at the shop each week.

But blessings are forever coupled with woe. Ann failed to wholly recover from the birth of our sweet Benjamin, who is now almost five years old. She labors in her breathing, and her condition has worsened as she continues to struggle to keep up with the children. We miss our Esther, who married her betrothed only two months ago and moved to Newport. Of recent days, Mary and Annie oft come to help their mother with the young ones. Mary has her own children, and Ann is overjoyed with her grandchildren but is oft saddened she is not up to playing with them. I pray each night for Ann's return to health, for I miss her free spirit. She is deprived of her joy of the forest and her garden. Her illness has been as a thief in the night, taking my vigorous and joyful wife from me.

I continue to contract use of the small home I built years ago, and I now own this house, our home in the woods, a house made grander with rooms added over the years. In spite of all my struggles with Captain Tallman, my land ownership and my standing in the community have bolstered my reputation. I am now a freeman of Portsmouth, since the year of our Lord 1678. There are times, late at night in the dark, when I recall the coalfields from whence I came, and am filled with wonder at my success.

It is a quiet fall evening as I ride my mare to the house and settle her in the barn. I see, by the buggy near the porch, that Annie is at the house.

"G'day, Annie. How is she?" I ask, tousling Benjamin's hair as he greets me.

"Yet weak. She is resting in bed and is tired. I took her some soup."

"Thank you, Annie. You should go home to your own husband. I will be fine here."

"Are you certain? I fed Benjamin and the others."

"Yes. I will see you soon. Go on home, dear." I help Ann into her buggy and turn back to the house.

Our room is dark and the curtains pulled, but Ann is awake.

"Thomas. Forgive me for not preparing your dinner. I am afraid it was a bad day. And you? Did you get Mister Pearson's gate made?"

"Yes, dear. How do you remember all these little things?" I ask her, stunned she has recalled his order.

"Oh, I believe it is because I have too much free time, and am waited on so diligently by you and my girls," she teases.

I smile, loving her light heart and persistent spark of wit. I kiss her forehead and pick up my fedyl. "I'll go play some music for the boys before bedtime. Would you have some rum or tea?"

"No. I will rest and enjoy your music."

I sit in a chair in the sitting room with the boys. Thomas sits at the desk with the candlelight, doing his schoolwork, while Richard, William and Benjamin follow me into the room and sit on the floor next to me with old Crabit. Robert is out in the barn doing chores as I play a tune on the fedyl, a tune that would oft bring a contented smile to Ann's face; it is a gentle lullaby.

"Papa, can I play? Please," William begs of me.

"Yes. Play the tune I taught you." William loves my fedyl, and I am heartened to pass down a tradition from my own Scottish roots.

After William plays a bit, I play an old favorite tune on the strings without the bow, as I am filled with a quiet peace, knowing Ann is listening. I hand the instrument over to William and rise to check on Ann, finding that she has drifted off to sleep.

Annie has left the pot of soup over the fire and I fix a bowl and sit with the children. Winter will be upon us soon. I will ask Martha to send her girl over to help Ann can some vegetables for our root cellar, though Ann's garden is untended and would likely be lacking. I need to get some help to replace Esther, and cannot rely on Mary and Annie to be here every day. Sweet Robert helps where he can, but we all know we need to do better.

The next morning, I ride into Newport, down by the docks, where slave trading is still openly negotiated each day, in spite of the writ restrictions. One of the traders has a number of newly arrived slaves, but I see a woman standing by the pier. She stands askew, as her foot or leg seems to have an old injury or malformation, her hair is grayed at the temples and there is sadness in her eyes. I approach her and, out of earshot of the trader, ask if she is willing to work as a housekeeper for me. It appears she is awkward with the English language, but she understands enough of my words to answer, "Yes."

"Well, I need a housekeeper and cook. In return I can provide you with food and boarding. Can you cook?"

"Yes, cook. Master, me man. Can you ... me man?" She pointed across the dock to a thin man who was unloading a skiff. He appeared to be about fifty years old, but looked strong.

"Yes, I could. I will have to purchase you both. Can he care for horses? Can he farm crops?"

"Yes, Master." I was not certain she understood, but I had little doubt the old man would help where he could.

"I will see if I can make the deal. You stay here."

I could afford the purchase of both, but still negotiated a good deal, as the trader knew well he may have trouble getting any value from a trade of these two. On the ride home to Portsmouth I try to explain to them that I do not own them but only wish their agreement that they work at my home for room and food and, eventually, a bit of pay. I believe the husband grasped my meaning. They are called Lucy and Abram, a name he said he was given when baptized in Barbados. Abram speaks fair English, and expresses gratitude and eagerness to work my barn and care for the animals.

I show them their quarters, Seamus's old quarters in the barn, and tell them they can fix the two rooms as they wish. I will send Ezekiel out here to help them get settled. I may even move Lucy or both of them into a room in the house if space permits, but imagine they may prefer their privacy.

"Come, come inside and I will show you the house and you may meet my dear Ann."

Chapter 48

Peter

I have not sailed to Europe for several years now, yet my heart again aches for the wooden deck beneath my feet and the sway of the sea. I crave one more trip to Barbados, but now my wife, Joan, is ill. Bedridden for a month, she becomes more frail each day, yet the house is full of children and old Obbah is still here, caring for all of us. In spite of all of the play and laughter amongst the children and flavors emanating from the kitchen, the house is filled with a somber darkness. The piano, brought home from Amsterdam years before, sits silent.

It is late winter, with the hope of spring before us. Snow hitherto clings to the meadow, but the ships yet come and go down the river. I am a grandfather, several times over, and focus my time at my apothecary. James and his son Charles now help to manage the shop for me, but I spend two or three days each week helping patients.

"Aye, Captain. How are you today?" calls Charles as I walk through the heavy door of my shop.

"Oh, Charles today is as good as any. Remind me to take ginseng home today for Joan. I am not certain what else to give her; she is so weak."

"What does the doctor say?" he asks.

"Nothing good. He thinks it is her blood, and we have had two bloodlettings at the house. There is each time a welcome return of her constitution, but it is short-lived."

"I do not know if you want to hear this or not, but this morn Thomas Durfee came for ginseng and some pennyroyal for his wife's vertigo. He says she is poorly and failing."

The news surprises me. I had not heard that Ann is ill, and the revelation saddens me. I am certain my silence speaks volumes to Charles, and he says no more. After all of these years, my wife, Joan, seems to be leaving me, and now to hear that my first wife, my Ann, is failing weighs heavily.

The backroom is well-stocked, with few needs, but I have a trader, Samuel Brooks, who gathers my goods on his runs to the old world and the islands. I no longer have my own ship, but Brooks sails where I ask. Over the years, I developed a beneficial relationship with Samuel's good sea captain, Nehemiah. He has, at my beckoning, added a young man to his crew, a strapping young man called Nathaniel from the docks in the parish of St. Michael in Barbados. I heard, through message from my old friend Modyford, that Marianne died of smallpox when her oldest boy Nathaniel was but sixteen; and I decided it was the least I could do.

I bid Charles good day as I leave the shop and ride my old mare back to Portsmouth. The snow is melting and the road muddy as I wrap by scarf tight against the persistent chill.

***

It is March when we bury Joan in the Tallman cemetery on the hill. I am filled with a hollow sadness, and am weary of the dark clothing and the even darker mood of the farm. I think this will be the summer I sail, with Brooks, again to Barbados. I will make ready my plans to leave in July as the seas calm and the days stretch.

Yet as the weeks pass, despair yet fills me. I cannot forget what Charles told me. As June comes upon me and I arrange with Brooks and Nehemiah to ready the ship for next month's journey, I cannot get the vision of Ann out of my head. Though I have seen her, in passing, a few times over the years, I have not spoken to her since the day she left our home. After so many years immersed in anger and vindictiveness over her transgressions, I have come to realize that some transgressions were my own. There are, and have been, those around me who have revealed that I was lacking in kindness; some even say that I have no heart. I have come to believe they may be right. Sitting at my desk one summer evening, the candle burning, I look up to see the pinks, browns and ivories of a form on the shelf. It is the old conch, the perfectly coiled shell I found on Dover Beach in Barbados all those years ago, and with the memory, remorse weighs heavy on me.

***

On a day midweek, knowing from the word of an old friend in Portsmouth that Durfee is usually at his tavern, I mount my mare and head toward town, turning left onto the road where sits the Durfee house.

It is a rainy day in June, the mud grabbing at my mare's hooves. The rain dwindles to a drizzle as I near the house where Ann lives. There is no buggy in front, but on a day such as this, the horses would be sheltered in the barn. I have never been to Ann's home, and it is strange to set eyes upon it. Before me is a fine house, not as grand as my own farm, but large, and with asymmetrical windows and roof. The long slope of one eave reveals Durfee has added on to the house. Dismounting my horse, I tie her to the rail and, not without some unease, walk onto the porch and knock at the door.

As I raise my hand to knock a second time, a gray-haired Negro woman opens the door.

"I am here to see Ann." The old woman stares at me and, stuttering, I add, "Mrs. Durfee."

The old woman looks at me, uncertainty on her face.

"Sir, do the missus expect you?"

"No. But I am family and would like to speak briefly with her. I hear she is ill. Is she well enough to visit?" I inquire.

"Yes. Come in. I will let her know you are here." She stands before me, as if awaiting a response.

I realize she knows not my name. "Tell her Peter Tallman is calling."

She walks into a room on the other side of the fireplace. Water drips from my boots onto the floor as I see the room around me has Ann's touch, the well-placed candlesticks, a basket of blankets, the blue-draped curtains and embroidered pieces on the chairs. I see there are no Asian carpets as in my home, making my footsteps harsh on the wooden floors. The room is dark, with no lit wicks or Betty lamps, but the soft elegance and comfort of the room are inviting. There are children's wooden blocks near the fireplace; and, in the corner, sits a fiddle, reminding me how my presence in this place would anger Thomas. Such anger may well be warranted.

The old woman returns, tells me to follow her and leads me to the room she had just left. The room is darkened, and the old woman pulls a heavy drape to the side as she leaves. I can see Ann is sitting in the chair next to her bed. It appears she has only left her bed and seated herself, wrapped in a dressing gown. Her hair is flowing down her shoulders, unkempt yet alluring, with a few curls turned gray framing her face, a face more pale and weary than I remember. On the other hand, her illness had failed to cloud the gaze of her piercing hazel-green eyes, eyes I have dreamt of.

"Well. It has been a long time."

Her voice is weak, but I am certain that is due to her malady.

"I am saddened to hear of the loss of your wife. She was good to our children."

"Yes. She was a good wife and cared well for the children." I realize my words and pray they will not offend as if a comparison. "I am certain you are surprised by my visit, but I have heard that you were ill, and I believe strongly that there are words, important words, unsaid."

"Yes, likely there are." Her gaze, confident and firm, remains on me.

There is no other chair in her room, so I stand near the window to enhance my sight.

"Ann, I have thought long and hard of the painful times between us. I have come to know that my actions were oft unkind, and I have come to beg undeserved forgiveness. In spite of my ill tempers and poor choices, I know you were a good wife to me and did not deserve my retributions. I do not want these bitter feelings to remain between us."

"Peter …."

Oh, the sound of her saying my name! Oh, how it stirs my heart and comes near bringing tears to my eyes.

"I forgave you years ago, Peter," she continues. "You are the father of our children." She pauses, but I can see she is not finished speaking, but merely catching her breath. I wait, with a newfound patience and a breaking heart.

"I have found peace and happiness in my life here. I have the love of my children. I pray that you, too, have found happiness."

I am not certain how to respond to her plea. The happiness Ann speaks of is unknown to me. I think briefly of all those wasted years, seeking only my father's approval, my own pleasure, power and wealth.

"Peter, I know your true mistress was always the sea. You were never happy but when you were sailing and trading. I could not compete with such a powerful mistress." She smiles at me, a smile that lights her face, and I see her beauty yet.

"You are a wise woman, Ann. The thrill of the waves did call me oft, and still I crave the sea; but my sailing days are near done." I hear the tinge of sadness in my own voice, startling myself.

"Peter, you need not worry about ill feelings. There are none. Years before, Thomas was very protective of me, but we are beyond that now, and we are happy. I do wish the same for you, Peter. You were, in my youth, the love of my life, and now we both know life is much too brief. May our God bless you."

My eyes well and I sense the taste of salt on my tongue. My own selfishness had consumed me; I never truly saw that this woman was too good for me.

"I love you, Ann." The words slip out before I can hold them, but they are now spoken and irretrievable; they are from my heart, a heart I have held too tightly. I know I have likely overstayed my welcome, assuming any welcome at all.

"I shall be going. Thomas is lucky to have you," I say, and I am again surprised how easily the words leave my mouth. "I pray for your health, Ann. You shall forever be in my prayers."

"May God bless you, Peter." And there, there on her enchanting face, is a faint smile as I leave her room. It is a smile etched with serenity, a vision now engraved on my soul for all my remaining days.

Part III

The rivers bound the island tight
Against the great sea's storm and might.
The years had passed and families bound
With threads of love and loss rewound,
Through and through, the struggles faced
Had woven families, e'er interlaced.

Chapter 49

The year is 1757 in the town of Portsmouth of Rhode Island, and the tensions between the colonies and the king rise as the French and Indian War rages to the north. Lydia Dennis, a young woman with her chestnut tresses pulled and pinned into curls and green eyes laughing, stands before her mother, Sarah Durfee Dennis, the granddaughter of Thomas and Ann Durfee. Lydia wears a gown of stunning embroidery with rich stitching of purples and greens on a pale silk. It had been her great-grandmother's wedding dress. Lydia's mother had recounted the story of Ann's wedding in the parish in Barbados so many years ago, a story passed down through her aunts and great-aunts, as was the dress.

Sarah pins a silver and pearl coil in Lydia's locks, capturing a stray curl into her braids. The pearl hairpin had been a gift from Grandpa Durfee to his beloved Ann. The day is still but chilled, blessedly without snow. Evergreen fills the air with the flavors of the looming Christmas holiday, as fir wreaths and berries dress the town's homes.

"I know, dear, thy dress is a bit exquisite for the Quaker ceremony, but it is Grandmother's. I wish I had known Grandmother. Aunt Ann has told me so many stories, but I do know thou have Ann Durfee's beautiful green eyes and her reverence of nature. Thou look elegant, Lydia, and thy young man is a good man. I am so happy for thee, for our families," she says, and she hugs her daughter long.

"Mum, look at this dress! I care not that it is ornate, Mum, for it is the most beautiful dress I have ever seen. This will be a day I shall never forget, I am certain." Her excitement rings through the room, echoing like a dinner bell springing from wall to wall. "Is the carriage ready?"

"Yes, your pa is hitching the horses now. I am certain, dear, that this will be one of many days thou shall never forget."

Lydia twirls around, flaring the skirt and holding out her arms. Her mum laughs and reaches for their woolen capes and gloves. The ceremony will be at the Fish home. All parties decided this arrangement was best because the Fish home is large, with a grand formal sitting and dining area. Their house sits on the hill where old Strange Lot used to live, next to the old Tallman mansion overlooking the river. The friends of the Quaker meetinghouse will be there to witness the ceremony.

As Sarah goes to find her daughter Ruth, Lydia walks outside to still her nervous excitement. Lydia's pa, dressed in his best clothes, is walking toward the house with the horses, so Lydia walks over to the trees. The forest has been her favorite playground, a refuge, as far back as she can remember. She recalls how the raccoons and deer, unafraid, would not run from her when she was alone; yet when she shared those encounters with her brothers, they laughed at her, so those times became her private cherished moments. As she walks among the barren birch trees, careful not to catch her dress, she hears something, a faint noise, almost lyrical.

"Lydia."

She turns toward the sound of the voice, an unfamiliar voice, but sees nothing and suspects she heard the leaves rustling on the ground. Then comes a whisper, the words ringing distinct but transparent.

"Sweet Lydia, on your own journey ...." It is as if the words floated through the branches, now barren, and then there is a rustling, followed by quiet.

Chills run up her spine. For a moment she is lost in the reverence of the forest. She still sees no one standing amongst the white birch, but she knows in her heart it is her great-grandmother's voice she has heard, a woman she never met. She has heard the tales. Suddenly, in the present, she stands straight, full of confidence, and with her great-grandmother's words echoing in her ears, she is certain that all will be well. A young quail sprints from a bayberry thicket, scurrying, through the dried leaves, deeper into the woods. Lydia begins to spin with joy, but then stops as she remembers the hem of her dress amongst the brambles, and sees her mother waiting.

Sarah takes Lydia's hand, and, with Ruth, they climb into the carriage and ride toward town. Her pa will bring her brothers just behind them.

***

At the Fish home, David is dressed and eager in anticipation of his wedding ceremony. His mother, along with friends and the help, have been busy all day preparing foods and readying the formal room, now filled with seating and ribbons and a few well-placed wreaths and berries fit for the holiday wedding. David adores his Lydia, a sweet young woman he met in town when he was but sixteen. Now a young man, a wheelwright in Portsmouth, he is ready to start a family and wants, more than anything in the world, to live the rest of his life with Lydia at his side. The announcement of their impending marriage has been posted, and now the day is upon him.

David knows well the significance of this ceremony. His great-grandfather had been an early freeman of Newport and Portsmouth, and a well-known trader. His father descends from the Fish family, early Quaker descendants of the island. His white shirt is pressed and he wears a dark wool jacket, but the smile on his face gleams as his finest asset. He paces the wooden floor, stopping often to gaze out the window, awaiting the arrival of the Dennis family.

The feast will be grand, and the house is filling with the members of their Friends meetinghouse, as well as other family. At last he sees the Dennis carriage, and he runs out to the porch.

"Lydia. Missus Dennis. I am so happy thou are here. Look! The sun is shining and this is surely a grand day." He reaches out his hand to first help Missus Dennis from the carriage, then Lydia and her sister.

"Mother has been cooking all week for a grand celebration."

Sarah puts her arm around David and hugs him.

"David, I am so grateful to gain a new son such as thou. I believe thy excitement for this day matches Lydia's." She smiles. "Let me go find thy mother and see how I might help."

Lydia discreetly takes David's hand and smiles, a smile filled with anticipation and radiance.

***

The ceremony is brief, as is the Quaker way, with the bride and groom seated before the group, present to witness the pledge and partake in the celebration.

David breaks the sudden silence in the room. "In the presence of God and these our Friends, I take thee, Lydia, to be my wife, promising with divine assistance to be unto thee a loving and faithful husband as long as we both shall live." With his promise said, he takes Lydia's hand.

Lydia smiles, looking into David's eyes and seeing his serious expression, and she recites her vow. "In the presence of God and these our Friends, I take thee to be my husband, promising with divine assistance to be unto thee a loving and faithful wife as long as we both shall live."

The deed is done. There is a short prayer, led by David's father, Daniel Fish, and the celebration commences. There are so many kisses and hugs, intermingled with soups, roasted lamb and quail, greens, breads, berry-filled tarts and puddings.

Lydia wants only to be alone with her David, but spends the afternoon receiving congratulations. She will go home with David this evening, to their own home, a home he has built with his brothers and friends on land he purchased at the edge of town, not far from the old Durfee house. He has prepared long for this day, and Lydia cherishes him all the more for it. He is a handsome man, tall, with blue eyes, and his hair is long and the color of sand. Those charming looks had first caught Lydia's eye when she was but sixteen, although it was David's kind heart that had sealed their fate. Her mother had schooled her repeatedly in the importance of the way a man treats a woman, and it has served her well.

Late in the evening, the crowd has left and the family lingers, the candles burning their wicks low about the room, flickering openings in the darkness. David's mother, the granddaughter of Captain Peter and Joan Tallman, has hosted a warm and festive celebration, and as the Dennis and Fish families visit with each other, Jemima Fish turns to her son and Lydia.

"It is time for thee to leave. This is thy night, thy celebration," she says, and she puts her arms around both David and Lydia, pulling them together and hugging them tightly. Sarah walks over and kisses both her daughter and new son-in-law.

"Go. Go. We love thee and will see thee soon," adds Sarah, turning back towards the family.

David helps Lydia with her cape, and they walk out of the house, full of laughter and love, and climb into David's small buggy. The night is dark, so dark the sky is sparkling with stars, the moon new and absent from sight. David guides his horse tentatively through the blackness, down the country road toward town.

"Look, David. Look at how bright the stars shine this night."

Pulling back on the reins, he slows to a stop as the road curves, and looks up.

"They are amazing. There are thousands of them. And look at how they shine on us, David." David searches for Lydia's lips, kissing her deeply, overcome with tenderness and anticipation.

About the Author

A Thousand Stars is Sandra Fox Murphy's first novel. She has been writing poetry since she studied the beatnik poets in Marin County, California, in the 1970's, and she has written several short stories, and more poetry, since she retired from the U. S. Geological Survey in 2009.

Born in Delaware, Sandra grew up in a military family, living throughout the country and in Portugal. She began her federal career at the North Island Naval Air Station in California. In the midst of her career and raising children, she graduated from The University of Texas with a B.A. in English and French literature. Sandra now lives in central Texas and is working on her second novel.in between road trips.

Made in the USA
San Bernardino, CA
12 March 2016